DEMON

WITCH

Also by Geoffrey Huntington

Sorcerers of the Nightwing

DEMON WITCH

BOOK II

THE RAVENSCLIFF SERIES

GEOFFREY HUNTINGTON

10 ReganBooks
Celebrating Ten Bestselling Years
An Imprint of HarperCollinsPublishers

This is a work of fiction. Names, characters, places, and incidents either are the product of the author's imagination or are used fictitiously. Any resemblance to actual events, locales, organizations, or persons, living or dead, is entirely coincidental and beyond the intent of either the author or the publisher.

ReganBooks
An Imprint of HarperCollins*Publishers*
10 East 53rd Street
New York, NY 10022-5299

Copyright © 2003 by Geoffrey Huntington
ISBN 0-06-059551-5 (pbk.)
www.reganbooks.com

First ReganBooks paperback printing: July 2004
First ReganBooks hardcover printing: July 2003

Printed in the U.S.A.

10 9 8 7 6 5 4 3 2 1

FOR
BRIGID, LIAM, SIOBHAN,
MELISSA, MATTHEW,
AND
DAYNA

CONTENTS

CONTENTS

◆—◆

THE BURNING
OF A WITCH
A.D. 1522

I**T TAKES SIXTEEN LOADS** of peat and fifty bundles of fresh green wood to burn a witch.

"When it's green," the Guardian explains to the boy, "it burns longer."

Men with shirtsleeves rolled up their hairy arms are laying the wood around the stake. The square is thronged with people cheering them on in their task. The execution of traitors, after all, is always a great public occasion, and a burning at the stake is the most festive of all. All around the bedazzled boy, vendors in silly jester's hats hawk roasted chestnuts and steaming fried apples. Spider monkeys turn somersaults while their owners play merry little tunes upon their lutes.

"There!" someone from the crowd calls out. "There she comes!"

A shout rises up as the cart carrying the witch trundles into view over the cobblestone road. "Burn the she-devil! Burn the witch! *Burn! Burn! Burn!*"

The boy turns, his eyes wide.

Isobel the Apostate looks back at them all with a cold, quiet disdain. Her black eyes flash as the crowd parts to make way for her cart. Strong men fall to the ground at the sight of her, overcome by her terrible beauty. If not for her wrists being bound by that strange golden chain, the boy knows they would all be in great danger. Yet bound as she is, the witch can no longer harm them, no longer summon the demons from the Hellhole to do her bidding, the demons that will terrorize the villages of northeastern England no more.

Her green velvet dress is torn and soiled. Her black hair is loose, tumbling down to her waist in disarray. Once, she was a noble lady with a vast estate who claimed descent from the blood royal, who dared to quarter her arms with those of King Henry the Fourth. For such audacity alone, the judges decreed she should die.

But there are sins far worse than treason.

"Look, over there," the boy's Guardian points out to him. "Do you see that man? The one with no legs, propped in the chair? 'Twas under his home that the witch discovered the Hellhole. Without any regard to him who lived there, she opened the portal between this world and the one below." The Guardian pauses. "You see the result. The man is fortunate. His wife and sons did not survive the cataclysm."

"But the golden chain . . . ?"

"It has the power to keep her from escaping, from turning all of us here into toads and rats and skunks." The Guardian lifts his eyes to the gray, cloudy sky. "At least, I pray that it does. I pray that the noble Sorcerers of the Nightwing, God be praised, have at last found the means to contain her."

The boy watches as the witch is led from her cart to the center of the square. The crowd surges forward. Insults and curses rain down upon the woman, whose neck now begins to snap back and forth, finally reacting to the taunts of the crowd. Her teeth gnash wildly. She growls, hissing like a cat cornered by a pack of angry dogs.

"Get up there, boy," the Guardian tells him. "You must bear witness."

Two platforms stand to the right of the square. They are filled with men from the king's court. Statesmen and clerics. The Archbishops of York and Canterbury. The Duke of Norfolk. The king's brother-in-law, the Duke of Suffolk. Even Cardinal Wolsey. They have all come to see the destruction of Isobel the Apostate, the most feared sorceress in all of Europe, a lady whose courtiers were not knights and gentlemen but the very beasts of hell.

She is shoved toward the pillory by her guards, where she is forced onto her knees to face her judges. A pointed hat is placed on her head, on which is inscribed the words HERETIC, WITCH, APOSTATE. Her death sentence is proclaimed, and a cheer rises from the crowd.

"Will she be allowed to speak?" the boy asks, looking up at his Guardian.

"Oh, no. For all that the last words of the condemned have long been a tradition in this realm, Isobel the Apostate is far too dangerous a prisoner. Even secured by the golden chain, what terrible catastrophe might she bring down upon us with her final words?"

But though she may be denied speech, the witch can still scream.

It is a horrible sound, and many in the crowd cover their ears. The witch's screams echo like those of a banshee off the walls of the square. Forcibly she is led to the pyre, snarling and twisting all the way.

"It wasn't supposed to end like this, you see," the Guardian explains, leaning down and whispering to the boy. "It was supposed to end with Isobel crowned as queen of England. From there, with the English navy at her command, it would have been an easy step for her to rule the world, the demons of the H͟ ͟ ͟ at her side."

The boy watches as the witch is push͟ ͟ ͟ ͟eps of the platform to the stake.

"But 'twas her own kind who tu͟ ͟ ͟ ͟er to the king. Her own Nightwing brethren lo͟ ͟ ͟ upon her evil and trapped her. It was they, far more than any of the king's men, who consigned her to this fate. And do you know why it was done so, boy?"

The boy's eyes remain riveted on the witch.

"Because true power can never be found through the pursuit of evil," the boy replies, never removing his gaze. "True power comes only from good."

His Guardian smiles. "Yes, boy. You have learned well. You will make a noble sorcerer. Now watch. And learn from the death of the Apostate."

She is tied to the stake with the same kind of golden chain that binds her wrists. Her black eyes continue flashing, looking at each and every face in the crowd, as if committing them all to memory.

Her gaze falls upon the boy.

He gasps, pulling back from the power he sees there.

Her eyes dance as she takes in the sight of him. She laughs, a cackle the boy will not soon forget. On his shoulder the grip of his Guardian tightens. "Fear her not," the Guardian whispers. "Her time has come."

The executioner lights the wood piled up around the base of the stake. Once more, Isobel the Apostate screams.

"Think not that I perish here!" the witch cries out into the crowd, defying the order against speech. "Think not that you have won!"

The boy feels his Guardian's hand tremble.

"This is not the end of Isobel!"

The flames spring into roaring life, caught by the peat. Like malevolent imps, they pop and crackle and jump upward. A spark ignites the witch's dress.

"She burns!" someone in the crowd shouts.

The fire below her grows in heat and intensity. It is so strong that even several feet away the boy and his Guardian can barely stand the heat on their faces. Thick sheets of pitchy smoke appear, obscuring their view. Soon the whole square is as black as night, and the crowd begins coughing, turning away from the pyre. The foul stench of burning flesh assaults their senses. From the heart of the darkness the witch screams again. It is taken by many as her cry of death.

"So must perish all of the king's enemies!" proclaims the executioner.

But then the wind shreds the smoke and there is a glimpse of the witch. The boy can see her, with her arms upstretched, free of her chains as the flames consume her body. Her eyes are wide and she is smiling.

"Does she perish?" the boy asks his Guardian, tugging at his robe. "Does she really perish?"

The Guardian does not reply.

Later, when the flames have died down, there is nothing left of the body of Isobel the Apostate. The king's men declare that so great was the fire that the witch was consumed completely, reduced to mere cinder and ash.

But the Nightwing know better.

For the boy reports to them that as he watched, the witch transformed herself into a great bird, a creature of gold with a tremendous wingspan that rose majestically above the flames with a resounding call of triumph. Then the bird diffused with the smoke, disappearing into the gray skies over the square.

"Like a phoenix," the boy's Guardian says, a great and shattering awe in his voice, "Isobel the Apostate has risen from the flames to live again."

FIVE HUNDRED
YEARS LATER

ONE

❖

THE NEW CARETAKER

FOR SEVERAL SECONDS the wind howling through the trees sounds like the tortured scream of a woman, overwhelming everything else.

Devon March listens. There's another sound. A sound behind the wind.

A car's engine. Tires spinning.

Trudging up the long cliffside driveway that leads to the great house of Ravenscliff, Devon has suddenly found himself caught in a fierce winter storm. The snow comes down in sheets; in just a few moments the driveway has become slick with ice. Just a couple hours ago, when Devon headed down into the village, the afternoon was calm. The storm arrived suddenly, with a terrible severity, as storms here always do. Why else, as the people of the village below like to say, would the place be called Misery Point?

Now, through the snow, Devon strains to see where the sound is coming from. Only a few yards ahead of him, half obscured in the swirling whiteness, is a car— an old black Cadillac by the looks of it. Its wheels are indeed caught on a patch of ice, and it jerks in fits and starts, precariously close to the edge of the cliff.

Who could it be? Devon asks himself. He knows few of the villagers ever drive up here. Ravenscliff is like Dracula's Castle to them. And no one from the great house has a car like that.

Devon hurries his approach, but the snow is falling heavier now. The wind hits him face-first. The Cadillac continues trying to break free of the ice, spitting snow from its spinning tires, screeching like some animal with its leg in a trap.

"Hang on!" Devon calls. "I'll give you a hand!"

Just then the car does break free. It thrusts forward, suddenly and with horrible speed, only to pitch itself right over the side of the cliff toward the rocky shore two hundred feet below.

"No!" Devon shouts, his eyes wide in horror.

But he doesn't spring forward. Instead, he concentrates.

The Cadillac stops in midfall, as if drawn by a giant magnet to safety along the edge of the cliff. It settles on the road, still dangerously close to the precipice, but safe.

Devon smiles. Such things shouldn't surprise him anymore, but they still do. No matter how often he uses his powers, no matter how often he proves to himself that he's a sorcerer, he remains in awe of what he can do when he puts his mind to it.

Devon runs up to the driver's door. "Are you okay?"

There's no sign of life behind the blue-tinted windows.

"Hello?" Devon calls again, rapping on the glass. Still nothing.

He pulls open the door. He sees no one. Was the car driving *itself*? It's not such an odd thought, really. Stranger things have happened at Ravenscliff.

"My, my, my," comes a voice. "That sure was close."

From the floor of the car, under the steering wheel, creeps a little man. His small pudgy hands grip the leather seat as he hoists himself back up. He looks over at Devon with bright blue eyes. His hair is white; his short beard forks into two small points.

"Are you . . . okay?" Devon asks again.

The little man rubs his bearded chin, his eyes studying Devon. "Strange how the car stopped like that. As if something just pulled it right back from certain doom."

"Yeah," Devon says, uncomfortable about revealing his powers to a stranger. "But you should get out of the car. I'm not sure it's safe where it is."

"Oh, I have a feeling it's perfectly safe now." The little man's eyes twinkle. He's like a Munchkin, Devon thinks, dressed entirely in brown suede. "But I doubt I'll get her started again." The man reaches over to the passenger seat and grabs a purple sack, then hops down out of the car. "Poor Bessie," he says, patting the Caddy as he closes the door gently. "I'll be back for you. I promise."

Devon looks down at him. He can't be more than three and a half feet tall. His hair is as white as the falling snow, and his skin is very pink. He swings the purple burlap sack over his shoulder.

"Do you live up there?" he asks Devon. "At Ravenscliff?"

They both look off at the great house, standing there at the crest of the hill, black against the snow, the view of its spires obscured but not obliterated by the storm. Ravenscliff: fifty rooms and countless secret corridors, built of the blackest wood, and covered with the birds from which it takes its name, even in the storm.

"I do," Devon replies. "I live at Ravenscliff."

"Should've guessed," the little man says. "Shall we walk, then? Or might you be able to *fly* us there?"

Devon laughs, and they begin to trudge through the snow.

* * *

DEVON MARCH is not like other boys his age. At fourteen, he can claim to have been to hell and back, literally. He's come face-to-face with demons from the other side, and he's proven himself to be stronger than any of them. Ever since he was six years old, when the first filthy thing had crawled out of his closet, Devon has known his powers were unmatched by any human. That first demon—so blundering, so stupid—had tried to kill Devon's father. But the six-year-old had stopped the thing in its slimy tracks, sending it spiraling back down its Hellhole with one word: "No."

His father never explained *why* Devon had these powers—those answers would have to wait until after he'd come here, to Ravenscliff—but Ted March *did* teach his son that his powers weren't to be feared. His powers made him stronger than whatever might try to harm him, but only if he used them in the pursuit of good.

"But why do they want me?" Devon asked his father. "These things from the closet?"

His father had never given him a satisfactory answer. Devon just knew, from the time he was only six, that there were indeed things in this world—and others—that would try to harm him.

His closet was a Hellhole—a filthy gateway into the realm of the demons who had been cast there eons ago by the old elemental gods. From these portals the stewing, resentful creatures occasionally escaped, repulsive beasts with fangs and talons that stunk worse than any backed-up septic system or stagnant swamp. Devon had marveled at the strength he found in fighting the demons, overpowering them, kicking them back to hell. But never was he truly free of them. Even after Dad died and Devon was sent to Ravenscliff to live as the ward of the mysterious Mrs. Crandall, the things still pursued him. Here, in fact, they proved even more numerous.

But no longer was Devon so clueless about *why* they came for him. Here on the rocky cliffs of Misery Point, Rhode Island, Devon had finally learned the first part of the secret of his past, a secret his father had apparently been unable—or unwilling—to reveal. Ted March was not Devon's real father. Devon was, in truth, the scion of a long line of sorcerers—a revelation that had seemed extraordinary, of course, and uncanny, but also *logical*, in a strange kind of way. It had finally explained Devon's powers, as well as offering a reason for why the demons of the Hellhole had pursued him all his life.

For Devon learned he is not just any sorcerer, but a sorcerer of the noble Order of the Nightwing, founded some three thousand years ago by Sargon the Great in the land of Asia Minor. No wizard or warlock has ever had the power of the Nightwing, for their power derives from controlling the portals—Hell-holes, as they're commonly called—between this world and the one below. The demons want to open the portals and set their filthy brethren free, and they see Devon as the key to their success. They know, even by Nightwing standards, that the boy's powers are awesome. He is of the one-hundredth generation since Sargon the Great—long foretold as the mightiest of the mighty.

As he trudges up the path, he thinks of his great lineage. *The time comes soon,* the Voice in Devon's head tells him, *where you will have to live up to such promise.*

A trusted oracle ever since Devon was a child, the Voice can nevertheless sometimes remain stubbornly silent, as it does now, telling him nothing about this Munchkin trudging beside him in the snow. Except—

Not a Munchkin.

Gnome.

Devon has no idea what the Voice means—or what a gnome is—but he figures he ought to inquire about this man's business at Ravenscliff. The house has few visitors, and those who *have* dropped by haven't always been of this world.

"I'm Devon March," he says. "What's your name?"

"Bjorn Forkbeard, at your command, my good sir. Reporting for duty at the great house of Ravenscliff."

"Reporting for duty?" Devon stops walking. "What do you mean?"

"Why, I've been hired as the estate's new caretaker. I understand your last one met a rather untimely demise."

That's one way of putting it. The last caretaker, Simon Gooch, had fallen to his death from the tower of Ravenscliff after trying to kill Devon and unleash the demons from the Hellhole. Devon still wakes up with nightmares remembering what Simon did, reliving in his dreams that terrifying night on the roof of the tower. Was it really such a short time ago? It seemed *forever,* now that peace and quiet had settled over Ravenscliff and the things from the Hellhole had ceased their offensives. He's known Mrs. Crandall has been considering hiring someone to take Simon's place, but he wasn't aware she'd made a decision. Wasn't that just like her? Always so secretive and mysterious.

"Well," Devon says, resuming his stride, "welcome, then."

He grins to himself, recalling his own welcome to the great house just three and a half months ago, if welcome it could be called. The villagers had tried to warn him away, filling his head with the legends of Ravenscliff and its ghosts—legends he quickly found to be true, even if Mrs. Crandall tried her best to deny the great house's legacy of sorcery.

Now it's Devon's turn to greet a newcomer, and he decides to use the same words that had been offered him.

"You know," he says to Bjorn Forkbeard, "all you'll find here are ghosts."

"Oh, surely, surely," the little man says. "Why else do you think I have come?"

They've reached the front door. Overhead, perched within a gargoyle's mouth to find sanctuary from the snow, several ravens flutter their wings.

DEVON, I'm so glad you're back. I was looking for you and—"

Cecily Crandall, having heard them come in, stops in the doorway between the parlor and the foyer. Her mouth opens but her words fade away as she looks at the little man at Devon's side.

"My, my," Bjorn Forkbeard is saying, his eyes taking in the sight of the foyer, the grand staircase, the dozens of candles flickering everywhere. "It is more than I could have possibly imagined. Long have I heard the tales of this place. To think I, Bjorn Forkbeard, should ever stand in the house built by the great Horatio Muir!"

"Um, Cecily," Devon says, hanging up his coat, "this is the new caretaker."

"Ah," says Bjorn. "You must be Miss Cecily. Your mother told me all about you."

"Funny," Cecily says, approaching warily. "She didn't mention a word to me about *you*."

"May I see the parlor? I've heard so much—" He glances beyond the open doors. "Ah! Horatio Muir's collection!"

Bjorn hurries ahead to gaze into the parlor. Even from here, Horatio's "trinkets"—as Mrs. Crandall calls them—are apparent among the bookshelves: shrunken heads, skulls, crystal balls. At the far end of the room, beside the French doors leading out to the terrace over the rocky cliffs, stands a suit of armor.

"Devon," Cecily whispers, leaning close, "what's going on? I mean, why would Mother hire a *dwarf* as a caretaker? There's an awful lot of heavy work around here."

Not dwarf, the Voice tells him again. *Gnome.*

"He looks strong enough. Check out those arms."

Indeed, now that he's removed his coat, Bjorn Forkbeard has revealed surprisingly muscled arms and powerful shoulders. He's gazing raptly at the sights of the parlor, making little sounds of wonder.

"You seem to know a lot about this house and this family," Devon says, walking up behind him. "I suppose that's why Mrs. Crandall hired you."

"That is *not* the reason I hired him."

They all look around. Mrs. Amanda Muir Crandall is descending the great staircase. "But if he already has a working knowledge of the house," she says, "so much the better."

As usual, she's dressed as if she's planning to attend some affair of state with the president of France, instead of just hanging around the house on a Sunday afternoon waiting out a snowstorm. Her gown of blue satin trails behind her on the stairs, a strand of pearls is knotted at her bosom, and her golden hair is swept up to reveal a long, slender neck.

"Mrs. Crandall, I am deeply honored to meet such a gracious and noble lady." Bjorn gives her a little bow. She approaches to stand over him, looking down. He barely reaches her waist.

"Welcome to Ravenscliff, Mr. Forkbeard," she says grandly. "I see you have already met Cecily and Devon."

"Oh, yes, your daughter has certainly inherited your beauty and charm." Bjorn smiles over at her, then moves his gaze to Devon. "And Mr. March. I think I owe him a great deal."

"Really?" Mrs. Crandall's eyebrow arches at Devon. "And why is that?"

Devon braces himself. Mrs. Crandall has forbidden him to use his powers. She blames him for stirring up the mystical forces that made for such a bad time here a few months ago, when the demons got loose and the Madman tried to destroy them all. Even if Devon explains that he *needed* to use his powers to save Bjorn's life, he knows Mrs. Crandall will still be angry, so insistent is she that sorcery remain banned from Ravenscliff.

But the little man saves him, returning the favor. "Oh, yes. When my car couldn't make it up the driveway, it was Devon who led me here, offering me a warm and gracious welcome on such a cold and blustery day."

Mrs. Crandall gives Devon a look. Then she turns back to Bjorn Forkbeard. "Shall I show you to your room? It's off in the back of the house, behind the kitchen. You can set your bag there and then I'll give you a tour."

"Of course, madam." He turns to Devon and Cecily. "I am sure we will all be great friends."

They nod. The little man follows the elegant lady down the corridor, their shadows casting weird shapes upon the walls in the flickering candlelight.

"I SUPPOSE," Devon says, considering, "hiring a gnome as Ravenscliff's new caretaker shouldn't be so surprising. Nothing that happens here is ever ordinary."

"Gnome? What's a gnome?"

"I'm not sure exactly. But that's what the Voice tells me Bjorn Forkbeard is."

They walk into the parlor. The wind roars through the old house, a harpy trapped among the eaves. Hanging over the mantel, the portrait of Horatio Muir shudders from the assault. "Hang in there, Great Granddad," Cecily calls. "If sorcerers and demons haven't brought down this old mausoleum, I doubt a simple nor'easter will do it."

Devon looks out the glass terrace doors. Even in the cold and wind, a few ravens are out there, perched on the railings, big black birds with proud, shining eyes. A couple of them caw as they sense Devon's approach. He's come to feel a great deal of affection for the birds. When Horatio Muir built this house a hundred years ago, the birds were his constant familiars, and their presence was remarked upon far and wide. But after his descendants were nearly wiped out by the malicious power of the Madman, the Muirs repudiated sorcery, and the ravens abandoned the house for many years. Only when Devon arrived at Ravenscliff did the ravens return.

"The snow's coming down harder now," he reports.

"The first of the season," Cecily exclaims, coming up behind him. "They say the first snow is a magic snow."

There's a twinkle in Devon's eye. "Oh, yeah?"

"Devon." Cecily grins. "What are you thinking?"

He looks out into the swirling snow and concentrates. With his mind he begins to shape the snowflakes, as easily as if he were doing it by hand with fallen snow on the ground. He arranges the flakes into a bird—a raven hovering in the air, made of snow.

"Oh, Devon!" Cecily exclaims. "That is so cool." But then she frowns. "Mother says you're not supposed to do any sorcery. She says it could . . . stir things up again." A look of fear crosses her face, reflected in her large doe eyes.

"Well, she's wrong," Devon says. "I was down in the village today, talking with Rolfe Montaigne, and he said using my powers is a *good* thing. Natural. Part of my heritage."

Cecily looks around to make sure they're alone. "If Mother found out you were seeing Rolfe behind her back, she'd be furious."

"I know. But I *have* to learn more about who and what I am, Cecily. I have to learn more about the Nightwing."

"Have you read more of the books?"

"Yes." He can barely wait to tell her. "*The Book of Enlightenment* is awesome, Cecily. The Nightwing have been around for centuries, and the book tells how they came to be."

It's proven fascinating reading for Devon; some of the book he can even recite from memory. He clears his throat and begins: " 'Once, well before the coming of the Great Ice, the world was inhabited by Creatures of Light and Creatures of Darkness, battling each other for eons for dominion. Their masters were the elemental gods—of fire, of wind, of sea, of earth—omnipotent rulers of nature, neither good nor evil. As the ages passed, and the time of the Creatures faded farther and farther into the dim recesses of time, they came to be known as Angels and Demons.' "

Cecily rolls her eyes. "Yeah, whatever, Devon." She gets impatient with him when he starts sounding too lofty about his Nightwing heritage. "What does that have to do with you, and your powers?"

"It's simple," he explains. "Many wizards and shamans have come in touch with the old elemental Knowledge. But the most powerful have always been the Nightwing, for only the Nightwing have discovered the secret of how to open the Hellholes. And it's been long foretold that the one-hundredth generation—"

"Yes, I *know*, Devon. Rolfe thinks you're the one-hundredth generation since Sargon the Great." She says it kind of sing-songy, as if she's bored by the whole idea, or maybe a little jealous. "You know, I've been doing some thinking about that on my own."

"What do you mean?"

"If *you're* the one-hundredth generation, then *I* must be, too." Cecily smiles. "We're the same age, you and I. *And,* after all, my great-grandfather Horatio Muir was a very powerful Nightwing himself, if Rolfe Montaigne is right. Even Mother can't deny that now."

"Well, you may be right," Devon acknowledges. "You're probably one-hundredth generation from Sargon the Great, too."

But even so, Cecily holds no powers of the kind Devon possesses. In the years before either of them was born, a great tragedy happened at Ravenscliff. The Madman—a Nightwing gone bad—killed Mrs. Crandall's father, Randolph Muir. The Madman kidnapped a young boy, dragging him down the Hellhole, and threatened to destroy the whole family. Afterward, the family repudiated their Nightwing past. Now they attempt to live out their lives as ordinary people—or at least as ordinary as a life at Ravenscliff can be.

The family includes not only Cecily and Mrs. Crandall but Mrs. Crandall's senile, bedridden mother Greta Muir, who never leaves her room in the West Wing. There's also Mrs. Crandall's brother Edward Muir, a playboy wandering the globe whom Devon has never met. Devon has, however, made *quite* the acquaintance of Edward's eight-year-old son, Alexander, who lives at Ravenscliff under the guardianship of his aunt. One could say Devon and Alexander became very close very quickly. After all, it was Devon who plunged into the Hellhole to save Alexander, who'd been taken there by the Madman, back from the grave for yet another assault on Ravenscliff.

Even now, months later, Devon is staggered by the memory. Just thinking of it makes his knees go weak. *The Hellhole . . . the Madman.* He grabs the back of a chair to steady himself.

"You okay?" Cecily asks.

He nods. The wound on his leg, obtained in battle in the Hellhole, tingles just a bit, though it healed several weeks ago.

I went into the Hellhole, he says to himself, as if he still needs convincing. *I went into the Hellhole and made it back out alive.*

And the Madman, Jackson Muir, wayward son of Horatio, had been defeated.

I defeated him.

Cecily's getting impatient. "But what about your *past,* Devon? Has Rolfe made any progress in finding out who your real parents were? And what their connection to this house was?"

Devon sighs. "No, he hasn't."

"Well, what about your father's crystal ring? Have you gotten it to work yet?"

Devon withdraws the ring from his pocket and holds it out in his hand. A gold band with a crystal embedded in front. It had been Ted March's ring—Ted March, who Devon discovered was in truth a Guardian named Thaddeus Underwood. Guardians were charged with training and protecting the Nightwing sorcerers, and they possessed crystals that held great knowledge. But so far, his father's ring has told Devon nothing.

"Rolfe wonders if it's been damaged in some way. It doesn't work the way a Guardian's crystal should."

"Oh, Devon," Cecily says sympathetically, putting her arms around him. "I'm sure you'll find out the truth someday."

They stand quietly gazing out into the snowstorm. Still hovering there is Devon's snow raven, looking in through the glass at them. Beyond it, they can see the tower of Ravenscliff. In the topmost window a light suddenly appears.

Devon laughs. "There's that light again. Ever since I first came here, I've seen that light. But if I tell your mother about it, she denies it."

"Strange, isn't it? She's been forced to admit so much, but not that. She refuses to admit there's a light in the tower—or what she's hiding there." Cecily looks over at Devon. "Do you think she's up there now, showing the new caretaker whatever her secret is?"

Devon considers it. Simon, the old caretaker, had seemed very protective of the tower. Twice Devon had encountered him there. Simon, who had been in league with the Madman and his plan to open the portal of the demons.

"It's possible," Devon replies. "Maybe that's why he was hired."

"Bjorn clearly knows about this family's history of sorcery," Cecily says. "You saw how he admired all of Horatio's trinkets."

Devon nods. Bjorn Forkbeard was certainly no ordinary caretaker. Then again, Ravenscliff was no ordinary house.

The light in the tower disappears.

"What could be up there?" Devon muses out loud. "Whatever it is, it couldn't have anything to do with Jackson Muir. It would have disappeared when he was defeated."

Cecily shrugs. "This house has more secrets than we could probably ever discover."

"Look," Devon says, gesturing toward the French doors and smiling. "My raven's getting bigger."

Indeed, his snowbird has grown fatter, losing much of its shape, as snow has continued to accumulate on top of it. It struggles to keep moving its wings.

Cecily laughs. "Poor little thing. Maybe you ought to turn him into an eagle or something."

"What are you two looking at?"

They both spin around in surprise. It's Mrs.

Crandall, who's returned to the parlor. On the terrace behind them, the snow raven suddenly falls with a thud.

"We were—just—just watching the storm," Cecily says.

Her mother glares at her.

She knows we saw the light, Devon thinks.

"Come away from there," she says. "There's a draft."

Mrs. Crandall settles herself into her wingback chair opposite the fireplace, where her face reflects the glow of the fire. She closes her eyes, lacing the fingers of her hands together in front of her. She is beautiful. Despotic, stubborn, eccentric, but Amanda Muir Crandall is undeniably beautiful.

"Devon," she says, "I told Mr. Forkbeard that you would help him retrieve some necessary items from some of the higher shelves in his room. He's waiting for you. Would you attend to him, please?"

He approaches her. "Mrs. Crandall, how much does he know about this house?"

"Only what he needs to know to be an effective caretaker."

"Mother," Cecily says, "it's clear he knows about Horatio Muir and the sorcery. Don't deny it. You hired him because he has some experience with magic."

"Cecily, your imagination is running away with you."

"My imagination! You hired a dwarf with the name Bjorn Forkbeard! I don't need any more imagination than that!"

"Devon," Mrs. Crandall says, ignoring her daughter, "he's waiting for you."

Devon and Cecily exchange exasperated looks.

"And Cecily, will you please go up to Alexander's room and bring him down here? I want him to meet Mr. Forkbeard."

"Yes, Mother," Cecily says.

The mistress of the great house of Ravenscliff looks out the doors to the terrace. "The storm seems to be building," she says quietly. "I expect the lights will go out soon."

T HEY DO, only minutes after she's made the prediction. Power outages are frequent here on the isolated rocky point. The electricity sputters a few times, then fades out completely, leaving the house in that soft, blue late-afternoon light so peculiar to winter. If not for the candles kept perpetually lit throughout the parlor and foyer, the shadows that fall over the house would have been even darker and lengthier. But as it is, Devon and Cecily, parting in the corridor that leads to the kitchen, see well enough to give each other a quick kiss.

They are both fourteen years old, both in the throes of heady first love. At times Devon still thinks it's weird to find himself holding hands with a girl, to steal a kiss when no one is looking—especially not her imperious mother. But other times, it's different. He's knocked over by his emotions for her, startled by their intensity, and confused by their unpredictability.

If only Dad were still alive, Devon thinks as he turns toward the door. He could've talked to his father about these feelings. Devon had been able to talk to his father about anything.

Since coming here, he's learned to find his own way. There's been no one to guide him, no one to offer any advice. Except for Rolfe Montaigne, who was himself the son of a Guardian and who has all the Nightwing books—but Rolfe is the first to admit he doesn't have all the answers.

"Cecily," Devon calls back into the foyer, "tell Alexander no tricks on Bjorn."

Devon remembers all too well the boy's antics upon his own arrival at Ravenscliff. Neglected by his father, deprived of his mother's care at an early age, Alexander is a troubled boy, with a mind that can be pretty devious. But since their time together in the Hellhole, Alexander and Devon have forged a much stronger bond. The younger boy now considers Devon his only true friend in the dark old house.

"You know Alexander never listens to a word I tell him," Cecily calls down from the stairs. "In fact, he'll do just the opposite of what I say. I suggest *you* bring it up with him." On the landing above, her look changes to one of concern for Devon. "Be careful in there with that dwarf, okay?"

"*Gnome*, Cecily. Not dwarf."

"Whatever. What else does that Voice thing have to say about him?"

"Nothing," Devon says with disappointment. "But I'm sure if Bjorn Forkbeard meant me any harm, the Voice would warn me."

"Still. Be careful." She shivers a little, then turns away from the banister.

Devon heads through the kitchen toward Bjorn's room. This was once Simon's lair, and the place still repels Devon. Even months after Simon's death, some of his stench still remains.

But as Devon turns the corner he's pleased to see that the fragrance of the place has changed. It's sweet, crisp. Devon raps on the door and Bjorn is quick to open it. Behind him burns a tall, fat candle. A simple bed, a spartan bureau, and Bjorn's purple sack on the floor.

"What's that smell?" Devon asks.

"Sage," the gnome tells him. "Aromatherapy to cure whatever ails a place."

Devon smiles. "And this room sure was ailing."

"I always burn a little sage whenever I go to a new place. Drives out the old spirits."

"Is that all it takes? Wish I'd known that *my* first night at Ravenscliff. Would've saved me a lot of grief."

Bjorn nods. "You've seen your share of them, then. The ghosts."

Devon frowns. "Look, there's one thing you need to understand if you're going to make it here. You can't talk about the ghosts around Mrs. Crandall. Anything out of the ordinary she'll deny."

"But why should she? The granddaughter of Horatio Muir is hardly an ordinary woman."

"Try telling that to her. Even with everything that's happened in this house, she won't let anyone talk about it. She's a very stubborn lady."

"Well, I'm sure she has her reasons." Bjorn pulls open his closet door and points up to the shelves inside. "Will you be so kind as to fetch those things for me? Just a few items I'll be needing."

Devon sees bubble bath and shoe polish, bags of microwave popcorn and boxes of raisins, shaving cream and nail clippers—Simon's things. Devon shudders.

"Why don't we just drive into the village tomorrow and get you some stuff of your own?" Devon asks. "You ought to toss this junk."

"Waste not, want not."

"Suit yourself."

Bjorn examines the items as Devon places them on the bed. He rips open the box of raisins and knocks back a handful, but when he comes to the nail clippers he pushes them aside. "Won't be needing these."

For the first time Devon notices the little man's fingernails are long, pointed, and very thick. Smiling, the boy shuts the closet door. "Won't it be difficult for you to do your chores without breaking one of those?"

"You mean my nails? Oh, no, not at all. They're harder than stone, my boy. They don't break."

Devon sits down on the bed so that he's eye level with the little man. "Okay, so what's your story? Tell me what exactly a *gnome* is."

Bjorn Forkbeard grins. "Oh, you *are* the clever one. I knew it from the moment you saved poor old Bessie and me from a nasty spill over the side of that cliff. Are you some kind of enchanter?"

"I asked you first."

"Well," Bjorn says, "I was born in the village of Lokka, far in the north of Finland. My parents worked in a mine deep in the earth. I didn't see the light of day until I was seven years old."

"And how old are you now?"

"Would you believe it if I told you six hundred and sixty-two?"

"I would." Devon holds his gaze. "You're a Guardian, aren't you?"

"Oh, I wish I were. Guardianship is a noble heritage. But I'm just a caretaker." Bjorn narrows his blue eyes at Devon. "But tell me, my boy. What do you know about Guardians?"

"My father was one. Well, my adopted father was. I don't know much about my real parents."

"From what I've seen, they must have been very powerful sorcerers."

Devon nods. "Nightwing."

"Of course, if you are living in the house of the great Horatio Muir."

Devon looks around suddenly, cautious of the open door. "Mrs. Crandall would probably fire you if she caught you talking about all this with me. Fire you and lock me up in my room." He crosses his arms over his chest. "But if you've got answers, I'll take that chance."

"Me? I know nothing of your parents, my boy."

"I want to know what Mrs. Crandall showed you in the tower. Don't lie to me. I know she took you up there. I saw the lights."

"Oh, there is no reason to lie. She did indeed take me up there as part of the tour. And she told me no one else was ever to be allowed in the place."

"You saw nothing? Nothing unusual there?" Devon

leans in. "No clue that someone may have been *living* there?"

A queer little grin crosses the gnome's face. "What makes you think someone lives in the tower?"

"I've seen a woman there. Once I heard her calling my name."

"Ah, but Ravenscliff is the home of many ghosts. You've said as much."

Devon sighs. "It wasn't Emily Muir or any of the other ghosts that haunt this house. I've heard sobbing, too. Sobbing that was *human*."

"Then maybe Mrs. Crandall's mother? I met her only briefly on my tour. Poor confused lady. Perhaps she wandered . . ."

Devon can see he's getting nowhere. Either Bjorn is colluding with Mrs. Crandall or he's as clueless as Devon. He decides to change course. "Okay, another question, then," Devon says. "You know about the Nightwing. You know about this house's history of sorcery. Was that why Mrs. Crandall hired you?"

"But of course it is, my boy. Mrs. Crandall is a smart woman. Do you think she would hire just any caretaker to work here? Some ignorant soul oblivious to the workings of worlds other than our own? Oh no, that would never do. She searched high and low for me, I can tell you that much. She needed someone who knew about these things, someone who would not be frightened away."

Devon nods. "So are you really six hundred and sixty-two?"

Bjorn chuckles. "You believe whatever you want. That's the key, Devon. You have the power." He taps his skull. "Up here. You can make things happen."

"What do you mean?" Devon asks cautiously.

"If you want to find out what's in that tower, a locked door shouldn't stop you."

"You'd think not. But sometimes my powers won't work. I can prevent cars from falling over cliffs with my mind but I can't get the tower door to open. Sometimes I can even will myself to disappear and then reappear someplace else, but I can't do that with the tower. Believe me, I've tried."

"Then there's got to be another way." The little man looks around the room. Suddenly he points. "Through that door, for example."

"Uh, Bjorn. That's the door to your bathroom."

The little man shrugs. "So don't believe me. I just thought you would know there are other ways into the tower than those that are obvious." He sighs and moves to the door. "Well, thank you for your help, Devon. I must hurry now to begin my first task here as care-taker. That would be shoveling the front walk of all this snow. Then I'll have to do something about poor old Bessie stuck in the driveway."

Bjorn Forkbeard hurries out of his room, through the kitchen and back into the foyer. Devon can hear him putting on his coat and heading outside. For a moment he can hear the wind rushing into the house when Bjorn opens the door.

Devon starts to leave, then stops.

I just thought you would know there are other ways into the tower than those that are obvious.

He looks across the room.

Through that door, for example.

"That's ridiculous," Devon says softly to himself. "I know what's behind that door. It's just a bathroom. I helped clean it out after Simon died."

You can make things happen.

Devon approaches the door and places his hand on the doorknob. It's hot. That's never a good sign. He swallows, then turns the knob and opens the door.

He gasps.

It's not a bathroom at all—but a dark set of stairs.

There are other ways into the tower than those that are obvious.

"Could it be true?" Devon wonders aloud. "Could this lead me to the tower?"

But the stairs head down, not up.

You can make things happen.

Descending the first few steps, he senses no danger. The Voice is stubbornly silent. He takes a couple more steps, stops and listens, then takes a few steps more.

Only then does he see the yellow eyes at the bottom of the stairs, staring up at him.

Only then does he feel the sudden gust of heat.

Only then does he hear the scuttling and muttering of demons in the dark.

Only then does he realize—too late—

"It's a Hellhole!"

T W O

THE TOWER ROOM

SOMETHING LEATHERY brushes by his face. Devon pushes it away, trying to get his bearings. Below, an image is taking shape. And sounds. Voices. It's a crowd. He's no longer inside the house, but outside somewhere. Coming down the steps of a building into a square, and hundreds of people are gathering. People dressed in strange clothes.

"Burn the witch!" they're shouting. "Burn the Apostate!"

Devon's blood turns to ice with fear.

Apostate—that's what they called Jackson Muir, the Madman. He was a renegade Nightwing, shunned by his brethren for his evil ways. Could he be here, waiting for Devon in the Hellhole?

No way does Devon want to run into Jackson Muir again. The Madman would do everything in his power to make sure Devon never got out of the Hellhole again.

"Come," a man is suddenly saying to him, reaching a gnarled old hand out to Devon to lead him off the steps. The man is tall and hooded, in a long brown cassock. He looks like a monk, except he has a long white beard.

If I leave these steps, I'm trapped here, Devon tells himself, not sure if it's the Voice telling him this or just his own intuition.

"Come, boy," the hooded man urges him again, crooking a long bony finger. "Come with me."

"No!" Devon cries.

He turns on the steps. He tries to climb back up, but it's tremendously difficult, each step a willful defiance of the most powerful gravity Devon has ever encountered. It's like swimming against the tide, only a hundred times more strenuous. Devon literally grips his thigh and forcibly lifts his leg to move up one step, then another.

Behind him the sounds of the crowd fade away. He is back on the dark staircase and he can see the door leading into Bjorn's room.

He falls against it. It opens. He is indeed back in Ravenscliff, out of breath.

"Well, there you are," Cecily says, coming around the corner. "What were you doing in Bjorn's bathroom?"

He smirks at her, unable to resist a little sarcasm. "When you gotta go, you gotta go."

She looks at his face. "Devon, you're as white as a—"

"That was a *Hellhole,* Cecily!" Devon turns, pointing back through the door into what appears to be an ordinary bathroom again. "Bjorn tricked me into going into a Hellhole."

"Are you *sure,* Devon? I thought the only way into the Hellhole was through that bolted door in the East Wing."

Devon frowns. He had thought so too, but now he's not so sure. "Maybe gnomes can do some sort of magic. Maybe they can—"

"Shh, my mother's coming."

Mrs. Crandall appears in the doorway. "What are you two doing in here?"

"I was helping Bjorn like you asked," Devon tells her.

Her eyes survey the room, coming to rest on the bathroom door. "And did you get him what he needed?"

"Yes."

She looks sharply at Devon. "So why are you still here?"

Devon gives her a small grin. "Just making sure his bathroom was tidy."

Mrs. Crandall eyes him coldly. "Come away from here. Both of you."

She turns quickly, the satin fabric of her gown rustling down the corridor.

"She *knows*," Devon says. "She sent me here for a reason. She *wanted* me to go into that Hellhole. She and Bjorn planned it!"

"Devon! My mother may be weird, but she would never try to harm you!"

Devon doesn't answer. He just follows Cecily out of the room in silence.

He broods over the experience for the rest of the day. How insistent Mrs. Crandall had been that he go help Bjorn. *He's waiting for you,* she had said, just before sending Cecily upstairs, out of harm's way.

I know too much, Devon tells himself. *That's why she wants to get rid of me. After Dad sent me here to live, she tried to keep the secret of my Nightwing past from me. But now that I've discovered it, I represent a danger to her. She knows I have the powers that she and her family repudiated. Every day she looks out the windows and sees that the ravens—the signs of Horatio Muir's sorcery—have returned to the house because of me!*

Suddenly the truth seems clear to Devon.

Mrs. Crandall fears my powers will cause the Madman to return.

Devon knows that's always been her greatest fear.

The Madman killed her father, drove her mother insane, stole little Frankie Underwood into the Hellhole. She is terrified that he will come back for her and her family. He nearly succeeded last time with Alexander.

So she'll sacrifice me, if need be.

At one point he imagined Mrs. Crandall might be his mother. He laughs bitterly at the thought. At the time it had seemed logical: She has Nightwing blood, and Dad *did* send him here to live with her. For a time, Devon worried that such a situation would make Cecily his sister—a repulsive thought, given his budding romantic feelings for her—but the idea has lately come to seem increasingly absurd, especially after this episode. What mother would knowingly send her son into a Hellhole?

In the weeks since Devon had defeated Jackson Muir, he had begun to feel some degree of safety at Ravenscliff. He had even, for the first time since his father died, begun to feel a sense of home. There were Cecily, Rolfe, and the good friends he had made at school—D.J., Ana, Marcus. He and Alexander had become real buds, too, despite their initial hostility, and Devon had actually started to feel as if he had a family. After all the terrors of his first weeks at Ravenscliff, he had finally achieved a sense of security.

Not anymore. With the arrival of the gnome and

Mrs. Crandall's apparent treachery, Devon decides he will once again have to be on constant alert.

THE SNOWSTORM leaves two feet on the ground, but by the next morning the roads are all plowed. "Isn't that always the way?" Cecily asks. "A blizzard on the weekend but all clear by Monday. No day off from school."

D.J. picks them up in his car, an old red Camaro named Flo. He's a year ahead of Devon and Cecily in school, so he's got his license. D.J. is seen by most people as a bit of a rebel, with his black clothes and piercings, one through his nose and one through his chin.

"Hey, who's got the old Caddy?" he asks, noting Bjorn's car, now safely parked outside the garage.

"It's our new caretaker," Cecily tells him, climbing into the backseat while Devon slips in up front. "He's a dwarf."

"Gnome," Devon reminds her. "And he's six hundred and sixty-two."

"Get out," D.J. says.

"That's what he claims. He spent his childhood in a mine. He's got long fingernails hard as stone. Guess he used them for digging up diamonds or whatever."

D.J. shakes his head. "The weirdos never quit showing up at that house, do they, dude?"

Devon laughs. His friends went through the horrors of the past months with him, watching in terror as he plunged into the Hellhole to save Alexander. He knows he can trust them. Now that he's with his friends, Devon can relax and enjoy the kind of safety he no longer feels at Ravenscliff.

At school, Ana and Marcus are waiting for them. Marcus is neatly dressed as always, with a button-down oxford tucked smoothly into khakis. Ana's skirt is daringly short, even on such a cold day, and her boots are red vinyl up to the knee. She and Cecily are constantly in competition with each other, though close friends and confidantes of each other's secrets. To most of the kids at school each of the four is a bit of an outsider: D.J. because he dresses to shock and listens to thirty-year-old rock and roll; Marcus because he's the only openly gay kid in the entire school; Ana because she refuses to hang out with the cheerleaders, even though she's one of them; and Cecily because she lives at Ravenscliff, the legends of which everyone has heard.

Devon, on the other hand, is a bit of an enigma. He could've hung out with anyone he chose, especially after a couple dozen witnesses watched him beat off a demon at Gio's Pizza with one hand a few months back. Of course, only Devon knew it was a demon; the kids just thought it was some punk from the next village making trouble. A group of football players had jumped up from their table and roundly clapped Devon on the back. Even the upperclassmen hailed him in the hallways in the days that followed. But Devon, while friendly to everybody, chose to stick with Cecily and D.J. and Marcus and Ana. Now most of the kids at the school eye him a bit suspiciously, not quite sure just what his story is.

The five friends make an odd group, that's for sure. But they've become fiercely loyal to each other since living through the terrors of the Madman. During one fight with the demons from the Hellhole, Devon was even able to share his powers with his friends, and for a brief moment they all had the powers of the Nightwing. Devon will never forget how awesomely Cecily kicked demon-butt. It was like she was born to it. She *was*, actually. Like him, it's in her blood.

"Guess what?" Devon whispers to the group as they gather around his locker before class. "I landed in a Hellhole again last night."

"Oh my God!" Ana cries. "You've *got* to move out of there, Devon. Come stay at my house. My parents won't mind."

"Retract your claws, Ana," Cecily interjects. "Devon's not going anywhere, he can take care of himself."

D.J.'s scratching his head. "Dude, I thought you

learned your lesson last time. What made you go down one of those things again?"

"The new caretaker tricked me," Devon says. "He said it was a way into the tower."

"Are you sure?" Marcus asks. "I thought there was only one way into the Hellhole that exists under Ravenscliff, and that's in the East Wing."

Devon shrugs. "That's what I thought, too."

He looks over at Marcus. Once again, he sees a red pentagram hovering over his friend's face, but it disappears in seconds. It's been weeks since he last saw the pentagram on Marcus's face, and he still has no idea what it means. He worries that Marcus might be in danger. He'll have to talk to him about it when they're alone.

"I need to get over to Rolfe Montaigne's after class," Devon tells them. "I've got to read through some more of the Nightwing books. D.J., will you drop me there?"

The bell signaling the first class of the day sounds.

"You got it, my man," D.J. says, giving him a quick salute as he saunters off down the hall.

Devon watches Marcus disappear around a corner, then trudges off toward history class.

DEVON MARCH," Mr. Weatherby is asking, "maybe you can tell me why King Henry the

Eighth was so insecure on his throne in the early years of his reign."

Oh, great. He would have to call on me. With all that happened last night, Devon had given his reading assignment only a cursory glance.

"Well, um, because his father had, uh, usurped the throne," he stammers.

"Yes. Go on."

"And there were . . . other guys who had more royal blood than Henry."

"Precisely."

Devon breathes a sigh of relief.

"Which is why," Mr. Weatherby explains, turning to the class, "Henry was so desperate for a son and heir, to ensure the continuation of his dynasty. There were many people early in his reign who tried to position themselves as more rightful rulers. But the king . . ."

Mr. Weatherby drones on. Devon likes history, and especially English history, with its knights and kings and castles and high Celtic priests. He suspects his interests in these areas may have something to do with his Nightwing heritage. But today his mind is preoccupied with what he needs to talk about with Rolfe. Devon thanks God for Rolfe. He's the one hope Devon has for finally understanding his powers and the Hellholes.

But even Rolfe can only do so much. Rolfe Montaigne's father was a Guardian, trained in the special skills of teaching and protecting the sorcerers of the Nightwing. Rolfe had been in line to become a Guardian himself, but his father had been killed when Rolfe was just a young boy, one more victim of the Madman, Jackson Muir.

You'd think that would have been enough to set up some serious bonding between Rolfe and the Muirs, but instead Edward Muir had grown up envious of his father's preference for the stronger, swifter Rolfe. And the young Amanda Muir, before she married Mr. Crandall, had fallen in love with Rolfe, only to turn savagely on him when she caught him with another girl. So bitter was she, Devon has discovered, that she told the police Rolfe had been behind the wheel—*drunk*—when his car plunged over the cliff into the ocean several years ago. Rolfe survived, but two others, including the servant girl he'd been seeing, perished. Because of Amanda's story, Rolfe spent five years in prison for manslaughter.

Now Rolfe's entire being burns with a desire for revenge against the Muir family. If Mrs. Crandall knew Devon had been spending so much time with him, she'd come down hard on him.

Maybe that's why she set me up. Maybe she knows I've been sneaking out to see Rolfe . . .

No matter what his past—manslaughter, prison—

Rolfe has become a hero to Devon. Devon firmly believes Rolfe wasn't behind the wheel that night. The only problem is, Rolfe can't say for sure, because he *was,* in fact, drunk. He says he's haunted by the deaths of the two people in his car. They were both servants at Ravenscliff, a boy and a girl. The girl, Clarissa, has a gravestone out in the cliffside cemetery. Although her body was washed out to sea, somebody evidently thought enough of her to erect a memorial. Rolfe visits her grave, he says, torn with guilt over their affair and her death.

At one point Devon thought Clarissa might have had something to do with the Madman: He could have sworn he saw the ghost of the Madman's wife, Emily Muir, sobbing over Clarissa's grave. But Rolfe says Clarissa was just a servant girl, born long after Jackson Muir was dead. So Devon's put that theory aside—for now.

The rest of the Muir family history is just as troubled, and Devon wonders what it has to do with his own origins. Amanda Muir went on to marry a man she didn't love, who left her soon after Cecily's birth. Devon figures that's another reason to rule her out as his mother. He and Cecily are both fourteen, and there just isn't enough time between Devon's birthday and hers to allow for another birth. Unless, of course, the birthday Dad always told him was his is wrong. There's no birth certificate, after all.

Devon shudders. Whenever he starts thinking about his real parents, he becomes confused and upset. It can't be Mrs. Crandall; it just *can't* be! He likes Cecily too much to learn that she's his sister. That would just warp his mind. He consoles himself by remembering that they look nothing alike. Both Cecily and her mother are fair-skinned, and Cecily has shiny red hair. Devon is dark, almost olive, with deep brown eyes and nearly black hair.

Although Rolfe has been unable to solve the mystery of Devon's parentage, he *does* have his father's library of books and crystals, all of which have assisted Devon in assembling pieces of his Nightwing heritage. Devon's father—his adoptive father—had lived on the grounds of Ravenscliff before Devon was born. Rolfe knew Dad, and had loved him. That fact—even more than the books and the crystals—makes Devon feel a special connection to Rolfe.

"I know my roots are here," Devon says after classes let out for the day. The five friends are heading toward D.J.'s car. "I just *know* it."

"Well, there's that stone out in the cemetery with the name Devon," Cecily says as she slips into the backseat.

"Yeah, there really ought to be a record at the town

hall about who's buried under there," says Marcus, who's shoved in between Cecily and Ana.

"We looked," Devon tells him as he slides into the front seat beside D.J. and pulls the door shut. "The only person with the last name Devon in the Misery Point vital records was a lady who died long before I was born. So she couldn't be my mother."

"You know, bro, I think maybe you just dropped out of the sky," D.J. says, starting the car and squealing out of the parking lot.

"Hey, I have a thought," Ana offers.

"This ought to be good," Cecily says.

Ana ignores her. "Maybe the Nightwing don't have babies like regular people. Maybe they hatch out of eggs or something."

Cecily scowls. "Ana, you totally got the wrong genes. Instead of a brunette, you should definitely have been born a blonde."

"Hey," Ana says, pouting. "It's not so weird to imagine. Look at the ravens those Nightwingers always have around them. *They* come out of eggs."

"Well, I'm Nightwing, too," Cecily says. "Everybody seems to forget that. I'm just as much a Nightwing as Devon. And I was certainly *not* hatched out of any egg."

"But you got gypped with the power thing, Cess,"

D.J. says. "With your mom and uncle renouncing their heritage and everything."

She just snorts. "Maybe someday I'll get my rightful powers back. They're my birthright, after all."

"Consider it a blessing, Cecily," Devon says, and he's being serious. "At least you didn't grow up with the monsters in your closet being real."

They talk about other things for a while: How Jessica Milardo is breaking up with her boyfriend and the fact that Mr. Weatherby always wears shirts with pit stains. "It's so gross," Ana complains. "Like a fungus or something."

Devon laughs. He looks out the window as they head toward Misery Point. *The time comes soon,* the Voice tells him again, *when you will need to live up to the promise of your heritage.*

They've reached Fibber McGee's, the restaurant Rolfe owns on the craggy point. It's a very popular spot, drawing diners from as far away as New York and Boston. It's given the Muirs' restaurants a real run for their money, which was precisely the strategy Rolfe Montaigne had in mind when he returned to Misery Point after his five years in prison. Fibber McGee's is one of the few places open all year; most of the village's other establishments shut down for the winter. In May the population swells with summer residents and tourists. Now the town is mostly a deserted collection of boarded-up white clapboard buildings, braving the fierce Atlantic wind and ice.

"Thanks for the ride," Devon says, hopping out of the car.

"March on, Ghostbuster," D.J. says.

Devon peers into the backseat at Cecily. "If your mother asks, say I stayed after school for some extra help in geometry, and that I'll get a ride with someone else."

She nods in agreement.

"And Marcus," Devon adds, remembering the pentagram, "call me later, okay?"

"What about?"

"Just call me."

"How about *me*?" Ana says, batting her eyelashes ridiculously.

Devon knows Ana has a crush on him; she just won't seem to accept the fact that he and Cecily are an item. "Yeah, sure," he tells her, shrugging. "You can call me too, if you want."

"Not if I get the phone first," Cecily says, elbowing Ana in the ribs.

"Ow!"

They laugh. Devon watches as the Camaro roars off. He knows they're heading back to Gio's for pizza. They'll spend the day like any other group of kids.

Once again Devon resents this fate thrust upon him. Once again he wishes he could just be an ordinary boy.

Not that he isn't intrigued by his Nightwing blood, and not that he doesn't find his powers awesome at times. But he's tired of living in fear and doubt. He wishes he could do normal things, like joining an intramural basketball team after classes. He didn't transfer to this school until October, so it was too late to get on the cross-country team, but in the spring he'd like to try out for junior varsity baseball. And maybe the school play.

But he doubts he'll ever have time for any of that. Instead he's got to head to Rolfe's and pore through ancient texts and hold magic crystals in his hand, while his friends get to hang out and eat pizza.

He's greeted by Roxanne, Rolfe's lady companion. "Well, good afternoon, Devon March," she says, her strange golden eyes taking him in. She is strikingly beautiful, tall with deep brown skin and the twist of a Jamaican accent. "I suspected we might see you today."

"You always seem to know when to expect me, Roxanne."

"You are hungry. I will have the chef whip you up some food."

She's right, he *is* hungry. She must be clairvoyant—ESP or whatever they call it. Rolfe says Roxanne is very wise. An "intuitive," he called her.

"Rolfe is in his office," Roxanne tells him. "You go ahead in."

There are only a few diners in the restaurant, out-of-towners braving the snowy cliffs, probably down from Newport. Devon passes by them, heading toward Rolfe's office. He hopes they'll be able to go back to Rolfe's house, where the books and crystals are kept. At the very least, he hopes Rolfe will have the time to listen to his story.

He knocks lightly on the door. "Come in," Rolfe commands, his deep, resonant voice instantly taking the edge off Devon's anxiety about the day before.

"Devon!" Rolfe greets him warmly. "Back again so soon? Any trouble?"

"Well, maybe," Devon says.

The man rises from behind his desk and gestures for him to sit in an easy chair off to the side. Rolfe is a tall, dark man with piercing, deep-set green eyes. He's in his midthirties, with the swagger of a man who's made his fortune the hard way and totally on his own. Five years in prison didn't break him. They merely steeled his resolve to become as successful as he could when he got out. Just how he made his fortune is a bit mysterious: He's regaled Devon and his friends with talks of oil rigs in Saudi Arabia, hidden jewels in the pyramids of Egypt, strange connections in China and Japan.

All that matters is that Rolfe is here, now, and that he's the only one who can help Devon find any answers.

"Tell me what's happened," Rolfe says, sitting opposite Devon.

"There's a new caretaker at Ravenscliff." He pauses. "A gnome."

"A gnome? What's a gnome?"

"I was hoping you'd know."

Rolfe shakes his head. "Maybe in one of my father's books back home."

"Well, anyway, he's this little man, and he tricked me into going into a Hellhole."

"*What?*"

"I was trying to get information out of him. He knows all about Horatio Muir and the history of the Muir family's sorcery. When I brought up the tower, he suggested I get there through his bathroom."

Rolfe makes a face. "Through his *bathroom*?"

"I know it's weird. Just listen, okay? So I opened the door to his bathroom and there were steps leading down. I saw and heard and felt demons, Rolfe. The heat. It was intense."

Rolfe stands. "Devon, there is only one way into Ravenscliff's Hellhole, and that's through the portal in the East Wing. I am sure of that. And that portal was sealed by your own powers when you came out of there after rescuing Alexander."

"Then what was the staircase I went down? I *saw* things, Rolfe—"

Rolfe eyes him. "What kinds of things?"

"There were people gathered, calling for the burning of the Apostate." Devon holds Rolfe's gaze significantly. "That's what they called Jackson Muir, remember? The *Apostate*. The heretic, the renegade sorcerer. There was a man there, trying to lead me down off the stairs and into the crowd."

Rolfe is shaking his head. "That was no Hellhole. But if it's what I suspect . . ."

"What, Rolfe? What do you suspect?"

"I need my father's books."

"Then let's go, Rolfe. Let's go to your house."

The older man sighs. "My car's in the shop. It's not ready for another hour or so."

Devon knows that hiking to Rolfe's place, poised far off on the precipice of one of Misery Point's steepest cliffs, would take far too long.

"I could try my trick," Devon offers. "But it doesn't always work."

"I suspect it might this time," Rolfe says, "since you'd be doing it in the pursuit of knowledge. But whether you can take me with you, I don't know."

"Want to try?" Devon asks.

Rolfe nods. He reaches over and grasps both of Devon's hands.

The boy closes his eyes and thinks of Rolfe's den, its three walls of glass overlooking the white-capped sea, its fourth wall covered from floor to ceiling with books. Books of knowledge. Books of Nightwing history. And when he opens his eyes, he's there, and Rolfe is with him.

"That is so cool," Devon says.

"Yes," Rolfe admits, laughing a little, "it sure is."

He's already approaching his bookshelves, running his hand along the spines. From the skulls wedged in between the books, black eye sockets stare out at Devon, the ancient Knowledge somewhere within.

"Here," Rolfe says, pulling down a book. "An encyclopedia of sorcery, written by the Nightwing Johann the Wise in Holland at the turn of the first millennium. It remains the standard."

He blows the dust off the book and begins flipping through its pages.

"What are you looking for?" Devon asks.

"*Gnome*," Rolfe says. "Ah, here it is." He begins reading: " 'A subterranean creature, responsible for guarding the Nightwing's treasures, be they jewels or knowledge. Clever with potions and remedies. Physically very strong. Can live many hundreds of years. Mostly found in Scandinavia and Russia.' " He holds the book open for Devon to see. "Look, here's a drawing of one."

Devon agrees that the gnome etched there does indeed look like Bjorn Forkbeard, with his powerful shoulders and pointed fingernails.

"He said he was six hundred and sixty-two years old," Devon says. "I guess he wasn't kidding. And he said that he was born in a mine in Finland. This fits, Rolfe."

"Curious that Amanda should hire a creature such as this to be Ravenscliff's caretaker," Rolfe muses. "It's similar to how she kept that scoundrel Simon all those years." He pauses. "Of course, I imagine she couldn't hire just any old caretaker, not for a house like Ravenscliff."

"What do you think she's hiding in the tower, Rolfe? I'm sure that's why she brought Bjorn in—to guard whatever it is, just as Simon guarded it."

"I can't imagine," Rolfe says. "But it must be very important. Perhaps dangerous."

"Do you think it's another Hellhole?"

He considers the idea for a moment, then shakes his head. "No. I remember the great cataclysm that killed my father and Amanda's father, too. There is only one way into the Hellhole, and that's in the East Wing."

"Then what was that staircase in Bjorn's bathroom?"

Rolfe sighs. "The answer to that won't be found in any of these books." Rolfe moves away from the bookcase, looking out over the sea. The waves crash against the rocks below with a ferocity that always seems to make him melancholy. Devon suspects whenever Rolfe looks down at the rocks he thinks of the two young people killed there, in his car, their bodies washed out to sea. Even if he wasn't driving, he had been drunk—and Devon doesn't think Rolfe will ever fully absolve himself of responsibility for their deaths.

The boy comes up and places his hand on his friend's back. "Rolfe, what are you thinking about?"

"About all the secrets, all the knowledge, that was lost when the Madman took the lives of my father and Mr. Muir." He turns around to look at Devon. "Information you need now and answers I can't give you. There was so much tragedy after that cataclysm. None of us were ever happy again."

"You would've made a great Guardian, I'm sure."

Rolfe eyes him sadly. "You think? Even though you know what I did?"

"It wasn't your fault, Rolfe. You weren't driving."

"Amanda says I was."

"She lied. She was angry at you and wanted revenge."

A small smile creeps across Rolfe's face. "Yes, as I want revenge against her now. I'll get it too, Devon. I'll drive them out of business, and you can come live with me."

Devon struggles with Rolfe's need for revenge. He can understand his desire to pay back Mrs. Crandall for her lies, but Devon wouldn't want any harm to come to Cecily or Alexander. Driving the Muirs out of business would no doubt affect them, too. As ever when Rolfe starts in about all this stuff, Devon decides to change the subject.

"So tell me about the staircase, Rolfe. What do you think it was, if not a Hellhole?"

Rolfe sighs. "I remember something—something which fascinated me as a boy."

"What was that?"

"I remember stories about how Horatio Muir built a Stairway Into Time. It was a magical staircase that appeared and reappeared in various places throughout the house. It was a stunning achievement of Horatio's master sorcery. It allowed him to go back through time to consult with the great Nightwing of the past. It could also take him into the future."

"Awesome," Devon breathes.

"But when sorcery was repudiated at Ravenscliff, the Stairway Into Time was presumably lost forever. But if what you say is true, I suspect it's back. *You've* allowed it to exist again, Devon, because you are a sorcerer with all your powers intact."

"So it wasn't a Hellhole . . . it was a *staircase through time*."

"That's my guess," Rolfe says. He looks back out at the sea. "But I don't know whether Bjorn knew you would manifest it or whether there was anything specific he wanted you to learn from it."

Devon considers something. "So do you think I was foolish in thinking Mrs. Crandall wanted to kill me?"

"Devon, my friend," Rolfe says, resting his hands on the young man's shoulders. "I'd put nothing past that woman. I advise you to remain on your guard."

ONCE MORE Devon is able to will himself and Rolfe back to the restaurant, where he wolfs down the chicken salad sandwich and French fries Roxanne brings in to him. "One other thing," he asks Rolfe between bites. "Have you figured out why I can't get my father's ring to work?"

Ted March had left behind a crystal ring. Every Guardian holds a crystal that contains knowledge needed by the Nightwing. Devon had learned a good deal from holding the crystal of Rolfe's father in his hands—and had had some terrifying visions as well. But his own father's ring has proven useless.

"No, I'm sorry, Devon," Rolfe tells him. "Possibly it

was damaged in some way. Or maybe it's holding back for some reason. I'll keep reading up on the crystals."

Outside it's gotten dark and a sharp cold wind blows in off the harbor. Devon's tired and doesn't feel like making the long hike back up to Ravenscliff. He tries to will himself there, but as ever in cases like this, his sorcery fails him.

It's not meant to make things easier for no greater purpose, the Voice reminds him. *You know that.*

Yeah, yeah, Devon answers back. *But it sure would be nice once in a while.*

So he makes the long haul up the cliffside staircase, hurrying through the snow-covered cemetery, where the angel with the broken wing marks the gravesite of the Madman. Devon glances quickly at the marble obelisk in the center with the name DEVON etched into it. What does it mean? Is there any connection to him?

Inside the house, he shakes the snow off his boots as eight-year-old Alexander Muir comes bounding down the stairs. "Devon!" he shouts. "You're home!"

"Hey, buddy, what's up?"

"We're putting up the Christmas tree," he calls. "Bjorn chopped one down this afternoon from the woods on the estate. It's a real tall one."

It's nice to see the boy so animated. When Devon had first arrived at Ravenscliff, Alexander had been gloomy and despondent, a sour-faced puck full of malevolent mischief. But he's brightened over the last few weeks, and Cecily gives Devon most of the credit.

"You want to help decorate it?" Alexander asks, tugging at his hand.

Devon gives the boy's hair a tousle. "Sure," he says. "What d'ya think, I'm some old Scrooge?"

It will be Devon's first Christmas without his father. He watches with some sadness as Cecily unpacks the boxes she's lugged up from the basement, boxes filled with ancient glass ornaments. She sets them around the blue spruce standing tall in the parlor. Devon wonders what became of the little ornaments he and his dad had made every year out of pinecones and popcorn, then wrapped carefully and stored in the garage. Dad's lawyer cleared all that stuff out. He probably just threw it away.

"You miss your dad, huh, Devon?"

Devon looks at the young boy. It's as if Alexander can read his mind.

"Yeah," Devon says. "I guess I do."

Alexander hangs a glass icicle on a tree branch, then sits down on the couch next to Devon.

"My father promised he'd come home for Christmas," the boy says, "but Aunt Amanda says we shouldn't expect him."

Devon feels a wave of compassion for Alexander. Here the kid had been trapped in a Hellhole while his father was off living the high life traipsing across the Côte d'Azur. Edward Muir rarely wrote or called to check on his son. An occasional postcard or some expensive gift from some exotic place was all that ever arrived for Alexander. Devon doesn't think the boy has seen his father in nearly a year.

"He promised to take me on a safari when I'm ten," Alexander tells Devon. "He's been on them lots of times. Giraffes and elephants and rhinos—he's seen them all."

And you've seen a lot more, kiddo, Devon thinks. But thankfully, the boy has no memory of his time in the Hellhole.

That night, Devon falls asleep thinking about his father. He has a dream. He can hear his father calling to him through the fog that drifts in over the cliffs from the ocean. Finally he can make out Dad on Devil's Rock, the very edge of the Muir estate, where the land drops two hundred feet to the sea, where the Madman's wife, Emily Muir, plunged to her grisly death.

"Devon," his father is calling. "The tower. The secret is in the tower."

D EVON SITS UP in bed. His father's voice still reverberates in his ears.

"The tower," someone says. "We've got to leave the tower."

Devon realizes the voice is not that of his father. It's coming from far away, a conversation between two people. But why can he hear it so clearly up here, in his bedroom with the door closed? It's as if he's suddenly developed superpowered hearing.

"Just come with me. It will be all right."

"But where? Where are you taking me?"

"Just come along. Trust me. It will be all right."

Devon creeps stealthily out of bed and toward his door. He listens. The voices are gone, but he can hear footsteps now, coming downstairs.

I can hear what's going on in the tower, Devon realizes. *Somehow I'm tuned in and can hear what's happening in there.*

He sneaks out into the corridor. The house is nearly pitch dark. Devon slowly makes his way to the landing that overlooks the foyer and the entrance to the tower. Crouched behind the railing in the dark shadows of the night, he sees the door open and two figures emerge. He can barely make them out, but now he's certain the voice he heard had been Bjorn's. One of the figures is very small. It must be the gnome.

The other figure is sheathed in white. That's all he can discern. He's seen a figure in white in there before, a figure he took to be a woman.

They disappear below the landing into another part of the house. Devon's ability to hear them fades away. If he tries to pursue them, he runs the risk of being discovered. He should just go back to bed. If Mrs. Crandall catches him—

Then he realizes Bjorn left the door to the tower ajar. Devon knows he has to take the chance. He's powerless to open the door when it's locked. This is the opportunity he's been waiting for. He wills himself down to the foyer below. He slips quickly through the shadows into the tower.

He's made it this far before. Weeks ago, he'd snuck in and made it halfway up the curving stone stairwell before Simon assaulted him. But the experience had at least given Devon the knowledge that a door exists three flights up. A door to a room he's convinced holds a secret into his past.

With every breath he's sure someone will catch him. He tries to will himself to simply appear in the room, but he can't. *I have to work for this,* he reasons. *I have to work to find out who I am.*

Having no light, Devon must rely on the weak blue moonglow that comes in through the tower windows. He feels his way, step-by-step, his hands inching up along the wall, his palms detecting cracks in the stonework and the occasional furry spider.

He finally arrives at the door to the tower room.

Once he dreamed of finding the Madman in here. Now, instead, he thinks he will find something else: the secret of who he is. And, crazy as it sounds, the prospect scares him even more than finding Jackson Muir.

As he opens the door he realizes it's just a room. A small, plain, round room with a bed, a bureau, a table, and two chairs. The bed has been stripped and the bureau is empty. Devon looks out the window and can see the terrace off the parlor below. Yes, this is the very window where he's seen the light so many times, where once he saw a woman—a ghost?—who called his name.

There's nothing in the room to indicate who it was that Bjorn just whisked away. Devon feels some disappointment settling in, then notices something on the floor. He stoops down to pick it up. In the dim moonlight he sees it's a doll. A naked, pink plastic baby doll—whose head suddenly falls off its body. A gigantic brown spider crawls out onto Devon's hand.

That's when the hideous laughter fills the room.

THREE

———◆———

A HOMECOMING

DEVON DROPS THE DOLL and shakes the spider off his hand. The laughter continues— not laughter he has heard before, not the laughter of the Madman, but rather, from the sound of it, the laughter of a Madwoman. It is high and shrill and cruel.

He steels himself. "Show me your face," he commands.

"My face?" comes a voice as the laughter subsides. "You dare to look upon my face?"

"Yes, I dare."

"Foolish boy. Once before you looked upon my face. Oh, yes. I remember you. Watching with your bright young eyes . . ."

"Who are you?" Devon demands again.

"Are you accustomed to talking to yourself in the middle of the night?"

But this is a new voice. Devon turns. Bjorn Fork-beard stands in the doorway, smiling.

He runs his little hands together. "Which ghosts are you communicating with, my boy?"

Devon says nothing. The gnome approaches him, smiling in apparent interest.

"Poor old Emily Muir, perhaps? I read about her just tonight in the family history book. How she jumped to her death from Devil's Rock—"

"I'm not sure *who* I was talking to," Devon tells him, "but it was no one as kind and gentle as Emily Muir, I can tell you that."

"Then who?"

Devon scowls at him. "Why don't you tell me?"

"But how would I know?"

Devon draws himself to his full height over the gnome. "I want to know who you just took out of this room."

Bjorn's face registers confusion in the moonlight. "I don't know what you're talking about, my young Nightwing child. I simply heard all this shouting up here and came to investigate."

"Don't lie to me, Bjorn. I saw you with someone, someone you brought out of the tower. I can see now that you're hiding things from me, just as Simon did. Who are you in league with, Bjorn? Tell me, because I'll find out."

Bjorn gives him a stricken look. "My boy, I owe you my life. I'm not working against you. Believe me."

"Then why not tell me who's been living in this room."

The gnome smiles sadly. "I can't tell you things I don't know."

"Then tell me what spirit haunts the tower? Whose laughter did I hear? Who is the woman who spoke to me? She said she'd seen me before. Who is it, Bjorn?"

The gnome shudders, looking around. "I truly do not know, my young friend. But if there's a malevolent ghost in this room, we had best leave. Quickly."

Devon sighs, knowing he'll get no more out of Bjorn. And suddenly he does feel the heat in the room rising. There is indeed a hostile entity here—one that he is sure he will meet again.

As they are heading out of the room, Devon stops and picks up the headless doll. "Who did this belong to? Do you know that much at least?"

Bjorn gazes at it with sad eyes. "Some child from Ravenscliff's past, I imagine. Just leave it where you found it, Devon. Best not disturb the room further."

Devon complies. They head back down the stairs. Bjorn secures the door with his key and advises Devon to say nothing of this episode to Mrs. Crandall. "I don't think she'd be very pleased with either of us," Bjorn says. It's the first thing the gnome has said that Devon believes.

WHEN DEVON was a boy, the Christmas season was a time of much joy and wonder for him. His father always made the most of it, with wreaths on the doors and candles in the windows. They'd hike up into the woods near their home in Coles Junction, New York, and chop down a tall pine, bringing it home to decorate with strings of popcorn and those big old-fashioned Christmas bulbs. Dad would make a pot of his cinnamon brew, as he called it, a secret concoction of various syrups and herbs that all the kids in the neighborhood loved. Devon remembers how his friends Tommy and Suze loved nothing more than hanging out at Devon's house at Christmastime, with all its lights and scents. Dad would be smoking his corncob pipe, just like Santa Claus.

In truth, Dad kind of looked like Santa Claus, with his round red cheeks, white hair, and twinkling blue eyes. He had no beard but was a rotund, jolly old fellow all the same. After his death, Devon had been stunned to learn from Rolfe that Dad had in fact been several hundred years old, not an unusual age for a Guardian. Ted March, Coles Junction mechanic, had in reality been Thaddeus Underwood, Nightwing Guardian.

Yet as much as Dad looked like Santa Claus, there were never many presents under the tree. Oh, he made sure Devon got something he wanted: a train set one year, a Batman utility belt when he was seven, and a CD player their last Christmas together. They never had a lot of money, which was another reason coming to Ravenscliff had been so staggering for Devon. Here his bedroom is nearly as large as the entire house he and Dad had shared in Coles Junction.

Still, he'd give anything to be back there right now. He'd willingly give up these strange powers and his noble Nightwing bloodline just to be an ordinary kid again, back with Dad, hanging out with Tommy and Suze.

But that would mean leaving Cecily and D.J. and Marcus and Ana. If only he could take them with him, back to his old life.

The Christmas preparations at Ravenscliff have made him melancholy. Sitting on the couch watching Alexander hang Christmas stockings on the mantel, Devon notices how incongruous they look under the somber portrait of Horatio Muir. That's when Devon realizes there's no stocking for him.

Alexander seems to pick up on this, too. "Hey, Devon, didn't you bring your stocking?"

He shakes his head.

"Well, you have to make one, then. My aunt Amanda fills all our stockings with lots of candy."

Cecily has come into the parlor. "As if you *need* any more candy, pork chop," she says.

Alexander sticks his tongue out at her. He is definitely on the chubby side, though Devon thinks he looks healthier since he's been getting out of his room more. Alexander used to sit and brood in front of the television set, all day, but now Devon gets him outside, sledding down the hills on the estate behind the tennis court.

"I don't need a stocking," Devon says. "I'm too old for all that stuff."

"Of course you need a stocking," Cecily says. "I'll make you one."

"*Muchas gracias,*" he says, smiling.

Bjorn is suddenly behind him. "Mister Devon, you have a visitor," he says.

"A visitor?"

"Yes." Bjorn gestures into the foyer. Devon sees Marcus standing there, wrapped up in his parka and scarf.

"Hey!" Devon calls, leaping off the couch to greet his friend. "What's happening?"

"You said you wanted to talk to me," Marcus says.

"When I called, you said it would have to wait until we were alone."

Devon nods, looking over his shoulder to make sure they're out of earshot. "Come on into the library with me, okay?"

They hurry down the corridor. Once settled into the dark room, heavy with the musty fragrance of old books, Marcus takes off his coat and looks Devon straight in the eyes. "What's up? I can tell it's something bad."

"Well, not necessarily bad. It's just something . . . about you."

"Me?"

"Yeah." Devon pauses, not sure how to put it. "Listen, I have to tell you something. But I don't want you freaking out."

"Is this about the demons? The Hellhole?"

"No." Devon's not sure about that, actually, but he doesn't want to alarm Marcus. "Look, the very first time I met you I saw something on your face. And lately I've seen it again."

Marcus frowns. "What? Like a zit?"

"No. A pentagram."

"A *pentagram*? What's that?"

"A five-pointed star with a circle around it."

"Devon, I've never put a star on my face. Maybe D.J. would do something weird like that, but not me."

"It wasn't actually *on* your face. It was *over* your face. It was like a vision."

Devon sees the realization light in Marcus's eyes. Too much has happened for anyone to doubt Devon's ability to see things beyond the scope of an ordinary kid.

"What does it mean?" Marcus asks, a little flicker of fear in his voice.

"I thought maybe you'd have some clue."

"Clue? Like what?"

"I don't know. Does your family have any magic in its past?"

Marcus laughs derisively. "*My* family? I don't think so. My dad's a plumber. We're hardly Nightwing like you, Devon."

"Well, I just figured I had to tell you. I looked up the meaning of the pentagram in one of the books at Rolfe's house. It's a good symbol. It's used for protection against evil spirits. So really it shouldn't freak you out. Maybe it means you're somehow protected."

"And maybe it means I'm marked for something to happen," Marcus says gloomily.

"So I shouldn't have told you about it?"

"No, you did the right thing." Marcus smiles. "You know, I really admire you, Devon. I hope you know that. You're the bravest kid I know."

Devon blushes a little.

"And I want to thank you for always being totally accepting of me. You know, you've never made me feel different or anything."

Devon gives him a little smile. "Well, I know something about what it's like to grow up feeling different, Marcus. I know what it's like to feel as if there's nobody else like me in the whole entire world."

Marcus smiles. They shake hands, pledging to find the reason behind the pentagram. As he watches his friend leave, Devon thinks that despite the fact that Marcus is gay, he's got a far more normal life than Devon can ever hope to have.

Unless, of course, that pentagram turns out to mean something sinister.

CHRISTMAS EVE ARRIVES, and a light snowfall delights Cecily, who'd been hoping for a white Christmas. The house smells wonderful, with the aroma of baking cookies wafting into the parlor. Bjorn has spent all day in the kitchen preparing an elaborate feast of turkey and cranberry stuffing; in addition to being just about the strongest man Devon has ever known, he's also a master chef. Still, Devon's wary of him. He eats very little.

What kind of life is this? Devon gripes to himself.

Now I've got to worry that maybe some gnome is going to poison me, with Mrs. Crandall's blessing.

Later, the matriarch of the house has them all up to her mother's room for a rare visit with Grandmama, who looks at each of them with yellow, rheumy eyes, seemingly not recognizing anybody except her daughter.

"Are you my beau come to call?" the bedridden old woman asks Devon.

"No, Mrs. Muir," he tells her. "My name is Devon." He looks at her intently. The others are fixing a bouquet of flowers on the other side of the room. "Does that name—*Devon*—mean anything to you?"

"Devon," she repeats. "Is that the name of my beau?"

He sighs. The old lady's eyes reflect nothing he can see. It's very sad, actually: If Devon had ever suspected Greta Muir might be the powerful sorceress who saved him from Simon on the roof of the tower last fall, he now considers such a thing impossible.

She's so frail when Mrs. Crandall helps her stand that she can barely take the few short steps to a chair, where she's handed a couple of brightly wrapped Christmas gifts. Her trembling hands cannot figure out how to open them. Cecily moves in beside her to do it for her: One is a sweater, the other a shawl.

"Are they from my husband?" Greta Muir asks,

becoming slightly agitated. "Where is he? Where is Randolph?"

Devon feels tremendously sad for her. *Your husband died in the Hellhole,* he thinks to himself. *That's why you went mad. That's why your family renounced its glorious Nightwing past.*

Poor Mrs. Muir falls asleep in her chair. Her daughter helps her back into bed.

"You children go downstairs," Mrs. Crandall tells them. "I'll join you momentarily."

"Grandmama sure is one crazy old bat," Alexander says as they head down the corridor.

"Show some respect," Cecily scolds.

The little boy thumbs his nose at her.

In the parlor, the three young people take their places on the floor under the Christmas tree. Mrs. Crandall arrives and agrees that each may open one gift. Alexander gets a book, *Tom Sawyer;* Cecily exults over a pair of jeans; and Devon finds a pair of ice skates in the box marked for him. He thanks Mrs. Crandall; he'd been actually wanting these, hoping to get a chance to skate on one of the frozen ponds on the estate. She smiles down at him warmly and says, "Merry Christmas, Devon."

He looks up at her eyes. Is that actually compassion he sees?

Could she have really tried to kill me? Rolfe said not to trust her, not to put anything past her.

But Devon remembers how tenderly she'd treated him when the demons wounded his face, and how she had held him after Simon had tried to kill him. Is she friend or foe? Does she care for him somewhere down deep under that icy exterior? Or does she want him out of the way, because he represents all that she wants to disown about her family's history? He wishes the Voice would tell him for sure, but as it so often does, it remains silent.

"There's nothing under here from my father," Alexander observes, peering under the low-hanging branches of the tree.

Mrs. Crandall frowns. "No, there isn't." Devon can tell she's angry at her brother for forgetting his son—yet again. "I'm sure his gifts are just late getting here. You know the mail is very slow at Christmastime—"

Just then the front doors of Ravenscliff open into the foyer. A swirl of snowflakes blows in on a gust of wind. Devon turns. A man has entered, his arms loaded down with packages.

"Ho-ho-ho," the man cries. "Meeeeeerrry Christmas!"

There's a moment of stunned disbelief in the parlor. Devon looks at the faces of Mrs. Crandall, Cecily, and Alexander. They're frozen, emotionless. But suddenly Alexander breaks the silence, jumping to his feet and shouting, "Dad!"

"It's my uncle Edward!" Cecily exclaims to Devon, standing herself now and running into the foyer after Alexander.

Devon rises automatically. Only Mrs. Crandall remains seated, in her wingback chair, her face stony.

"Speak of the devil, huh?" Devon offers.

She turns her eyes to him. "Not an inappropriate choice of words, Devon."

"How's my boy?" Edward Muir is asking. Having deposited all the brightly colored packages on the floor of the foyer, he's scooped Alexander up in his arms for a fat kiss. Edward Muir is a big man, tall with broad shoulders, as fair and golden-haired as his sister. But his eyes dance where hers are cold and guarded, and when he smiles, large dimples indent his rosy cheeks.

"Dad! I knew you'd come!" Alexander cries.

"You didn't think I'd miss Christmas with my loving family, do you?" He sets his son down and turns to Cecily. "Hello, Kitty-cat. How you've grown!" He embraces her fondly.

"It's so good to see you, Uncle Edward," she says. "You always bring so much lightness into this house."

"And it can usually use it," he says, his eyes moving past the children into the parlor to settle on his sister. "Merry Christmas, Amanda."

"Welcome home, Edward," she says, but Devon can sense no conviction in her voice.

"Dad, you've got to meet Devon," Alexander says, pulling his father into the parlor by the hand. "He's my best friend."

"Yes, yes," Edward Muir says, looking down at Devon now. They shake hands. "Amanda wrote me about her new ward."

"It's good to meet you, sir," Devon says.

"Now, now, there will be no 'sir' among friends." He smiles. "Call me Edward. I'm sure we'll be good pals, Devon."

Devon smiles. He wishes Edward Muir had been at Ravenscliff when he first arrived here. His warmth and friendliness would have made a marked difference in those first few weeks.

Edward has turned now to his sister, who still hasn't risen to greet him. "Dear Amanda," he says. "I'm sorry I didn't phone ahead to tell you of my plans, but I wanted to surprise you." He looks around at all of them. "For I have a *big* surprise."

Mrs. Crandall eyes him warily. "What is it *now*, Edward? Another new business scheme to take the world by storm, only to end up costing the family fortune a few tens of thousands of dollars?"

He laughs, ignoring her. "I note you hired a new caretaker, Amanda. An interesting man. I met him outside. He's bringing in my bags. So strong for such a little fellow."

Mrs. Crandall's expression doesn't change.

"Ah, look," Edward Muir says, "here he comes now."

Devon turns. Bjorn is carrying in several bags through the front door. But he's not alone. Behind him comes a woman dressed in a floor-length mink coat.

"Darling," Edward Muir says, gesturing for the woman to join him in the parlor.

Now Mrs. Crandall stands up, her eyes wide, her lips pursed tightly.

"I want you all to meet my fiancée," Edward Muir says. "My son Alexander, my niece Cecily, my new friend Devon, and of course, my dear sister Amanda." He smiles, gazing at the woman with adoration. "This is the woman I intend to marry. Morgana Green."

"Hello," Morgana offers in a quiet, respectful voice. She's beautiful. Short dark hair and enormous brown eyes. Devon looks quickly from her to Mrs. Crandall, then down at Alexander. Both of them stare in shock.

"Might I remind you, Edward," Mrs. Crandall says, not bothering to welcome Morgana to her home, "that you are already married."

He dismisses her with a wave of his hand. "A technicality. Ingrid is a hopeless case. Her doctors have told me that many times. So I've already put the divorce into motion."

Devon instinctively puts an arm around Alexander's shoulder. This is, after all, his mother they're talking about. Devon knows that Ingrid Muir has been institutionalized for years, and that Alexander can barely remember her. But still, it must be difficult to hear one's father describe one's mother so callously. Devon begins to suspect there's something more, something cruel, behind Edward Muir's outward charm.

"I hope you will all come to like me," Morgana says. She has some kind of accent to her voice, but Devon can't quite place it. "Especially you, Alexander."

She stoops down to meet the boy at eye level. They shake hands.

"I know I could never replace your real mother," Morgana says kindly, "but I'd like to be your friend."

Alexander says nothing.

Edward has turned to his sister. "And how is *our* good mother?"

"The same," Mrs. Crandall says, her eyes not moving from Morgana.

Edward beams, dropping an arm around his fiancée. "Nevertheless, I'll want to introduce Morgana to her."

"She's asleep for the night." Mrs. Crandall looks off

toward the fireplace. "So tell me, Edward. How long do you intend to stay here this time?"

"Long enough for the divorce to go through at least." He grins. "Of course, I want to be married here at Ravenscliff." He spreads his arms wide. "The ancestral home."

Devon watches as Morgana blushes.

Mrs. Crandall stiffens. "Well, if you're going to be here, you can help me with the ancestral *businesses*, too," she says, moving away from the group to stare out onto the terrace and over the rocky cliffs beyond. "You know we have competition now."

"Oh, yes, you wrote me all about that. Rolfe Montaigne is still causing trouble."

"There's talk he's thinking of opening another restaurant, and sponsoring his own fishing fleet." Mrs. Crandall sighs, not looking around. "Tell me, Morgana. What line of business are *you* in?"

"I'm a dancer," Morgana says.

Devon catches a quick smirk from Cecily.

"Ballet?" Mrs. Crandall asks, but they already know that's not the answer.

Morgana hesitates in her reply, so Edward fills in for her. "I met Morgana in a club in Monte Carlo," he says. "Her reputation as a performer is celebrated." He looks over at her fondly. "She has quite the act."

"I can imagine," Mrs. Crandall says, her voice dripping with disdain. "Well, you can show her the house, Edward. And afterward, I'd like to speak with you. *Alone.*"

"What—no Christmas festivities?" Edward asks.

"We've opened our presents for the evening and now it's getting late." Mrs. Crandall looks at Morgana. "I'm sure you'd like to freshen up and get settled. I'll have Bjorn bring you up a pot of tea."

"Thank you," Morgana says.

Devon feels for the young woman. He knows just how cold Mrs. Crandall can be. He was a newcomer to this family once, too, and until he became friends with Cecily, he'd felt very alone here. He decides he'll befriend Morgana. She's only in her early twenties, it seems, and despite the mink, which Devon imagines Edward bought for her, Morgana seems unpretentious and sincere. And so pretty. Especially those big dark eyes. Not unlike Devon's own.

Edward takes Morgana upstairs, Bjorn following with their luggage. The Christmas gifts he'd brought with him will be opened tomorrow morning, Mrs. Crandall insists. For now, Alexander and Cecily settle them under the tree. Mrs. Crandall moves out of the room soundlessly, like a cat, disappearing to whatever part of the house she goes to when she wants to be alone. It's clear she is not happy with Edward's return, or his decision to marry Morgana.

"So," Devon asks Alexander, "what do you think of your dad's surprise?"

"I don't like her," he says bitterly.

Devon scowls. "Alexander. She seems very nice."

"No. She's *not* nice." The boy crosses his pudgy little arms over his chest. "Not nice at all."

"Listen, buddy, I know it must be hard, with your own mother still out there and all. But maybe you ought to give Morgana a chance."

"No," Alexander spits.

Devon hasn't seen him so petulant in months. He's acting mean-spirited and stubborn, like he did in the weeks after Devon first arrived.

"Well," Cecily says, "all I can say is I hope that mink coat is faux fur. I mean, how tacky is that? I *hate* fur coats. The senseless slaughter of innocent animals for human vanity—"

"I'm sure your uncle bought it for her."

"It doesn't matter. She's *wearing* it." She huffs. "And what kind of *voice* was that? That's no accent I ever heard."

"She's from Europe," Devon says. "She could be—I don't know—French."

"That was *not* a French accent. Or an Italian accent. Or Spanish." Cecily scoffs. "She's just making it up, trying to sound exotic. When she's just some low-class stripper."

"Why are you so *down* on her?" Devon looks at Cecily strangely. "Neither one of you is giving her a chance."

Cecily scrunches up her face. "You *like* her, don't you?"

Devon feels defensive. "Yeah, I do."

"Just because she's pretty. So a pretty face can just blind you to the fact that she's some gold digger trying to get my uncle's money?"

Devon laughs. "You sound just like your mother, you know that? It's obvious that's what *she* was thinking, too."

Cecily just rolls her eyes.

"I'm going to bed," Devon tells her, fed up with her childishness.

"Wait." She stops him, pressing her hand on his chest. "Let's not fight on Christmas Eve."

He shrugs. "I wasn't fighting. I just want you to give her a chance. It's hard being a newcomer in this house. Believe me, I know."

Cecily promises she'll try. Alexander, however, makes no such vow.

THAT NIGHT, all Devon can dream about is Morgana. It's a dream that, even as he's having it, he feels embarrassed about. She walks into his room and opens up her mink coat, to reveal only a black negligee. She purses her lips and calls his name. Devon wakes up flushed and bothered.

"Man," he whispers into the night. "She sure is something."

He can't get back to sleep. He tosses and turns. The clock beside his bed reveals it's almost one in the morning. He finally decides he needs a glass of water, so he tiptoes out of his room and into the hushed corridor. From the landing at the top of the stairs he sees the parlor door is ajar. There's a light inside, and people are talking in there. He's pretty sure it's Mrs. Crandall and her brother. He's also pretty sure they're talking about him.

It's stuff I need to know, he tells himself. *So where's my superhearing now?*

The Voice surprises him by answering: *Maybe you have something else instead.*

Devon doesn't know what the Voice means, but looking down at himself he suddenly understands. He sees his slippers, and the sweatpants and T-shirt he'd been sleeping in—but not himself! It's as if his clothes were walking by themselves.

I'm invisible!

"Whoa," Devon says, and his voice sounds strange to his ears, coming from lips he can't see.

Okay, he thinks, *this is absolutely the coolest thing yet. I didn't even know I did it. It just happened!*

That's because it will enable you to find out what you need to know, the Voice tells him.

"Duh," Devon says to the Voice.

Lately, the Voice has been coming less and less, and sometimes it tells him things he already knows, or things that are obvious. Of course he knows that being invisible will give him the ability to slip into the parlor undetected and eavesdrop on their conversation. He knows that might be a totally rude thing to do, but he's got to discover the truth about his past one way or another.

So he pulls off his T-shirt and his sweats and kicks off his slippers, hiding them behind a curtain. It feels weird to be walking naked down the stairs, because he can still feel his body, just not see it. He can still make sound, too, he discovers, when one of the steps creaks under his foot. He's going to have to be careful.

Mrs. Crandall looks up when he enters the parlor. He has to open the door slightly to fit through. It's clear, though, she's not onto him. She walks right past him and shuts the door. Now he's trapped in here with them.

Devon takes a deep breath, fearful of letting it out and being heard. As softly as he can, he pads over to the far wall and leans against it, watching but not being seen.

"So he's discovered all about the Nightwing, then?" Edward is asking.

Mrs. Crandall nods. "Thanks to Rolfe."

"Perhaps we can get him to renounce his powers, like the rest of us."

She shakes her head. "As ever, you're a fool, Edward. Don't you realize that Devon's sorcery allowed him to save your son from the Madman? If we got rid of his powers now—"

Edward scoffs. "But Jackson Muir can't come back again."

"That's what we thought the last time."

He shudders. "We ought to burn this house to the ground." He smiles wickedly. "Better yet. *Sell* it. We could make a killing."

"That's just like you, Edward. Not caring what might befall new occupants of this house."

He laughs. "Better them than us."

Mrs. Crandall watches him with contempt as he pours himself another brandy. "And do you really think we could simply be free of our past by leaving this house? It would follow us—just as I'm sure it has followed you, in all your travels around the globe."

Devon can tell by Edward Muir's expression that she's right. Despite his desperate flight from this house, it's clear that Edward has never been able to put the tragedies far from his mind. He walks over to the French doors and looks out into the night.

"I notice there's no light in the tower," he says.

"It's been taken care of."

He smirks at his sister. "Oh, really? And how was that accomplished?"

"Never mind. I've seen to it."

He holds his brandy snifter up to her in mock salute. "Dear sister, you are the most capable woman I know."

"I've *had* to be. Since you walked out and left me with guarding this house on my own."

"Has it been that much of a burden?" he asks sarcastically.

She eyes him coldly. "Are you planning on taking Alexander with you after you marry that woman? I expect you'll start globe-trotting again after the wedding."

Edward laughs. "Take Alexander *with* me? Dear sister, you willingly assumed the boy's guardianship. I can't be saddled with an eight-year-old boy."

"But now you'll have a wife. And she seems to want to be involved with Alexander."

Edward shakes his head. "Alexander will stay here. I don't want him."

Devon's heart breaks for his little friend.

"How much have you told her about the sorcery?" Mrs. Crandall asks.

"Nothing at all. Do you think I'm crazy?"

"Crazy like a fox." She sighs. "Be careful, Edward. I don't like her."

He makes a face. "What's not to like? She's sweet. Kind." His lips curl upward. "Not to mention beautiful."

Mrs. Crandall sniffs. "In a common sort of way."

"You know, Amanda, bitterness does not become you."

"Good night, Edward."

She turns and walks imperiously out of the parlor. Her brother chuckles to himself, refills his brandy, then saunters out himself.

Just in time, too: Devon's become visible again. He's not sure why—maybe because he was concentrating on their conversation and not on staying invisible. But he knows one thing very well: He's now standing stark naked in the middle of the parlor and his clothes are up behind a curtain on the landing.

But before he can decide what to do—make a run for it, try his disappearing-reappearing act—he's startled by a voice.

"You looking for these?"

In the doorway stands Bjorn Forkbeard, holding Devon's clothes in one hand.

Devon lunges at him, snatching his sweatpants as the gnome chortles to himself.

"How did you know I was here?" Devon asks, now slipping his T-shirt over his head.

"Because you weren't in your room, and I came looking for you." Bjorn's face turns serious. "Thought I should tell you something. Something you ought to check out."

"What's that?"

Bjorn leans in close to him, his little face intent as it looks up at Devon. "There's some kind of disturbance at the Hellhole in the East Wing. I can hear it. Trust me, I can hear things like that."

"What are you talking about?"

Bjorn's face has gone white. "May the Gods preserve us," he says, listening to something only he can hear, "but I think something's trying to get out of the Hellhole."

THAT'S ABSURD, Devon keeps telling himself, as he heads upstairs. The Hellhole is sealed. The door is bolted. And if there *were* some demons about to escape, Devon feels confident the Voice would've warned him.

He tries willing himself into the East Wing to check on things, but nothing happens. Surely his powers would work if they were in any danger. So Bjorn must be wrong.

He *must* be.

Either that or he's lying—for some devious reason of his own.

Still, Devon wishes he knew of a physical way into the East Wing, just to reassure himself that the door into the Hellhole is still bolted, still impenetrable. But the East Wing has been sealed off from the rest of the house. Devon has wanted in there as much as he's wanted into the tower. There are books there—books he needs to read—and a portrait of a young man in the clothing of the 1930s who looks just like Devon. For many reasons, Devon has wanted to get into the East Wing. It holds many secrets for him, but his powers just can't seem to get him through Mrs. Crandall's locked doors.

Walking down the corridor toward his room, he can't deny the gnome's words have unnerved him. Bjorn knows that Devon is the only person left in the house who could possibly fight off a demonic attack. But maybe his warning was a trap—like the one that led him onto the Stairway Into Time. Devon still isn't sure he can trust Bjorn. He wishes the Voice would tell him something more.

But when he opens the door to his room, he doesn't need the Voice to tell him anything. He feels the sudden blast of heat and the throbbing pressure—a demon is near.

Devon braces himself. His heart starts thudding fast in his chest.

"Devon?" comes a scared little voice.

He looks down. Crouched beside his bed is Alexander.

"I'm scared," Alexander says, near tears. "The bad things that happened before. They're coming back."

Devon kneels beside him. The heat in the room is definitely overpowering. The little boy is sweating and trembling in his pajamas. Devon puts his arms around him and pulls him close.

"I'm going to fight them, Alexander," Devon promises. "I'm going to send them back to their Hellhole."

"I don't think so," Alexander says. "Not this time."

Devon stiffens. The boy's voice—cold, low. Not his own.

Devon looks down just in time to see Alexander's lips part, revealing a mouthful of yellow fangs. He sinks them deep into Devon's left shoulder, hitting bone.

Devon screams.

FOUR

A VISION OF BLOOD

THE PAIN is excruciating, but Devon manages to push the creature off him. It's not Alexander. Once more, Devon realizes, cursing himself, he's been tricked by a demon disguised as something else. He watches in horror as the thing shifts its shape, elongating itself like a lizard, its bones pushing out of its flesh. It becomes a seething, decomposing reptilian corpse, crouched down on all fours as if to spring.

"Back to your Hellhole!" Devon commands as best he can, his right hand clutching his shoulder, trying to stop the blood.

"I don't think so," the demon says again in its own voice, a deep, scratchy sound.

"I am stronger than you!"

But even as he says it, Devon falls, his head weak from loss of blood.

The thing begins to creep toward him. "Are you really so strong? Then prove it. Open the door in the East Wing, and let them free. They're restless behind it. Listen. You can hear them. Set them free, Devon March. Then you will have the power of the world to command!"

"Never," Devon rasps, but his head is spinning.

The demon looms over him now, his fangs dripping yellow saliva. "Then I will have you," it says, and grips the boy's arms with its bony talons.

Suddenly the windows of Devon's room unlatch and swing inward, and the air is filled with the sound of angry flapping wings. Ravens—dozens of them, hundreds even, squawking and shrieking and descending upon the demon. Their beaks peck at its decaying flesh, and though it tries to fight them off, they are eating the thing alive.

Or dead, whatever the case may be.

"Nooooo!" the demon cries, now entirely covered in a black mass of furiously pounding wings.

Devon manages to sit up. "Back to your Hellhole," he commands again, in a far weaker voice. The thing disappears, and the ravens swarm back out the window en masse. A few of their brethren lie dead on the floor, legs upraised. Devon picks one raven up and holds it gently in his hand. He gazes down in gratitude at the dead bird.

The door to his room suddenly flings open. It's Cecily. "Oh my God!" she screams. "Devon—you're bleeding!"

He manages to nod his head. For the first time he realizes his shirt is drenched in blood.

"They're back," he tells her weakly. "The demons are back."

"Mother!" she shouts. "Mother! Uncle Edward!"

Mrs. Crandall and her brother are soon in the doorway, in their robes, with Morgana peering timidly over Edward's shoulder.

"Dear God," Edward says, horrified. "What's happened?"

"The demons," Devon whispers.

Edward stoops down to look at him severely. "Are you certain?"

"Look, I've had run-ins with them before. I know what I'm talking about. If not for the ravens—"

Edward stands. "Wouldn't you know it? I come back and this place is still the stinking horror it's always been."

"I've got to check on Mother," Mrs. Crandall says.

"Please!" Cecily is furious. "Can't you people think of something besides yourselves? Devon is bleeding to death! We've got to call Doctor Lamb!"

"That won't be necessary," comes a voice.

They look around. They can't see who's speaking at

first until Bjorn Forkbeard appears, pushing between Mrs. Crandall and Morgana in the doorway.

"I've been trained to deal with this sort of wound," the gnome says. He carries a little black bag and stands beside Devon to study his shoulder. "First we need a tourniquet to stop the bleeding."

"I could've told you that much," Devon says.

Cecily yanks the case off Devon's pillow and hands it to Bjorn, who fastens it around the wounded shoulder.

"Now," the little man says, opening his bag, "I have certain herbs here—"

"Herbs?" Cecily asks. "Shouldn't we be taking him down to the emergency room to get stitches? And some kind of tetanus shot?"

"You could, if you want to waste all that time," Bjorn says. He withdraws a small vial filled with a green powder. "Where I grew up, we were always running into these things. The mines we worked in went right through some major Hellholes. So we gnomes learned to be prepared."

He shakes a bit of the powder over Devon's shoulder.

"That should stop the bleeding," he says.

Devon's watching him with great interest. *The treatment will work,* the Voice tells him. *Do not fear it.*

But how much had Bjorn known about the demon's attack in advance? Can Devon truly trust him?

He looks toward the doorway. *Well,* Devon thinks
to himself, *I suppose for the moment I can trust him
more than I can Mrs. Crandall or Edward Muir, neither
of whom bothered to stick around long enough to make
sure I was going to be all right.*

Why was checking on their mother so important?
What connection did the senile old woman still have to
the demons of the Hellhole?

"Somebody needs to get into the East Wing,"
Devon says. "If the portal is opened—"

"Is that where you think it came from?" Cecily asks.
"Whatever attacked you?"

"I don't think the Hellhole here at Ravenscliff is
open," Bjorn says, wrapping Devon's shoulder now in
a bandage. "My sense is only that they are restless inside. Something is disturbing them. Perhaps *trying* to
let them out—but it is not yet opened."

Cecily's perplexed. "Then where did the thing that
attacked Devon come from if not there?"

"There are many Hellholes all over the world, and
some are open," Devon explains to her. This is information he's learned from Rolfe. "Many demons are
loose upon the earth, and their goal is to get their filthy
brothers and sisters set free. We just happen to live over

one of the largest Hellholes in the world. So they're particularly interested in getting into this one."

They're startled then, not by any horrific cry, but a small sob. They turn. In the doorway still stands Morgana, her face white. She's crying.

"I—I didn't know you were still there," Devon says.

"All of this talk," the pretty woman cries. "Hellholes. Demons. And your shoulder—and those dead birds! What kind of a house have I come to?"

Devon's immediately on his feet. He's surprised at how much the pain has eased from Bjorn's treatment. He takes Morgana's hands in his own. She's small, about his height, and it just breaks his heart to see her so scared. What must she think of all this? And how wrong—how *very* wrong—of Edward Muir to bring her to Ravenscliff without telling her of its sorcery.

"I know it all sounds bizarre," Devon tells her tenderly. "It did to me, too, when I first came here."

She looks at him imploringly. "What kind of family am I marrying into?"

Devon gazes into her dark eyes. How truly beautiful they are. In fact, he's suddenly aware that he's never seen a more gorgeous woman—not any supermodel, not Roxanne, not even . . . Cecily . . .

He feels an immediate twinge of guilt and drops Morgana's hands. But he can't take his eyes off her.

"I think you need to talk with Edward," Devon tells her. "He owes you an explanation. It's not my place."

She manages a small smile. "You're a very decent young man, Devon. Thank you." She kisses him on the cheek and then walks off down the corridor, presumably in search of her fiancé.

"Well," Cecily says, her voice icy, "you certainly seem smitten."

"Cecily, she was scared! Come on! You've been through this before. She hasn't."

"You ought to lie down, Devon," Bjorn tells him. "You've lost a good deal of blood."

Devon sighs, sitting down on the edge of his bed. He's suddenly aware of the blood on the floor and feels slightly nauseous. "I need to talk with Rolfe," he mumbles.

"In the morning." Bjorn helps him remove his bloody shirt. "Cecily, fetch a cloth and some warm water."

They clean Devon up and get him into bed, Cecily insisting that they should still call Doc Lamb, their family practitioner. Devon assures her that the Voice tells him he's going to be fine, that Bjorn's treatment will do the trick. She reluctantly agrees, just as her mother comes back into the room. Devon is suddenly very sleepy, but he manages to answer her when she asks if he's okay.

"Just peachy," he whispers. "Thanks for your concern."

"I *was* concerned, Devon, and still am. But once I knew Bjorn could treat you, there were things I needed to do. Important things."

"Like what?"

"Like making sure the portal in the East Wing was secure," she says reluctantly.

"And is it?"

"My brother reports it is," she says.

"That's good." He starts to doze off, then opens his eyes again. "You were smart in hiring Bjorn. You knew we'd need his skills."

She doesn't reply. "Just rest, Devon." She places her hand on his head. "I suppose it's rather awkward to say right now, but Merry Christmas. Sleep well."

He falls asleep. He dreams not of demons, but of Morgana, her brown, liquid eyes and soft, inviting lips . . .

THE NEXT DAY his bed is bouncing with his friends.

"Hey, watch it," Devon says, laughing. "Remember I'm wounded here."

Ana is attempting to fluff his pillows behind him.

"Poor baby, bedridden on Christmas Day. Do you want some more eggnog?"

"He's fine," Cecily tells her. "I've been bringing him eggnogs and coffeecakes and popcorn balls all day."

"Yeah," Devon says, laughing. "It's not the shoulder that hurts anymore, it's the stomach."

Marcus is sitting on the edge of his bed studying him. "I don't like what this suggests, Devon. The demons are restless again. Why?"

D.J. had been leaning up against the bureau, tossing a ball into the air and catching it, not wanting to fuss over Devon like the rest of them. Now he turns his attention to his friend. "Yeah," he agrees. "That does rattle my brain a bit. Last time it was that crazy Jackson Muir who got 'em all stirred up. What about now?"

"I don't know," Devon admits.

"Maybe it's that dwarf," Ana says, shuddering. "He gives me the creeps."

"He's a *gnome*," Cecily corrects her. "But I don't think he's a bad guy. I'm pretty sure Bjorn is on our side. Look how he treated Devon's shoulder."

"He could be pulling a fast one," D.J. warns. "These things are clever. Remember how one of them disguised itself as me."

Devon nods. "That's why I really need to talk with Rolfe some more. There's so much about the relationship between the Nightwing and the demons that I don't understand."

Cecily sighs. "Mother and Uncle Edward are worried. I can tell."

"Well, if anything happens," Devon promises, "I'll do what I did before. I'll give you guys the powers of the Nightwing to fight them off."

Marcus smiles weakly. Devon knows he's concerned about the pentagram, what it means. That's one more thing he'll have to bring up with Rolfe.

There's a light tapping at the door. Cecily gets up and pulls it open. It's Morgana, carrying a tray with a pot.

"I thought our patient might want a little hot cocoa," she says.

"Thanks," Cecily says, "but he's filled up with eggnog."

"I'd love some cocoa," Devon says. "Thanks, Morgana."

Both Cecily and Ana shrink back as the older woman carries the tray over to the side of Devon's bed. They scrunch up their noses at each other. Morgana doesn't appear to notice. She walks sensuously across the room, her shapely legs encased in black tights, worn under a long, torn sweater that's nearly falling off one shoulder. She sets the tray down on a side table and pours Devon a cup of cocoa.

"Tastes excellent," Devon says, grinning up at her. "Oh, hey. Have you met my friends?"

Morgana flickers her dark eyes up at them. "No. Not yet."

"This is Ana Lopez," Devon says. Ana barely nods. "And this is Marcus Johnson." Marcus smiles. "And finally, this is D.J. Kerwinsky."

"Very pleased to make your acquaintance," D.J. says, leaping forward, nearly stumbling. He shakes her hand, suddenly grinning like a fool, forgetting any of his usual cool reserve.

"And yours, too, D.J.," Morgana purrs. Devon notices she bats her long eyelashes just a little bit. "And yours, too, Marcus," she says, turning her eyes back to him.

Marcus just smiles again.

"Did you talk with Edward?" Devon asks her. "Did he explain about all—this?"

"It's rather hard to believe," Morgana says, looking around and her voice trailing off.

"It's okay," Devon tells her. "My friends know all about the demons."

Morgana sighs. "Edward says there is some kind of door in the East Wing. A door that leads to . . ." She wraps her arms around herself and shudders. "I just can't say it."

"I know it's hard," Devon says. "But if you're going

to marry into this family, you're going to have to know about the sorcery. The Nightwing and the Hellholes. Mrs. Crandall tried to keep the secrets from me, but it was impossible to live here and not find out."

Morgana smiles kindly down at Devon. Her eyes brim with tears. "Oh, do hurry up and get better, Devon. I have a feeling I'm going to need your friendship *desperately* in this house."

Devon promises. She kisses him on the forehead, then hurries out of the room.

After she's gone, the room is quiet for a moment. Then D.J. lets out with a whoop. "Oh baby!"

Cecily makes a face over at him. "Okay, so like you only made a *total* fool of yourself, D.J."

He ignores her. "That is one hot babe," he says to Devon.

"Yeah, she sure is," Devon agrees.

"Well, I didn't like her the moment I saw her," Ana says.

"For once," Cecily says, looking over at her, "we're in agreement on something."

"You two are just jealous," D.J. says. "Because I'll tell you. That Morgana is *hot. H-O-T.*"

"D.J., you surprise me," Cecily deadpans. "You can spell."

Devon looks over at Marcus, still sitting on the edge of the bed. "What did *you* think of her, Marcus?"

He pauses. "Well, she's certainly beautiful. And she seems very nice."

"So what's the problem?" D.J. asks.

"No problem," Marcus says, but he seems unsure.

"She's a gold digger," Cecily says. "Trying to get my uncle's money. Mark my words, they'll be divorced within a year and she'll have a big fat settlement."

"She seemed very sweet, Cess," Marcus says.

"You're supposed to be gay, Marcus. You're not supposed to be taken in by her."

Devon rests his head back into his pillows. Yes, Morgana is sweet. So sweet that he can't seem to get her out of his mind for the rest of the afternoon, and all through the night. When he wakes up the next morning, he's still thinking about her. About a dream he had—a dream in which Morgana once again came to him, and this time she kissed him, right on the lips.

It's not something he shares with Cecily. Oh, no, not at all.

NEW YEAR'S comes and goes. Devon, his shoulder pretty much healed, attends a party at Jessica Milardo's with all his friends, but Mrs. Crandall insists he and Cecily be home no later than 12:30. "I can't wait until I'm fifteen," Cecily gripes as they come back through the front doors of Ravenscliff, the grandfather clock in the foyer reading 12:29. "I'm going to demand more independence."

Devon laughs. As if one could demand *anything* of Amanda Muir Crandall.

He takes off his coat and hangs it on the rack. There's still a little pain when he lifts his arm, and there will definitely be a slight scar, but it sure beats having stitches and his arm in a sling for several weeks.

Cecily looks back at him as she starts to climb the stairs. "D.J. seemed kind of out of it tonight, didn't you think?"

"Yeah," Devon agrees. "Even for D.J., he seemed quiet. Hardly talked at all."

"Wonder what's bothering him?"

Devon shrugs. "You never know with Deej. He goes off into his own world sometimes."

Cecily stops on the stairs and turns around. "You don't think—?"

Devon laughs. "What? That some demon's disguised itself as him again? No, I would've felt the heat. Whatever's bugging D.J. is nothing like that. Maybe he had a fight with his parents."

Outside, the snow is starting. Devon hears the long, shrill howls of the chill winter wind screeching through the eaves of the house. The shutters outside his window have come loose; Simon was supposed to have fixed them, but never got around to doing it before taking his swan dive off the roof of the tower. Devon will have to ask Bjorn to attend to it. On nights like this, the shutters bang and crash all through the night.

Or maybe I can fix them myself, Devon thinks.

He suddenly throws open his window. *Sure, I can,* he tells himself. *Aren't I a sorcerer of the noble Order of the Nightwing? A couple of loose shutters shouldn't be—*

His thoughts suddenly stop. He makes a little sound in his throat as he looks down. There's movement below. A sudden blast of heat hits his face.

"Oh, man—" Devon gasps.

Crawling up the side of the house are *scorpions*—at least, big, black-purplish things that *look* like scorpions. Hundreds of them. *Thousands!*

Devon instinctively slams his windows shut and takes a step backward. The heat and pressure in the room ratchet up unbearably. Within moments, hundreds of the horrible things are tapping at the glass of his windows, their swishing tails menacing him from the night. They look in with their tiny, black, beady eyes. They're at least a foot long, and they cover his windows, trying to break in.

"Back, I order you," he says, but his voice is weak. The things repulse him. They remind him of cockroaches. "Back to your Hellholes."

But just as it hadn't worked with that other demon,

once again Devon's command proves ineffectual. He knows why. Both times he'd been surprised and scared. He feels *fear*. That's precisely how they can overcome him. If he's scared, his powers fail him. Sargon the Great himself had warned him against that; he had scornfully called Devon the "Abecedarian." The beginner. The novice. The *amateur*.

"Oh yeah?" Devon says to himself, feeling a growing sense of indignation. "I've been inside a Hellhole and back out again, Mr. Sargon I'm-So-Great. Can you say the same?"

Just then the scorpion things break through his glass. Hundreds of them pour into his room, moving at speeds unimaginable. They are soon spreading out across his floor, climbing the posts of his bed. Devon backs off into a corner, fighting off his fear.

"Did you hear me, you filthy things? I've been to hell and back. And that's precisely where I'm sending you!"

The scorpions stop in their advance but do not retreat or disappear. A few are munching through Devon's backpack on his desk. "Hey!" he shouts. "You can have the geometry book but claws off my Palm Pilot!"

With one sweep of his arm he finds he can destroy them. The backpack munchers suddenly explode in clouds of purple dust. "Nice work," Devon tells himself. "Now keep it up."

The other creatures are beginning to back up slowly, an agitated vibration spreading through them.

"Go on, get out of here!" Devon commands, full of confidence now. "Go back to hell or you'll be purple powder like your friends!"

They begin scurrying back up the wall and out the window, down the side of the house to wherever they came from. But Devon is on them quickly.

"Not so fast for one of you," he says, reaching down to grip one of the hideous things by its enlongated abdomen. He lifts it from the ground, its tail coiling defensively. "I order you not to sting," Devon barks. The thing falls limp in his hand.

"I think I'm going to keep you, study you awhile." Still holding the demon in his left hand, Devon pulls open his closet door. The thing's siblings are almost completely gone now, scurrying as fast as they can over the broken panes of glass. The snow is blowing in from outside but Devon pays no heed. He dumps his dirty laundry out of his duffel bag, drops the scorpion-thing inside, and cinches the top with the drawstring. "I order you to remain in there," he tells his prisoner.

"I'm stronger than they are," he reminds himself, a little grin spreading across his face. "I'm stronger than they are, and they know it." He pauses. "So long as I am not afraid."

*　*　*

[116]

BUT JUST WHY have they started coming for him again? What does it mean?

The next afternoon Bjorn is fixing Devon's window. "You know, Bjorn, when I first came here," Devon says, feeling more and more that he can trust the caretaker, "I seemed to have stirred up the demons because they sensed I was Nightwing—that I had the power to open that portal. But I showed them I was stronger than they were. In fact, stronger than the Madman, Jackson Muir himself, and so they went away. Why have they returned? What do they hope to get from me?"

"Maybe the same thing," Bjorn tells him, hammering Devon's shutters into place. "After all, the demons want nothing more than to give their disgusting kin free rein on the earth once again."

"But if I didn't open the portal for them the first time, why would I do it now?" Devon sighs. "Something else must have gotten them riled up. I've got to talk with Rolfe."

Bjorn levels his small round eyes at him. "Mrs. Crandall has given me strict orders never to take you there."

"I don't need a ride," Devon tells him.

"Well, the cliffside staircase is covered in ice. And the road down to the village is slippery and still pretty snow-covered—"

Devon grins, feeling cocky. "Just watch this."

He concentrates. He wills himself to disappear and reappear at Rolfe's house—but nothing happens. He looks up at Bjorn and blushes.

"Well?" the gnome asks. "I'm still watching. What was I supposed to see?"

"It should have worked," Devon gripes.

Bjorn smirks. "I think maybe you were doing a bit of showing off, wouldn't you say? And from what I know about the Nightwing, the powers won't work if you use them like that."

"But I really *do* need to get to Rolfe's."

"Then try it again."

And this time it comes easily for him. He closes his eyes and transports himself to Rolfe's house. He appears behind the sofa, where Rolfe and Roxanne are in the midst of an embrace.

"Yikes," Devon says. "Guess I should've called."

Rolfe looks at him sternly. "Yes. That would have been considerate."

Roxanne stands. She's smiling. "Worry not, Devon March. I had a sense you might be stopping by."

"Strange things keep happening," he tells them both.

Rolfe sighs. "All right. Come on over here and tell me."

"There was another demon attack," Devon says, moving around the couch. "A whole swarm of things that looked like scorpions. I was able to stop them. I even kept one."

"You kept one?" Rolfe asks. "Like a pet?"

"I'm hoping to learn something from it, though the thing appears to be pretty stupid."

"I suspect it is," Roxanne says. "Lower-life demonic forms are controlled by forces much greater than themselves."

This is the first time Roxanne has offered any input on the demons. Devon looks at her significantly.

"I admit to not being an expert on demonic lore," Roxanne tells him, "but I can intuit very well. Something is manipulating the demons. *Using* them for something."

"And only the Nightwing can do that," Devon says. "Right, Rolfe?"

Rolfe is nodding. "So unless it's you, Devon, then there's another Nightwing, with his powers intact, making trouble out there."

Devon swallows. "Jackson Muir?"

Rolfe looks out over the crashing sea below. "Could it be possible? How could he find his way back? He was sealed in the Hellhole."

"There are Nightwing all over the world," Devon says. "You've told me that. Maybe it's somebody else."

"No Nightwing of any honor would use the demons in this way," Rolfe tells him. "If it's a

Nightwing behind this, he must be an Apostate. Another renegade sorcerer like the Madman."

Rolfe stands and walks over to his desk. He pulls open a drawer.

"Here, Devon. Try this again."

Devon looks. In Rolfe's hand he holds Ted March's crystal ring.

"Dad's ring," Devon says. "But it's never worked before."

"A Guardian's crystal holds Knowledge, but it works like the Voice you hear in your head. It only shares Knowledge when you are ready to hear and understand it." He looks down at the ring. "I've been studying this ring for weeks. There's nothing wrong with it. I suspect you were simply not ready to learn what it had to tell you."

"And you think now I am?"

"Roxanne does. She told me so this morning."

Devon looks over at her.

"Yes, Devon March. I have sensed this. So your appearance tonight is not a surprise."

Devon lets out a long breath. "Okay, then. Let me put on the ring."

"Just be prepared," Rolfe says. "For anything. You remember what happened last time."

Devon did indeed. Using the crystal of Rolfe's father, Devon had been granted visions of the

Nightwing past. He had even met Sargon the Great. But somewhere in the midst of his astral voyage, he was snatched by the Madman and taken down to his grave—right into Jackson Muir's rotting coffin with the stinking remains of his human body. It's not an experience Devon wants to ever go through again.

"Pull it off my finger if I seem to be in any trouble, okay, Rolfe?"

The older man nods, handing Devon the gold band.

This was my father's, the boy thinks to himself.

He slips the band onto the ring finger of his left hand.

Please, Dad, let it work.

And don't let the Madman get ahold of me.

"HELLO, SON."

Devon spins around. He's not in Rolfe's den anymore. He's home—back home in the little house in Coles Junction where he grew up. His dog Max sits on his hind legs, looking up at him and wagging his tail.

And his father is standing across the room, his arms open wide.

"Dad!"

Devon is about to run toward him, but suddenly he

stops. This could well be a trick. Demons have disguised themselves as Dad before.

But there's no heat, no pressure, the sure signs of demonic presence. No odor, either: Sometimes the craftier ones have been able to conceal their heat, but never have they been able to hide their stink.

"Devon, it's all right," his father tells him. "But you are wise to be cautious."

"Dad? Is it really you?"

I'm wearing his ring. It's got to be him. Somehow—Dad is alive!

"Yes, Devon. Oh, son, how brave you have been."

Casting all doubts aside, Devon runs to his father's embrace. He is warm and soft, just as Dad always was, and he smells just the way he always did: slightly of oil and grease and a hint of Old Spice aftershave.

"I have seen the trials you have gone through, Devon, and my soul has cried for you. But you are proving to be a strong and noble Nightwing. I am very proud."

"Dad, are you alive somewhere? I mean, can we be together again?"

His father looks down at him compassionately. "I will always live in your heart, Devon."

"But I need more than that. I need you at Ravenscliff. Or let me just stay here with you. In our house. With Max and all my old friends."

His father smiles sadly. "You cannot stay here, Devon. This is but the stuff of memory."

Devon can't hold back the tears. "I need you, Dad."

"And I will always be there for you." He cups his son's chin. "Do you still carry my St. Anthony medal?"

Devon nods, patting his pocket where he feels the indentation of the medal. The tears drip off his chin.

"I have been with you through all your trials," Dad tells him. "You know that, Devon."

Again the boy nods. "Why did you never tell me the truth of what I was? Why did you send me to Ravenscliff to live?"

"It is your destiny, Devon, to find out the truth of your past."

Devon's suddenly aware that they're no longer in their house. Max is gone. They are standing outside Ravenscliff, looking up at the mansion from several yards away.

"This is the hard part, Devon," his father says, his voice thick and fearful. "I have come to you to show you something, Devon. To warn you of the danger that comes."

"What do you mean, Dad?"

"Look, son. Look up at Ravenscliff."

Devon obeys. And what he sees shocks him. The great house is in ruins. The tower is a charred stump pointing brokenly toward the sky. The great stained-glass windows are smashed; the front doors are torn from their hinges. Large sections of the walls have crumbled inward.

Devon begins to run toward the house. "Cecily!" he shouts. "Cecily!"

As he nears the ruined mansion, his nostrils catch the acrid odor of smoke. Small fires still burn, sending the occasional burst of flame from the debris. Devon is suddenly startled by a sound overhead: Demons like pterodactyls soar over the smoldering house, screeching in triumph.

And inside, as he runs through the gaping, broken front doors, Devon finds a sight far more gruesome: Cecily lying dead in a pool of blood at the foot of the stairs.

FIVE

——◆——

THE APOSTATE

C ECILY!"
It's no use. He tries to lift her but she is cold and stiff. He backs away in horror, stumbling into the parlor.

And nearly trips over the body of D.J., sprawled out in his own thickening spill of blood. Beyond him lay Ana and Marcus, their bodies broken and twisted into unnatural shapes. He looks around. The foyer and parlor have been destroyed. Chandeliers are smashed on the floor. Walls are ripped open. The glass face of the old grandfather clock is shattered, its hands stopped forever at a little after nine o'clock.

"No," Devon cries. "This can't be! Dad! Where are you?"

Just then a hideous thing leaps from somewhere onto the banister of the stairs. It's a horrible apelike creature, with a mouthful of fangs and blazing yellow eyes.

"We're free," the demon speaks in a voice low and scratchy. "The portal has been opened and now we all are free!"

"Back!" Devon commands. "Back to your Hell-hole!"

The thing laughs at him. "It is too late for that! We have won!"

The demon is joined in its laughter by a chorus of others, now all appearing from various parts of the ruined house. Skeletal creatures and slimy reptilian things and hairy brutes with claws—all of them gather to laugh at Devon. The terrible sound echoes through what is left of the great house.

"Who did this?" Devon demands. "Who had the power to open that door?"

"Why, you did, of course, Great One," the apelike demon replies. "Only you have that power!"

"No! I did not! I would never—"

"Yes, Devon, only you have the power to open the door," comes his father's voice.

Devon turns. His father stands sadly in the door-frame.

"I never did! Dad, I never did—"

"But you will," his father tells him. "You will, and your friends will die."

"This is a dream! Some crazy hallucination!"

Around him the demons hoot and holler again, like a gang of rowdy bikers.

"Get this ring off my finger!" Devon shouts. "I want to stop this!"

But try as he might he can't budge the ring. He's left surrounded by the beasts and staring at Cecily's cold, lifeless body.

"Please, Dad, make this not be true," he pleads, still struggling with the ring.

"Only you have that power, Devon. Only you."

"Join us," the ape demon urges. "Think of the power you will have. Others of your kind have joined us. You will not be alone."

The creatures begin advancing on him. Slithering, stumbling, dragging their cloven feet and spiked tails, the very stink of them clogging Devon's nostrils and making him gasp for breath.

"Never!" Devon shouts. "I am not an Apostate. And never will be!"

With those words he's able to pop the ring off his finger. It flies from his hand and rolls across the floor, coming to rest in the pool of Cecily's blood.

D EVON?"

Rolfe's voice.

"Devon, are you okay?"

"No," he says, unable to hold back tears. He staggers over to the couch and sits, covering his eyes. "It's too much. I can't deal with all of this."

Rolfe places a hand on his shoulder and stoops down so he's eye level with the boy. "What did you see, Devon?"

"My father." Devon lifts his eyes to find Rolfe's. "I saw my father."

"Thaddeus?"

Devon nods. "All I wanted to do was stay with him. But I couldn't. He showed me—"

His voice catches in his throat and he can't go on.

Roxanne sits beside Devon on the couch. She takes his hand in comfort.

"I saw Ravenscliff . . . it was totally destroyed," Devon says, composing himself. "Cecily was dead. All my friends, too. The demons were running all over the place. The house was theirs."

Rolfe says nothing.

"I suppose that would make you happy, huh, Rolfe?" Devon asks, feeling himself growing angry. "You'd like nothing more than to see Ravenscliff destroyed and that family brought down."

"No, Devon. I don't want any harm to come to Cecily or Alexander. You know that."

Devon fights off the sickest feeling in his stomach

that he's ever had. Worse than any flu. He feels he might vomit all over himself.

Roxanne touches his head. "Let me get you something," she says, standing and hurrying up the stairs to the kitchen.

"You do look a little green," Rolfe tells him.

"You would too if you'd just seen Cecily lying in a pool of her own blood." He tries to stand but he can't. "I've got to get back to Ravenscliff to make sure she's okay."

"Take it easy. I'm sure she's fine. If Thaddeus showed you the vision, it wasn't to frighten you, but to give you a warning. A heads-up on what *could* happen if we're not vigilant."

"You don't know the worst of it," Devon says as Roxanne returns, handing him a glass of ginger ale. He drinks it. It does indeed make him feel better. He thanks her, then looks back over at Rolfe. "*I'm* the problem, as always. It's me who's destined to open the portal and let the creatures out of the Hellhole. *Me.*"

"That's what Thaddeus showed you? That it would be you?"

Devon nods. "I've got to leave Misery Point. Get as far away from Ravenscliff as I can."

"Just slow down. There is no way you would ever willingly open that portal. If Thaddeus showed you that vision, it was to forewarn you that someone would try to force you—or trick you—into doing so."

"But who could do that? One of the demons?"

"Not likely. You've shown you're smarter and stronger than they are."

"Then who?"

Rolfe is silent for a moment. "Only another Nightwing could exert that kind of power over you," he says at last. "An Apostate who needs your help—the help of the one-hundredth generation since Sargon the Great."

"Then—then you think it's Jackson Muir, coming back."

Rolfe shakes his head. "Not necessarily Jackson."

"But you said Apostate. That's what he was called."

"Any Nightwing who uses his powers for evil becomes an Apostate. There have been many throughout history. There's no reason to think that there aren't others right now."

Devon feels strong enough to stand. He walks across the room to look down at the crashing waves below. The sun is setting. On the far horizon a lightning storm is starting to ignite.

"If there *are* bad Nightwing out there, isn't there any way we can find out who they are?" Devon asks. "Like isn't there a registry of all the Nightwing in the world or something?"

Rolfe smiles. "Possibly. But remember I've been out of the loop since my father was killed. I *do* know, however, that every twenty years there's a gathering of Nightwing called the Witenagemot. It's a word taken from old Anglo-Saxon England, where these gatherings first began over a thousand years ago. My father took me to one as a young boy. It was in Madrid, and all of the Guardians sat in awe as Nightwing from all over the world entered the great hall, all of them in their ceremonial dress."

"Cool," Devon says, allowing himself to feel a little more relaxed.

"Oh, it was." Rolfe walks up to join the boy looking out at the sea. "Nightwing from all over Europe, and China, and Africa. And of course, Randolph Muir, Amanda's father. I remember how resplendent he looked in his cape and medals. How proud my father was to serve as his Guardian."

"I want to go to one of those things, Rolfe. I need to meet others like me. Other Nightwing."

"You will. I'll have to find out when the next Witenagemot is held, and where." He sighs. "But for the time being, I don't have any way to know what Nightwing might be out there who may have gone astray."

"Perhaps it is not a living Nightwing," Roxanne says suddenly. "Perhaps it is one from the past."

Rolfe studies her. "Are you intuiting that? Is that clear to you?"

She frowns. "Not entirely. But it has come to me. I can't ignore the idea."

"When Roxanne gets these thoughts, it's good to listen," Rolfe explains to Devon. "I suppose it's possible. After all, Jackson Muir is dead, and he managed to come back."

"That's what I've been saying," Devon tells him. "The Madman isn't through with us. I just know it."

Roxanne has withdrawn a book from the shelf. "I feel it's important you read this," she says, handing the book to Devon.

He glances down at the cover. Raised gold letters read:

The Nightwing Genealogy of Horatio Muir

"These are Horatio's ancestors?" Devon asks.

"Yes," Rolfe says. "And to his credit, he recorded the black sheep of his family along with all the heroes and legends."

"Wear your father's ring as you read," Roxanne says. "It will help you see."

"No way," Devon says. "I can't put that thing on again."

Roxanne has retrieved the ring from the floor.

Devon looks down at it in her hand. There's blood on it. Cecily's blood.

"Fear is a Nightwing's greatest weakness, Devon," Rolfe reminds him.

The boy sighs. "If it means it can help me stop whatever it is that plans to kill Cecily, I'll do it." He takes the ring and slips it back on his finger. His mind remains clear as he sits down at the table and opens the book in front of him.

A LL HAIL Sargon! Sargon our leader! Sargon the Great!"

The words on the page come alive in Devon's mind as he wears his father's ring. He doesn't just *read* about the Nightwing—he *sees* them, too.

Sargon he's seen before. Sargon, the guy who started all this. Devon recognizes him, with his long red hair and beard, standing there in his tunic and sandals, his sword sheathed at his side. Devon reads that Sargon was born nearly three thousand years ago in the land of the Hittites in Asia Minor, now Turkey. At Termessos, the mighty city on the mountainous Mediterranean coast, Sargon set up a fortress of magic. He and his descendants protected the city for generations, with Termessos the only place in that part of the world to be left unconquered by Alexander the Great.

Devon sees Sargon now flanked by the mountains of old Termessos and surrounded by a group of people raising their gold goblets in his honor.

"All hail Sargon!"

"It's some kind of ceremony," Devon tells Rolfe and Roxanne. "I can see Sargon being honored. He's actually smiling." Devon laughs. "He didn't seem in nearly such a good mood when I encountered him."

In fact, at that time Sargon had given Devon a test—a test Devon had only partially passed. He had let his fear get in the way—*fear,* which is like a steroid to demons, pumping them up bigger and stronger and more difficult to defeat. That was when Sargon had called Devon "the Abecedarian." It annoyed Devon then, and it still rankles him now.

"I hope I get to meet Sargon again sometime," Devon says. "Tell him how I defeated the Madman and—"

"Read on, Devon," Rolfe interrupts, a little impatient. "We're looking for Apostates here. Nightwing who've gone bad. That's not Sargon."

Devon sighs and turns the page. He'll have to come back and do this again when he has more time. Wearing his father's ring, scanning the stories of sorcerers past, he's treated to some really awesome visions. On one page he reads about Brutus, a Nightwing who flourished in the last century B.C. Devon looks up to see an image of a dragon-headed ship with Brutus at the mast, as a scaly green sea beast roars up at him through the waves. Then there's Diana, ascending into the night sky, into the outer stratosphere of the earth, with all sorts of creatures made of light following her. Turning the page, Devon almost falls off his chair: a sorcerer named Vortigar, in full armor, is suddenly charging toward him on a white steed, surrounded by an army of other knights. It's like virtual reality gone wild.

Devon beams, ducking his head as Vortigar's sword comes lashing out—seemingly at him. But it impales another knight, who falls off his horse, revealing a demonic face behind the visor.

"Cool," Devon says. "Vortigar lived in the time of King Arthur, right?"

"Yes, Devon," Rolfe says.

"Can't I just watch a little of his fight?"

Rolfe shakes his head, smiling. "You can come back to that later."

Devon returns to the book. He flips through the next few pages. There's Brunhilde the Wise at the court of Charlemagne; there's Wilhelm in old Holland, teaching a roomful of young Nightwing painters; and then there's the first Witenagemot, a gathering of Nightwing that stuns Devon with its visuals: a castle draped in cloth of gold, the attendees all in majestic purple robes. Sorcerers of all ages and races present glowing crystals and magnificent jewels. The meeting is called to order by a white-bearded man named Wiglaf, whom Devon thinks he's seen before. But he can't quite place him.

"I'm only finding the good guys," Devon tells Rolfe.

"Keep reading."

Off the next page Erik Bloodaxe jumps out at him, axe held high over his head.

"Whoa!" Devon shouts. "Maybe this one's an Apostate."

The sorcerer's axe drips with blood as he lifts it from the guts of some guy. Devon understands how Erik, who looks like a Viking, got his name.

"It looks like he just killed a guy," he says. "He must be an Apostate."

"Look closer," Rolfe tells him.

Devon does. He peers into the vision as best he can to get a glimpse of Erik's victim. Talons instead of hands—Devon realizes it's a demon in human form. "Nope," he says, sighing. "Guess Erik's another one of the good guys."

But on the next page his vision darkens. The temperature in the room drops to nearly freezing. "Isobel the Apostate," Devon reads in a low voice. "It says it right here. She's—"

Laughter. A woman's laughter.

The whole room goes dark. Rolfe and Roxanne look around in alarm.

The laughter continues.

"I've heard that before," Devon says. "In the tower!"

"Are you sure, Devon?"

"It's *her*," the boy breathes.

Suddenly the room is engulfed in flames. Devon can no longer see Rolfe or Roxanne, only bright dancing orange flames. Devon recoils from the heat but keeps his eyes alert to learn what he can. He begins to discern images within the flames: huge flying demons soaring over an old village. The people are running out of their homes in fear, stumbling onto cobblestone streets and pointing up at the demons. The creatures dive into their homes, emerging with boxes and chests and even children in their claws. Devon notes from the architecture that it appears to be a village from the period he's been studying in school: Tudor England. But his studies never mentioned anything about Isobel the Apostate or the demons she let loose upon the people.

"Isobel the Apostate," Devon reads, trying to steady himself. "She was born in 1494, the only child of Arthur Plantagenet, a descendant of King Henry the Fourth. Her beauty and magic became legendary. She married a simple squire, Sir Thomas Apple, and, after bearing a son, had her husband poisoned. She opened a Hellhole, seized control of the demons, and directed them to ravage the countryside, making the people dependent on her and thus creating her own loyal army. Isobel's greed for power grew. She conspired with England's enemies abroad, promising untold riches if they would help her topple King Henry the Eighth and place herself on the Throne."

Isobel's laughter echoes throughout the room, causing him to stop reading. He gathers his wits and continues: "In 1522, the Witenagemot was held in England, and a secret meeting of the Nightwing decided Isobel must be delivered to the king as a traitor. It was largely the female Nightwing who overpowered her and subdued her with a golden magical chain. Isobel was condemned by the king's court and burned as a witch, but many claimed she rose from the ashes like a phoenix to seek refuge in the Hellhole."

Devon hears the evil Nightwing sorceress laugh again, but still he cannot see her.

Where is she? I've got to see her face.

Finally he makes out a figure within the flames. A woman, tied to a stake. She's burning alive, laughing as the flames consume her. Her skin is blackening and peeling from her face. Devon can smell her burning flesh. Worse, he can *taste* it.

He slams the book shut. The room returns to normal.

"It was too much," he says. "It was just too gross."

"But you saw enough to convince you it's Isobel the Apostate that we're dealing with?"

Devon makes a face. "It's more like I *heard* enough. I've heard that same laughter in the tower at Ravenscliff."

"Always that tower," Rolfe observes. "What does Amanda keep there?"

"Nothing anymore. I haven't seen a light up there in a while." Devon considers something. "But I did see Bjorn take somebody out of there. He denies it, but I'm sure it was a woman. Could it have been *her*—Isobel?"

Rolfe looks puzzled. "I can't imagine Isobel the Apostate allowing anyone to keep her locked in a room, or simply going along with some gnome who moves her somewhere else. Isobel was one of the most feared sorceresses of all time. She nearly toppled King Henry the Eighth from his throne. Even burning her at the stake wasn't enough to stop her evil. There have been legends ever since that her spirit has returned, still trying to gain mastery over the world."

Devon represses a shiver. "Sounds like somebody else we know. Jackson Muir."

Rolfe looks at him seriously. "Are you sure that was the same laughter you heard in the tower?"

"The very same. And the Voice is confirming it for me. I heard Isobel the Apostate. It must have been her in the tower all this time. It must have been her that I heard sobbing."

Rolfe walks over to stare down at the sea. The waves are growing more fierce, and the lightning on the horizon is becoming more intense. A thunderclap rolls in, louder than any of them expected.

It always storms when I'm here, Devon thinks. *It's as if whenever I discover any new truths about my Nightwing past, it stirs up the elements.* He kind of likes that.

"I don't know, Devon," Rolfe says. "Something must have been happening to Isobel to allow Amanda to keep her prisoner, but I can't imagine what that could be. Isobel is beyond mere flesh and blood now."

Devon shrugs. "Maybe there was some sort of spell put on her by Mrs. Crandall's father, or Horatio Muir, way back when."

"I suppose it's possible, but . . ."

"Well, however it's been managed, I'm *certain* that it's Isobel the Apostate who's been sending those demons after me, and not Jackson Muir." Devon smiles. "That much at least is some consolation."

Roxanne, up until now content to simply sit and listen, stands and approaches Devon. She smiles down at him, crossing her arms over her chest. "I suppose you feel that a woman cannot possibly be as formidable an adversary as a man. Even if she is an undead Nightwing sorceress."

He blushes. "No, I didn't mean that." He blushes harder. "Really. It's just that—"

"Isobel the Apostate has *five centuries* on Jackson Muir," Roxanne tells him. "Five centuries in which she's been able to perfect her powers. To hone her evil into a sword far sharper than anything the Madman could ever wield."

Devon swallows, suitably chagrined. "Yeah. I guess you're right."

Rolfe smiles. "The point is, Devon, we have a major problem on our hands. Once again we have a renegade Nightwing trying to open that portal in the East Wing. And clearly Isobel is looking to *you* to do the job for her."

"What stops her from doing it herself?"

"You sealed the door. Only you can open it."

Devon shudders. "In the vision my dad showed me, I *will* open it."

"Take that merely as a caution. What we need to do now is somehow find Isobel and defeat her."

"And how do we do that?"

Rolfe gives him a wry smile. "I have no idea."

"Great."

"You've got to remember, kiddo, I never got the training I was supposed to get as a Guardian. The

Madman killed my father before I learned very much. I've got to read more of these books. And try to find someone who may know more than I do."

"Any luck in finding other Guardians?"

Rolfe shakes his head. "But I suspect we might have a source of information close by."

"Who?"

"Your new caretaker. The gnome. He clearly knows a lot, and I'll bet he could find a Guardian for us."

"I don't know," Devon says. "Every time I start to trust him, something makes me back off. Remember I saw him with the woman from the tower. What if it *was* Isobel? He could be in league with her."

Rolfe sighs. "Your Voice tell you anything about him?"

"Well, it told me he was a gnome and that I could trust his healing remedy. But not whether I could trust *him*."

"How about you, Roxanne? Any intuition on Bjorn Forkbeard?"

"I'll have to meet him," she says. "Perhaps then."

They agree that the only course of action for right now is for Devon to return to Ravenscliff and stay on his guard. Rolfe pledges to find some answers, and they'll talk tomorrow. Once again Devon apologizes for interrupting them, telling the couple to go back to whatever it was they were doing. He snaps his fingers and disappears.

BUT INSTEAD of reappearing in his room in Ravenscliff as he intended, Devon makes it only as far as the cemetery at the edge of the cliff, at the far end of the Muir estate.

Why did I come here? Devon looks around. The storm is now overhead, although it hasn't yet begun to rain. Lightning crackles through the dark sky, and a bitterly cold wind whips his face. He tries willing himself to his room, but he can't. He hates it when his powers don't work.

He begins trudging through the tall grass. Much of the snow has melted, and the ground is a muddy mess. A particularly loud thunderboom startles him. He turns, as lightning illuminates the grave of Jackson Muir. The angel with the broken wing seems to glow. Devon approaches the monument. He's seen Emily Muir's spirit before, and she seemed sympathetic to his cause. Perhaps she can help him. Perhaps she can help them find and defeat Isobel the Apostate.

But Emily was just an ordinary woman. She had no powers in life. Why should she have them in death? Still, Devon cannot help but feel that she is important to understanding his past. Here, just a few yards away, he once saw the ghost of a woman, crying over the stone marked "Clarissa." He finds the grave now, gazing down at the single word carved into the granite. Why would Emily cry over the grave of Clarissa Jones? She was the servant girl whom Rolfe was hooking up with and who died when his car plunged over the side of the cliff. Her body wasn't even buried here. Like Emily herself, Clarissa had been washed out to sea.

There's got to be a connection between Clarissa and Emily and Jackson, Devon thinks. *And a connection to me. Why else would I see the spirit crying over her grave?*

He lifts his eyes from Clarissa's stone to the obelisk standing in the center of the cemetery. The one simply marked "Devon." No one seems to know who is buried under there. He's certain Mrs. Crandall is lying when she pleads ignorance. This, too, is a clue into his past. But what does it mean? How can he find out?

Devon sighs. He has no time to ponder all this now. The mystery of his past will need to take a backseat for a while, until they can figure out how to defeat Isobel the Apostate.

Unless, as he suspects, all of it is somehow intertwined.

The rain comes, lightly at first, then heavier. Devon hurries out of the cemetery and splashes onto the muddy path leading to the great house. He can barely make out its silhouette against the night sky. There are a few lights glowing from the downstairs windows. But the tower, as he's come to expect, is dark.

Where is Isobel? Could it be true that Mrs. Crandall has been hiding her? And how—and for what purposes?

Once again all his suspicions about the mistress of Ravenscliff come rushing back to his mind. *She did try to kill me,* he thinks. *She and Bjorn did try to send me down into the past*—a past he now recognizes as Tudor England, the time of Isobel the Apostate. *They wanted me to come under her power, so that she could force me to open the Hellhole.*

But why would Mrs. Crandall want that? That's the thing she fears most. As the rain begins to pummel him, he starts to run up the path, wishing he could make sense of things.

Why can't I just have a normal life? Why does it always have to be this way?

As HE NEARS the driveway, he spies D.J.'s car, its windshield wipers frantically swinging back and forth in a fruitless attempt to beat back the downpour. Someone's getting out of the passenger-side door. Devon squints through the rain. Is it Cecily?

Lightning flashes just then, and Devon sees it most certainly is not Cecily.

It's Morgana.

"Thanks so much again, D.J.," she's saying. "I really appreciate it."

"Hey, anytime."

Morgana hurries into the house.

D.J. starts to drive off, but Devon runs up into his headlights and flags him down.

"What's going on?" Devon asks.

D.J. rolls down his window, but just a bit. "What do you mean, what's going on?"

Devon makes a face, the rain slicking his hair down into his eyes. "I *mean,* what were you doing with Morgana?"

"She wanted a ride into town."

"But why did *you* take her?"

"What's the matter, Devon? You jealous? First you take Cecily, now you want Morgana, too?"

D.J. rolls up his window and screeches out of the driveway.

Devon is stunned. What was *that* all about? D.J.'s his best friend. Yes, Devon knows that D.J. once had a crush on Cecily, but he'd seemed to accept the fact that she and Devon were now dating. At least, Devon *thought* he'd accepted it.

But *Morgana?* First of all, she's six years older than D.J.—and she's Edward Muir's fiancée!

Devon hurries into the house, closing the door against the rain.

"Look at you, Devon March!" Cecily says, coming out of the parlor and into the foyer. "You look like a drowned rat."

"Thanks for the compliment," he says, pulling off his coat and hanging it on the coatrack. He shivers. "Did you see Morgana come in just now?"

Cecily scowls. "Yes. I saw her."

"Did she say where she was?"

"I don't engage with her." Cecily turns, walking back into the parlor. "I figure the less said between us, the better. Otherwise, I'll tell her I can see right through her dirty little scheme to bilk my uncle of his money."

Devon feels the need to rise to Morgana's defense again, but he puts it aside. Let Cecily have her childish feelings. "Look," he says, "I'm just curious because she was out with D.J."

Cecily spins on him. "D.J.?"

"Yeah. I just saw him drop her off."

Cecily's eyes nearly bug out of her head. "Wait until I tell Uncle Edward!"

"I'm sure it was harmless, Cecily. D.J. said he just gave her a ride into town."

"She doesn't need a ride into town! She has three cars in the garage to choose from! And Bjorn could've driven her! Or how about her fiancé? If she had wanted to go into town, why not go with Uncle Edward?"

Devon shrugs. "He's been down at the Muir cannery a lot, going over the books for your mother. Maybe he wasn't around."

"You're always defending her," Cecily snaps.

"Well, you're always *attacking* her."

She shakes her hair the way she always does when she's angry. "Well, I have homework to do. Good *night*, Devon."

"Cecily, wait. There's some stuff I need to talk to you about."

"Why don't you talk to *Morgana* about it?" She turns on her heel and hurries up the stairs.

"Geez," Devon says, flopping down on the couch. *What an immature brat*, he thinks. *I've never known Cecily to be so—so—juvenile.*

Why did she have such a visceral dislike of Morgana? Come to think of it, so did Ana. And Mrs. Crandall. All the women seem to hate her and all the guys love her. Except for Alexander, that is.

Devon looks up into the gray somber eyes of Horatio Muir's portrait, hanging over the mantel.

I mean, if Morgana really was a conniver, a schemer, a gold digger as Cecily believes, I think I'd know. But everything I sense about her is good. Mysterious maybe, but good.

And beautiful.

God, Morgana's beautiful.

"Hello, Devon."

He jumps. A hand on his shoulder. He turns around.

Morgana, in a pink angora sweater and tight black leather pants.

"Oh, uh, hi," he stutters.

"Your hair is soaking wet. You'll catch cold."

He smiles as she sits down beside him. "Yeah, I got caught in the rainstorm."

"It's quite the storm."

Devon looks over at her. "I saw D.J. gave you a ride."

"Yes. What a sweet boy. I happened to run into him when he was here this afternoon and mentioned how I was hoping to get a tour of the village. Edward's been so busy. And D.J. offered to take me. It was so nice of him."

Devon smiles. So it *was* perfectly innocent. At least from Morgana's perspective.

"Well," he says, "I think maybe D.J. might have a crush on you."

She blushes. "Oh, dear. You think?"

"He's harmless, don't worry."

Morgana smiles. "Oh, he's very nice. But not nearly as smart as you. I can tell."

Now it's Devon's turn to blush.

"Really," she says. "I am *so* impressed that you came to this madhouse and found your way on your own. After encountering all those hideous things." She wraps her arms around herself and shudders. "I can't imagine Amanda was much help to you."

Devon shrugs. "I guess I did okay."

"You *guess*? Devon, had it been me, with no one to talk to about it, I'd have been on the next bus out of this town." She looks over at him and her lips are trembling. "I still can't quite believe all the horror stories Edward has told me. He's only told me a little bit. He says that's all I need to know. But it's been enough to scare me out of my wits. I feel so confused and frightened."

She starts to cry.

"Oh, hey," Devon says, reaching over and placing his arm around her shoulder. "It's okay."

But he's not being honest with her. It is definitely *not* okay—not with yet another Apostate trying to open the portal and set the demons free. If Edward really loves her, he should get Morgana out of this house. *Now.* The rest of them here at least have sorcery in their blood: this is their heritage, the legacy with which they must contend, for good or bad. Morgana, on the other hand, is a complete innocent, pulled into this house of horrors without any forewarning.

She looks at Devon with imploring eyes. "How can

it be true what Edward tells me? About the door that leads into hell?"

"All I know is that it *is* true," Devon tells her. "And there *is* danger here."

Morgana wipes her eyes. "Edward's shown me some of the books about these Nightwing sorcerers. He says I need to know about them if I'm to be his wife. But that's all he'll tell me. I'm left so unsure of everything, with so many questions and fears."

"Look," Devon tells her, "I know it's none of my business, but if you have any doubts about this marriage, you ought to listen to them."

Her soft brown eyes find his. "You are wise beyond your years, Devon March," she says in a low, gentle voice, caressing his face with the back of her hand.

He feels his cheeks burn with embarrassment.

Morgana smiles. "Sitting here with you, I feel no fear. None at all. Why is that, Devon?"

He wants to kiss her. He wants to kiss her so bad but he knows he can't. He shouldn't. He mustn't.

He struggles to find his voice. "I can't promise you, Morgana," he says. "But I will do my best to protect you from anything in this house."

She looks as if she'll cry again. "Oh, Devon. I believe you will." She reaches over and kisses him quickly on the lips. "Thank you, Devon. Thank you for listening."

With that she stands and walks out of the room,

leaving Devon sitting there, hot and flushed, every fiber of his being on edge. He hurries upstairs to take the coldest shower he's ever had in his life.

H E'S TOWELING his hair dry when he hears the scratching from his closet.

That scorpion thing, he remembers.

He pulls on a pair of sweats and a shirt. *Maybe I can learn something from it. I've got it under my power now. Might as well check it out.*

It's repulsive. He pulls it out of his laundry bag and holds it away from his face. It stinks like rotting eggs. Its black tail quivers.

"So where is she?" Devon asks the demon. "Where is Isobel the Apostate? She sent you here. You must know where she is."

But the thing is stupid, one of the Hellhole's lower life-forms. It just wriggles in his grip.

"Do you have any intelligence at all?" Devon asks.

He studies the thing. He finds its tiny little eyes and looks into them. He begins to make out something, a tiny speck of light that grows larger as he gazes into it.

"Yes," he says, understanding. "I can use your eyes to see her."

He begins to make out a vision. Hundreds of scorpion demons, swarming over a floor. Devon tries to pull back, to get a larger view of the scene, but he can't. He's looking into the eyes of the scorpion and out from the eyes of another one like it, someplace else. He has to settle for its vantage point, low and indistinct. It's as if a tiny camera is strapped to the head of one of these things and Devon is watching on a video screen. His vision travels as the thing whose eyes he's hijacked crawls over its stinking brethren to reach a small clearing on the floor.

Devon recognizes the carpet. It's the old oriental rug in the East Wing.

That's where the scorpion demons are, he thinks. *The East Wing.*

And so Isobel must be there, too.

Yes, he's sure of it: There's the door to the inner room. It's open, and the scorpion through which Devon sees scuttles quickly inside. Devon recognizes the floor of the room. He could never forget it, not after being trapped in there months ago, convinced he would die. He feels the blast of heat against his face. He looks up, as best he can, as the scorpion hurries toward another door.

A metal door. The portal into the world of the demons.

The Hellhole.

Suddenly Devon's vision is rising. The scorpion is being lifted by someone, who then gazes into its eyes.

And thus looks directly at Devon.

He gasps.

They're eye to eye. He and Isobel the Apostate. He feels the evil pulsing from her black eyes. She starts to laugh.

She's here, in this house, he realizes. *At the very opening to the Hellhole in the East Wing!*

—◆—

SIX

A DEADLY DUEL

I'VE GOT TO GET up there," Devon says out loud. "I've got to get into the East Wing!"

"And just why do you need to go there?"

Devon looks up quickly. Edward Muir stands glaring at him, his arms folded across his chest.

"Excuse me, but haven't you ever heard of knocking?" Devon asks.

"The door was ajar. Not so smart for a young Nightwing-in-training—especially when he's got one of those filthy hellspawns in his hands." Edward makes a face of disgust. "Get rid of that thing."

Devon sighs. He's gotten all he can from the demon. "Back to your Hellhole," he utters, and the scorpion disappears from his hand.

He turns back to Edward Muir, who seems completely unimpressed with Devon's sorcery.

"I take it Mrs. Crandall has filled you in on everything that happened here," Devon says, "and all about my powers."

The older man nods. Gone is the twinkle in his eyes, the warmth that Devon had seen when he first arrived on Christmas Eve. He looms over Devon with a dark air.

"She's also told me she suspects you've been sneaking off to meet with Rolfe Montaigne," Edward tells him.

Devon says nothing to incriminate himself. "I'm sure you can understand my curiosity about who and what I am, and where I come from."

"I had hoped we could be friends, Devon. But if you're palling around with Montaigne—" His lips tighten in anger, little white worms of bitterness and resentment. "That murderer wants to destroy this family."

"That's not important now."

Edward becomes indignant. "Of *course* it's important. Montaigne is capable of anything. Poor Clarissa. Whenever I think of her, left to drown—"

Devon cuts him off. "What I'm trying to tell you is that this family faces a much more dangerous threat than Rolfe Montaigne."

Edward raises an eyebrow, distinctly irritated by such talk. "I suppose you mean the demons."

"Yes." Devon looks at him seriously. "That's why I

was saying I needed to get into the East Wing. Someone is trying to get that portal open."

Edward scoffs. "Look, Devon. I checked on the portal after the incident the other night. It's still bolted."

Devon is growing impatient. "Just because it's still bolted doesn't mean it will remain that way forever. Do you know who Isobel the Apostate is?"

Edward rolls his eyes. "All that Nightwing history bored me."

"Well, she was one of the worst of them all. Like Jackson, she used the demons of the Hellhole to make herself very powerful. She was burned as a witch in 1522. And now she's back."

Edward Muir laughs. "Is this what Montaigne's been telling you?"

"No. I saw it myself. I saw her just now—in the East Wing!"

Edward laughs again. "That's impossible."

"Why is it impossible?"

His face becomes serious. "Because we've made sure it's impossible."

"How? You and Mrs. Crandall keep saying things like that. But you renounced your powers. How can you do anything to prevent Isobel from doing whatever she wants to do?"

"You'll just have to trust me on this, Devon."

Devon shakes his head. "I don't think I can do that,

Edward. Too often I've been told everything here is safe, everything is secure, and then some stinking beasty crawls through my window and grabs me around the throat."

Edward Muir gives him a reproving look. "Well, there's a simple explanation for that. You're still practicing sorcery. That stirs things up. My sister forbade you from doing any of your little magic tricks, but just now I saw you send that scorpion demon back to its Hellhole. Why not just crush the blasted thing underfoot?"

Devon scowls. "Guess I didn't want to get the floor messy."

"You're a very brash young man." Edward gives him a small smile. "Rather reminds me of myself at your age."

"Please, Edward. Take me to the East Wing. Show me the portal is safe."

Edward sighs.

"You owe me," Devon says. "I saved your son from the Madman."

The older man grunts. Devon's not sure whether that makes much difference to Edward Muir. His cold "I don't want him" still haunts Devon's mind. Poor Alexander, stuck with a father like this.

But Edward gives in. "All right. Just don't tell

Amanda. She'd work herself up into one of her states, and neither one of us wants that."

THEY HEAD silently down the stairs. Thankfully the foyer and parlor are empty, the only sound the heavy ticking of the ancient grandfather clock. Edward pauses before the locked door to the East Wing and fumbles in his pocket for the key.

Devon can see he's trembling.

"This place holds a lot of bad memories for you," he says softly.

Edward eyes him. "Oh, not really. Just the image of my father being dragged to his death, and all of us thinking we were next. That's all."

He unlocks the door. With only a flashlight to guide them, they follow the corridor leading into the East Wing, then climb a set of stairs to the second floor. How well Devon recalls his last walk down this corridor—heading for the same place they're heading for now, except then he wasn't just going to check on the door. He was planning on *opening* it—and going *inside* the Hellhole.

He feels a little weak, as he always does when he remembers that episode, the most terrifying time of his life. He pauses a moment in the corridor, steadying himself against the wall.

Edward swings the flashlight around to find his face. "You okay?"

"Yeah," Devon says, and they resume walking.

The dust here is more than an inch thick in some places. The East Wing has been closed off for over two decades, and most of its furnishings removed. What's left are a few broken armchairs and dozens of rusty hooks on the walls.

A mouse suddenly scurries by, crossing Edward's foot. He reacts with a gasp.

"Damn things," he grumbles. "I've told Amanda we ought to call in an exterminator for this place."

Devon can't help but smile. He wonders what the exterminator would do if he encountered a nest of cretins other than rats and mice—ones with talons, forked tongues, and skeletal faces.

They turn into what was once an upstairs sitting room, where a grimy chandelier still hangs from the center of the ceiling. Simon had told him that this was Emily Muir's private parlor. How many tears had she shed here over her cruel husband, the Madman? Might it have been here, in this very room, that she made her fateful decision to take that final leap off of Devil's Rock?

But there's no time to ponder such things now. Just ahead is the place that they seek. A small inner chamber, with no windows, which Devon believes was once

Horatio Muir's private Nightwing library. He longs to read the books that are stored inside, but knows Edward would never permit it. Rolfe has many books that he's been reading, but these were Horatio's *own*. Devon can only begin to imagine what Knowledge they might contain.

"Edward," he says, as they enter the room. "Bring the flashlight over here."

The older man complies. Devon indicates a portrait on the wall, and the flashlight illuminates the face. It is the spitting image of Devon, dressed in waistcoat and knickers in the style of the 1930s.

"Resemble anyone you know?" Devon asks.

Edward moves the flashlight from the portrait to Devon and then back again. "I remember this portrait. It's been hanging here as long as I can remember." He pauses. "It *does* look like you, I admit that."

"Any idea who it is?"

"No," Edward says, and Devon believes him.

The older man swings the beam of the flashlight toward the end of the room. That's when the heat comes roaring at them, as if an electric heater had just been turned on full blast. Turning his face away from its intensity, Devon feels sick to his stomach. *This is where they live. The things that have haunted me all my life.*

On the far wall is the portal into the world of the

demons, a half-size metal door with a solid steel bolt securing it. Devon listens. He can hear the scratching behind the door, the whispers of the demons to be set free.

"You see?" Edward says, his voice trembling in undisguised terror. "It's still secure. Let's go. Let's get out of here."

Devon wants out, too, and bad—but he forces himself to stay in place. He takes the flashlight from Edward's hand and scans the room himself. The beam falls across the rolltop desk, the books on the floor, the bookcase filled with Nightwing lore. But he sees none of the scorpion things and no sign of Isobel the Apostate. The dust on the floor hasn't been disturbed.

"But she was here," Devon says. "I know it."

The Voice confirms it for him; Isobel the Apostate *was* here, in this room, desperate to get that portal open to harness the power of the creatures within. But the Voice also corroborates what Devon can already sense: If she was here, she's gone now.

But where?

"Let's go, Devon," Edward says, his voice shaking terribly.

Devon sighs. The older man snatches the flashlight back from him and heads back out into the sitting room, hurrying into the corridor beyond without even waiting for Devon.

"I'm telling you, she was here," Devon insists when he catches up with him.

"It's still sealed. That's all that matters."

They're heading back down the stairs toward the main part of the house. "Don't you still wish you had your powers?" Devon asks. "That way you wouldn't have to be so scared."

Edward stops suddenly and turns to face him. "I am *not* scared," he says defensively, and in his eyes Devon can see the same defiance he's seen in Alexander's. An overwhelming pride, a stubborn arrogance.

Devon simply shrugs. "I didn't mean to insult you."

Edward huffs. "You need to understand. I was never into the whole Nightwing tradition the way my father was. Not even as much as Amanda was." He pauses, remembering. "Or *Rolfe*. Oh, how *serious* he took it all. How *proud* he was to be a Guardian-in-training." He makes a sound of distaste. "I just wanted to be a *normal* kid. Can't you understand that?"

"Yeah," Devon admits. "I can understand."

"I just found all of that Nightwing training to be boring. All that talk of noble deeds. I was just a kid, wanting to have some fun." He laughs. "My father never let me use my powers the way I would've *liked* to. I would've liked to become my school's top athlete, but forget that. Or jump off the cliff and fly around to impress my friends. But *no*. Never anything fun like that."

"The powers don't work unless you really need them. They're not for show."

Edward makes a face at him. "Oh, Montaigne has been teaching you well. You sound just like him." He snarls at the memory. "Rolfe could do no wrong. He was just the *perfect* young boy in my father's eyes, because, see, he paid attention. He actually *cared* about all that Nightwing nonsense, about all that blather about the power of goodness and light. *Sissy* stuff, if you ask me. My father acted as if he'd rather *Rolfe* had been his son, and not me."

Devon says nothing. They resume walking.

"As a matter of fact," Edward says, as they lock the door to the East Wing behind them, "I'm not in the least bit sorry we renounced our powers." He laughs. "I don't think I would have made a very good sorcerer."

"Why's that?"

He grins. "Because I would've used my powers for my own gain. Wealth, women, privilege, control. I enjoy all of that enough now—imagine what I would have been like if I'd had the powers of the Nightwing." He smiles, more to himself than to Devon. "Oh, I definitely would've been an Apostate. Maybe not as bad as Uncle Jackson, but an Apostate nevertheless."

"Well," Devon says, "at least you're honest."

"Now, remember. None of this to my sister."

Devon promises. Watching the older man walk off,

Devon can only think that he's glad, too, that Edward Muir is not a sorcerer. One Apostate in the family is quite enough.

O N THE RIDE to school the next day, Cecily still isn't speaking to him. She sits in the backseat sulking as Bjorn chauffeurs them in his Cadillac. Devon's too tired to play any games with Cecily, so after a cordial "good morning" he makes no further attempt to win her over. He can tell his indifference just infuriates her more.

At school, Devon immediately seeks out D.J.

"He's not here," Marcus tells him as they stand at their lockers. "He's usually here by now, sitting out in his car in the parking lot blaring that ancient Aerosmith."

Devon admits it's unusual that D.J. is late. "Has he seemed weird to you lately?"

Marcus smirks. "With D.J., it's hard to tell. He listens to 1970s rock, washes his hair only once a week, and his latest piercing is in a place he can't show us."

Devon smiles. "No, not that kind of weird. That's normal weird. I'm talking like him being—oh, I don't know, angry or nasty."

Marcus nods. "Yeah, he *has* seemed moody. Since before New Year's, he's been really grouchy."

"I ran into him at Ravenscliff. He had been out with Edward Muir's fiancée."

Marcus makes a face. "Morgana? What's up with that?"

"I don't know. I talked to her, and she just considered it an innocent little trip into town. But I think it meant a lot more to D.J. He freaked out when I asked him where they'd been. Accused me of being jealous."

Marcus levels his eyes at him. "Were you?"

Devon is stunned. "What are you, *crazy*? She's eight years older than I am. And besides, she's going to marry Edward Muir."

Marcus folds his arms over his chest. "And then there's Cecily. You forgot to mention her."

Devon blushes. "Of *course*. Of course, there's Cecily."

He doesn't tell Marcus about his nightly dreams of Morgana. He's embarrassed about the dreams, feeling like a stupid lovestruck kid in awe of an older woman. Here he's trying to focus on a potential new round of demonic attacks and he's dreaming about Morgana Green. His dad was right when he'd predicted his teenage hormones were going to make him a little bit crazy.

He's still thinking about his father as he slides behind his desk in history class. Has it really only been a few months since Dad died? So much has happened since, and seeing Dad again by using his ring has left Devon feeling a new rush of grief. *If only I could talk with Dad, really talk to him, not just like I did in that vision. I want him here, with me, in the flesh, the way it used to be. There's so much we used to talk about. Dad could help me understand these stupid feelings I have for Morgana. I could talk to Dad about anything.*

"Mr. March?"

He looks up quickly. Mr. Weatherby is looming over him.

"I asked you a question."

Devon groans. Once again, he was a little too busy to do his homework.

"I'm sorry. Would you repeat it?"

"I asked you who was the chief rival claimant to the throne of Henry Tudor."

He suddenly remembers what he'd read at Rolfe's house, and Rolfe's words: *She nearly toppled King Henry the Eighth from his throne.*

"Isobel the Apostate," Devon blurts out.

Mr. Weatherby makes a sour face. "Isobel the What?"

"I—I thought I read about her. Somewhere."

His teacher arches an eyebrow at him. "Not in this text, you didn't."

Devon shrinks back in his chair a little. "No. I guess not."

"Can anyone else tell me? Someone perhaps who did their reading assignment and didn't sit around all night watching *SmackDown!*?"

Devon scowls. *Yeah, only if The Rock starts wrestling demons.*

Some snot-nosed classmate guesses the right answer—Edward, earl of Warwick—and Devon does his best to listen to the remainder of the lecture. After all, they're studying about a period of time in which Isobel was very much alive. He might actually learn something important.

After class, he approaches Mr. Weatherby. "Are you sure you never heard of Isobel the Apostate? I was sure I read somewhere that she tried to get Henry's throne."

The teacher sighs. "I consider myself an expert on Tudor England, Mr. March. I have never come across that name. But, just to indulge you . . ." He walks over to his bookshelf and withdraws a large book. "This is a definitive account of the reign of Henry the Eighth. There was much more to his reign than simply chopping off the heads of his wives, you know."

Devon waits as he consults the index.

"The only Isobel I find is Isabella of Castile, who was certainly no Apostate." Mr. Weatherby slams the book shut. "She was as good a Catholic as they come, and the very woman who sent Columbus to America. Now, does that satisfy your curiosity?"

Devon sighs. "Yeah. That should do it."

"If you come across a text that says otherwise," Mr. Weatherby calls after Devon as he leaves the classroom, "I should enjoy seeing it."

Devon just smirks. How he'd love to bring in the Nightwing history books and push them into Weatherby's arrogant face. That would sure shake up his notions of who did what in the past.

ONCE MORE, Cecily cold-shoulders him on the ride home. Devon had been hoping D.J. would show up so they could all head over to Gio's. He wants to talk to them all about Isobel. But D.J. has been absent all day.

The mystery of where he's been is solved once they pull into the long driveway at Ravenscliff. There, once more, just outside the front doors, is D.J.'s red Camaro.

"What is going *on* with him?" Cecily barks, jumping out of Bjorn's car and pushing through the front doors. "Is he crazy? *D.J.!*"

They spot him carrying cardboard boxes up the stairs.

"D.J.!" Cecily calls again. "What are you doing here?"

"I'm helping Morgana with some stuff she bought."

"You missed school for that?"

"Yeah," he says, turning away from her. "What are you gonna do? Tell my mother?"

Morgana now appears on the landing from the upstairs corridor. "Oh, D.J., you are a doll. Thanks so much for getting all this stuff from town."

"No problem," he says, grinning idiotically at her.

"Just put it with the rest of the stuff in my room."

"Aye, aye, captain."

Cecily turns to Devon. "Can you believe that?"

"Oh," Devon says. "Are you speaking to me now?"

Morgana has spotted them and she starts down toward them. "Devon, Cecily," she says. "How was school?"

Cecily meets her at the foot of the stairs. "What are you doing with D.J.?" she demands.

Morgana looks surprised. "I'm just—well, he offered—he got some things for me in town."

"And why couldn't you do it on your own?"

Morgana tries to smile. She's clearly taken aback by Cecily's aggressive grilling. "I don't know my way," she says. "And navigating that steep driveway frightened me."

"Does Uncle Edward know you're spending all this time with a sixteen-year-old boy?"

"Hey," Devon says, coming up behind her. "Cool down, Cecily."

"I will *not* cool down!" She spins around to glare at

him. "I can see right through this schemer even if you can't." She turns back to Morgana. "I don't buy your sweet and charming act for one instant, not that fake accent or phony smile. And don't think I won't tell my uncle how you've been messing around with D.J."

With that, she brushes past Morgana and runs up the stairs.

"She didn't mean that," Devon stutters. "She's just—"

Morgana bursts into tears.

"Why do they all hate me? Amanda, Cecily, Alexander. They all hate me!"

She covers her face with her hands and sobs into them.

"Hey, hey," Devon says, putting his arm around her and escorting her into the parlor. She's still crying uncontrollably as he settles her down onto the couch. He sits close to her. She smells wonderful: *Lilacs,* Devon thinks.

"I came here hoping I could fit in," she says, struggling to catch her breath. "But everyone hates me. What did I do?"

"I don't hate you," Devon tells her.

She looks at him. Her eyes are red and puffy, her mascara streaked down her cheeks. "Thank God for you, Devon."

She puts her arms around him and pulls him in

close. He looks over her shoulder to see D.J. glaring down at them.

"What's the matter?" D.J. asks.

"Cecily just said some stuff," Devon says.

Morgana pulls back, wiping her eyes. "Perhaps I was wrong to ask you to help me," she says to D.J.

"Wrong? No way." He hurries to her, dropping to his knees before her. He takes her hands. "Morgana, don't listen to Cecily. She's a spoiled brat."

"Uh, hey, D.J.," Devon says, "there's no need to start calling Cecily names."

"You know what, Devon?" D.J.'s voice is mean, condescending. "I can handle this. I'm here now for her. You can just run along."

Devon feels himself grow indignant. "You? *I've* been the one who's been comforting her. I've been the one to—"

"You've been the one to what?" comes a new voice.

All three of them look up. Edward Muir stands in the doorway.

"Oh, darling," Morgana says, standing and rushing to him. His arms encircle her possessively. "These boys were just reassuring me. They've both been so kind."

Edward looks at them with suspicion. "Reassuring you about what?"

"It's nothing," Morgana says. "Some silly misunderstanding with Cecily."

"Has my niece been giving you any trouble? If she has, by God, I'll talk to Amanda and—"

"Oh, no, no," Morgana pleads. "Don't do that. I wouldn't want to get her into trouble. I want her to like me. I want her to accept me."

"Come on," Edward says, clearly uncomfortable continuing this conversation in front of Devon and D.J. He ushers her off down the hallway toward the library.

The two boys just look at each other without saying anything for several seconds.

"I thought we were friends," Devon finally says.

D.J. sighs. "We are."

"You haven't been acting that way. You've been acting like I'm some rival for Morgana."

D.J. walks over to the large glass windows that look out on the rocky cliffs below. "So I admit I've got it bad for her. I've been acting like a jerk." He slams his fist into his palm. "It *killed* me to see Mr. Muir walk away with her."

"D.J., she's too old for you. And she's engaged."

His friend shakes his finger at him. "There's something between us. I know there is. When I look in her eyes, I see it. She has feelings for me."

Devon feels himself growing absurdly jealous—and he remembers Marcus's pointed question this morning, inquiring into that very thing. *Why do I feel this*

*way? It's Cecily I care about—so why do I feel I could be-
come as hooked on Morgana as D.J.?*

"Look, Deej," Devon says, "keep a level head on
your shoulders. You never lose your cool. Even when
you've had demons coming at you, you've been steady.
You've got to know what you're thinking is impossible."

D.J. grimaces. He puts his hands to his ears and
seems to try to crush his head between them.

"I just feel like I'm going crazy sometimes," D.J.
says. "I really like her, Devon. More than I've ever liked
any girl."

"Hey, buddy, it's going to be okay," Devon says.

D.J. says nothing. He just turns, terribly torn, and
runs out of the house. Devon hears his car start and
screech out of the driveway.

*I've got to stay focused here, Devon tells himself. I
can't be getting caught up in a soap opera with Morgana.
I've got a renegade Nightwing to defeat—or else that vision Dad showed me, with Cecily facedown in a pool of
blood, might just come true.*

UPSTAIRS, he finds Alexander in the playroom.
His concern for the boy has grown ever since he
made the discovery about Isobel. The last time an
Apostate tried to open the Hellhole, Alexander's life

was the first to be put in danger. Devon figures checking in on the boy is a good thing.

"Hey, buddy," Devon says.

Alexander's scrunched down in his beanbag chair
reading comic books. "Hey," he replies, barely lifting
his head in greeting.

"Why so glum?"

The boy just shrugs.

"I heard your aunt say she was talking with the
school. Looks like you're going to start in a couple of
weeks."

Once, before Devon arrived at Ravenscliff, Alexander had attended a prestigious boarding school in
Connecticut. But he was expelled after setting fire to
the curtains in the cafeteria. Since then, the boy has
just hung around the house, reading comic books, eating too many cupcakes, and getting sucked down the
mouths of Hellholes. Finally Mrs. Crandall has decided the best thing is to send him to the local Misery
Point public grammar school.

"I'm sure I'll hate it," Alexander says.

Devon stoops down beside him. "Not necessarily."

"I hate being a new kid."

"I do, too, but it worked out okay for me. Look at
the friends I made. D.J., Marcus, Ana . . ."

Alexander just shrugs again.

"Something's bugging you," Devon says. "What is it?"

"Nothing."

"Come on. I thought our days of keeping secrets from each other were over."

Alexander puts down the comic book and looks Devon in the face. "I hate her," he says plainly.

"Who?" Devon asks, but he's pretty sure he knows.

"Morgana."

"Why, Alexander? She is so nice. She really wants to be your friend."

"She's taking my father away from me."

Devon shakes his head. "No, she's not. She wants you all to be a family."

Alexander just flops back in frustration. He says nothing further, as if Devon couldn't possibly understand.

Devon considers something. "How often have you seen your Dad since he's been back?"

Alexander doesn't reply.

"I thought you guys were going to Boston—"

"It'll never happen." Alexander sits up. "I hardly see him at all."

Devon knows this is the real issue—the real reason why the boy resents Morgana so much. After missing his father so fiercely, Alexander has been left out in the cold, ignored by the father he adores. It's easy to blame

Morgana, but Devon knows it's Edward Muir's own selfishness that's the true cause.

Alexander stands and walks over to the window. "I wish I knew where my mother was. I'd write to her and tell her not to let my father divorce her. That way he could never marry Morgana."

Devon comes up behind him and places a hand on his shoulder. He really feels for Alexander. He knows how important a father's love is. Everything Devon is today he directly credits to Dad. His father had been the exact opposite of Alexander's—devoted, caring, compassionate—even if, as it turned out, he hadn't been Devon's biological parent. Still, he has more credibility as a father than Edward Muir could ever attain.

"Hey," Alexander says, looking out the window to the driveway below. "Isn't that Rolfe's car?"

Devon looks. Sure enough, it's Rolfe's Porsche. What would he be doing here? He knows he's persona non grata at Ravenscliff.

It must be very important, Devon thinks. *He must be here to give me some information.*

But if he hopes to see Rolfe privately, those hopes are quickly dashed. Alexander lets out a whoop and runs out of the playroom, heading for the stairs. Alexander thinks Rolfe is pretty cool, and somewhere, deep down, even if the boy can't recall all the details,

Devon's sure Alexander knows Rolfe played a part in saving him from the Madman.

"Hey, wait up," Devon calls after him. "Don't let everybody know he's here."

But it's too late. As soon as they emerge onto the landing overlooking the foyer, they see Rolfe has already encountered another member of the household.

Edward Muir has a pistol leveled straight at Rolfe's head, and he's grinning.

"I should have done this years ago," he says, and pulls the trigger.

Devon screams.

SEVEN

CRYING IN THE NIGHT

N O!" Devon shouts, suddenly leaping like an antelope over the banister and down to the first floor below.

Edward Muir leans his head back in laughter, cackling wildly. Rolfe still stands glaring at him, arms crossed over his chest.

The gun wasn't loaded.

"Brave little Nightwing boy to the rescue," Edward says, laughing. "No need to get your powers all aflutter."

"You haven't changed, Edward," Rolfe says.

Devon catches his breath as Alexander comes running down the stairs. "That was cool, Devon. Do it again!"

"Go up to your room, Alexander," his father orders.

"No. I want to see Rolfe. Can I go for a ride in your car?"

Rolfe tousles the boy's hair.

Edward Muir seethes. "The last thing in the world I'd ever permit is for you to get into an automobile with this man. Now, go upstairs, Alexander!"

The boy pouts, but he obeys.

"Now state your business, Montaigne, and get out of here."

"I came to see Devon."

"It's forbidden," Edward tells him.

"By whom?" Rolfe asks.

"By me." This is the voice of Amanda Muir Crandall, who, in her usual catlike manner, has appeared without any of them noticing. She stands over them, glaring down from the landing. "Devon is my ward, Rolfe, and you know I have given strict orders that there be no communication between the two of you."

She comes down the stairs, elegant and grand. All eyes watch her. Her brother backs off a bit, surrendering to the authority of his sister. She holds her chin high and gathers herself up imperiously to stand in front of Rolfe.

"As beautiful as ever, Amanda," Rolfe says, and Devon thinks he's being sincere.

"I'm going to have to ask you to leave, Rolfe."

"Please," Devon says. "If he came to see me, it must be important. Something about Isobel—"

"Isobel?" Mrs. Crandall asks, looking over at him.

"Isobel the Apostate. She was a Nightwing from the sixteenth century who—"

"I know perfectly well who Isobel the Apostate is," Mrs. Crandall says, cutting him off. "What possible connection could she have to Mr. Montaigne?"

"Maybe if you let me talk, I'd tell you," Rolfe says.

Her eyes are cold and full of hatred. So many years of bitterness toward this man she once loved. "You will do no such thing," she says. "Once again, I am asking you to leave."

"I've seen a vision of Isobel the Apostate," Devon blurts out. "She's trying to open the Hellhole."

"Isobel the Apostate has been dead for nearly five hundred years," Mrs. Crandall snaps.

"Death didn't stop Jackson Muir from coming back," Devon reminds her.

"Enough of this. I forbid this kind of talk. Nothing can happen here. The portal cannot be reopened. We have seen to that."

"*How* have you seen to that, Amanda?" Rolfe asks. "How is that possible? You have no powers. Only Devon—"

She steams. "Do I need to call the police to force you off my property?"

Rolfe sighs. Devon can tell he's not going to press further. There's only so far one can go with Amanda Muir Crandall before she inevitably wins. Rolfe turns to leave, but not before making eye contact with Devon. They'll have to meet later, away from these hostile forces.

But just as Rolfe opens the door, he runs almost headfirst into Morgana, who's coming in.

"Oh," she says. "I'm sorry!"

"Please," Rolfe says, clearly surprised. He immediately lays on the charm. "The blame is entirely mine, for not seeing such a beautiful lady."

She blushes. "I'm Morgana Green."

Edward Muir is suddenly behind Rolfe. "And my fiancée."

"Oh?" Rolfe looks at him, a wicked little smile playing with his lips. "Does your wife know you have a fiancée?"

Edward grabs Morgana by the arm and pulls her inside. She seems frightened and confused, and Devon feels sorry for her, yet again.

"That's none of your business, Montaigne."

"Edward, you're hurting my arm," Morgana cries.

He ignores her. "Go on, Montaigne. Get out of here."

"The lady said you were hurting her arm," Rolfe says, growing angry.

"What I do in my house is my business," Edward shouts, his face turning red.

"Edward!" Morgana seems to be in terrible pain as he keeps his grip on her arm. "You're hurting me!"

"Let her go," Rolfe demands.

"How dare you give me orders?"

"Edward, please!" Morgana cries.

Devon hardly sees what comes next, as it happens so fast: Rolfe hauls off and punches Edward right in the jaw. Edward flies backward, landing hard on his butt.

"I'm calling the police!" Mrs. Crandall shouts.

"What lie will you tell them this time?" Rolfe yells at her. He turns to Morgana. "I hope your arm is all right, ma'am. I'm sorry to have met you under such circumstances. If ever you need a friend, and in this house I suppose that to be inevitable, please remember that my name is Rolfe Montaigne."

With that, he's out the door.

Only then does Edward Muir stagger to his feet and make a great show of seeming to run after him, Morgana begging him tearfully to stay with her. "Please, Edward, no more fighting," she says.

He takes her in his arms. "Darling, that man is the personification of evil. He killed two young people from this house, years ago, and spent years in prison for it."

She looks toward the door. "He seemed so—kind."

"Devon," Mrs. Crandall says, "I'm sorry you had to

witness that unfortunate incident. But perhaps now you see the kind of a man Rolfe Montaigne really is. Violent, unpredictable."

"He was defending Morgana," Devon says.

"She needs no defense against me," Edward huffs. "Come along, darling." He escorts Morgana toward the study.

Mrs. Crandall approaches Devon. "Rolfe has filled your mind with nonsense, Devon. I assure you there is no need for fear in this house. The sorcery is over." She narrows her eyes at him. "Isn't it?"

"You know it's not," he tells her. "You saw the attack in my room. And there have been others."

"Then you must have been practicing your powers again, Devon, when I have forbidden it. That's the only thing that would stir up the creatures."

"I tell you. I've heard Isobel the Apostate here. And I've *seen* her now, too. In the East Wing."

He can see that his words trouble her, but she won't give him the satisfaction of admitting that. "Go do your homework, Devon. We'll talk about this later. Right now I'm too upset about Rolfe."

She moves off, gathering her long dress in her hands and walking quickly up the stairs.

They're like ostriches with their heads in the sand, Devon thinks, watching her go. *What's it going to take to convince them? A demon sitting down with us for breakfast? The house in flames? Cecily facedown in a pool of her own blood?*

Devon just lets out a long sigh and heads up to his room.

MRS. CRANDALL is right about one thing: He had better do his homework. Mr. Weatherby is giving them a quiz tomorrow, and Devon wants to make sure he passes. Of course, he first tries willing himself to disappear and reappear at Rolfe's. Whatever information he'd tried to deliver must have been very important, given that he risked coming here. But Devon's powers don't work, and the Voice says simply, *Not this night.* Devon takes that to mean he has a little time before Isobel makes her next move—time enough to study for his history quiz.

He dreams again of Morgana, as he has every night since she arrived. In this dream, she comes to him with tears in her eyes, tears that he kisses off her face, before finding her lips and kissing her deep. It goes on this way all night, until he feels her softly stroking his face—

"Devon," she says.

"Oh," he moans, taking her hand and kissing her palm. "You're . . . so . . . beautiful . . ."

"Oh, Devon, what a sweet thing to say."

He keeps kissing her palm.

"I'm sorry I've been so moody."

He opens his eyes. It's Cecily—sitting on his bed—and Cecily whose palm he's kissing.

"Cecily!" he shouts, suddenly self-conscious, sitting up in bed. "Cecily!"

She smiles. "You were dreaming about me. You are so sweet, Devon."

He gulps. "Yeah. God, what time is it?"

"Time for you to get up if you don't want to be late for school. I just came in to apologize for the past few days. I've been so irrational."

He sighs. He feels sweaty and runs his hand through his hair. "It's okay. It happens."

"I don't know what it is about Morgana that just makes me so hostile toward her. She's really perfectly nice. I don't know why I feel the way I do."

Devon's conscious of morning breath. He hops out of bed, hurrying over to his bathroom where he brushes his teeth. Cecily stands in the doorway watching him.

"Alexander's been really hostile to her, too," he says, between spits of toothpaste. "But I figured out why. Edward has barely spent any time at all with the kid since being back, and Alexander blames Morgana."

Cecily nods. "Uncle Edward is unusually devoted to

her. What *is* it about her? D.J.'s got that stupid crush, too?"

"Who can explain hormones?" Devon tries to laugh, but his dreams remain still too vivid for him. "Hey, Cecily. I've got to shower now. I'll see you downstairs."

She smiles. "Okay." She reaches over and kisses his cheek. "Thanks for calling me beautiful."

He manages a small smile in return. If she only knew . . .

After she's gone, he hops into the shower. Cecily's right to wonder just what it is about Morgana that has nearly every male who meets her worshiping at her feet. She's beautiful, to be sure, but it's more than that. It's as if she's the most beautiful woman in the whole world—the most beautiful woman who ever lived.

"Not as if," Devon says dreamily under the shower. "She *is*."

I CAN'T GET HER out of my mind," D.J. says at school, leaning against his car, smoking a cigarette.

"You really ought to quit, you know," Devon tells him. "Not to sound parental, but it is pretty nasty."

D.J. grunts. "I tried. Then I got caught up with these feelings about Morgana. Dude, she's all I think about."

"I know." Devon notices Cecily and Ana approaching. "Don't bring it up around Cess. It'll just get her started."

"Will you give us a ride home after school today, D.J.?" Ana asks.

"He may have *errands* to run for his lady love," Cecily says.

"I'll be *glad* to drive you all home," D.J. says, making a face at Cecily. "Flo is at your service."

"Good," Ana says. "Maybe we can go to Gio's. We haven't been there in a while."

"That's cool, too," D.J. says, showing Cecily just how agreeable he can be.

The first bell rings. They all head off to different classes. Devon thinks he does very well on his history test, naming all of the wives of Henry the Eighth. In the corridor between classes, he stops at his locker to get his geometry book and is joined by Marcus, who has the locker next to his.

"How's my face today?" Marcus asks.

Devon looks. "Clean. No pentagram."

"Why do you think it appears sometimes and not always?"

"I'm not sure. Maybe I'll start keeping a record of when I see it, and see if the dates mean anything."

"Cool."

"Excuse me, Devon March?"

Devon turns. It's one of the secretaries from the office.

"Yes?"

"This was just dropped off for you." She hands him a white envelope. "It's marked Urgent."

Marcus looks over at it. "What could it be?"

"It must be from Rolfe," Devon guesses. "It must be about what he came to tell me last night."

He tears the envelope open. But the note inside is not from Rolfe.

It's from Morgana.

Dear Devon,
Please meet me at Stormy Harbor after you get out of school. It's very important. Keep this just between us, okay?

Morgana

Marcus has read the note over Devon's shoulder. "What does she want?"

"I don't know." Devon looks up from the note. "Look, Marcus. Don't tell Cecily or D.J. about this, okay? They're all heading over to Gio's after school. Go with them and tell them that I can't go, that I have to do something else."

"Like what?"

"I don't care. Tell them I have to—I have detention or something."

"Detention? For what?"

"Be creative!" Devon looks back at the note. Morgana needs him. *Just between us.* He likes that. He can't believe how much he likes that.

"What is it about this Morgana lady?" Marcus asks. "You and D.J. are in la-la land whenever she walks by."

"You wouldn't understand, Marcus. It's a heterosexual thing. Imagine she's, I don't know, Brad Pitt or something."

"I don't care who it was. I wouldn't get like that over anybody."

"Get like *what*?" Devon asks, feeling defensive. "I just want to see what's up. So will you cover for me or what?"

Marcus sighs. "Yeah. I'll cover for you."

Devon can't stop staring down at the note for the rest of the day.

Just between us.

Man. He loves that.

H E MAKES a wild dash for the bushes behind the gym after his last class lets out. "Please let this work," he whispers, closing his eyes. "Please!"

When he opens them, he's behind Stormy Harbor, out near the Dumpster.

"Yes!" he shouts, punching the air with his hand. "I'm getting the hang of this!"

The bistro is fairly empty. In the summertime, he's been told, this place is hopping with tourists from morning until night. But in the cold days of late January, it's mostly local fishermen, sitting with their brews and fried clams, swapping tales of the sea under the old nets and life preservers that hang from the ceiling.

"Hey, Devon," the waitress, Andrea, calls out. "Long time no see. Thought maybe the spooks up at Ravenscliff had eaten you alive."

"Not yet," he tells her, smiling inwardly at how close to the truth Andrea is. He likes her. She's straightforward, down-to-earth, only a few years older than he is. She's lived in Misery Point all her life.

"I told you your very first day in this town to watch out for the ghosts up there," Andrea says. "So if anything happens, don't say you weren't warned."

"No, I sure won't say that." He looks around the place. There, at a table far in the back, sits Morgana, alone. Devon looks back at Andrea. "Will you bring a platter of calamari and a large Coke over to that table?"

She lifts an eyebrow and smirks. "Dating older women now, Devon?"

"No." He can feel himself blush. "She's Edward Muir's fiancée. We're just—talking."

"Uh-huh." Andrea moves off to put in his order.

Devon heads over to the table. Morgana stands when she sees him, her eyes brimming with tears. "Oh, Devon. Thank you so much for coming."

"Sure," he says. She gives him a quick kiss on the cheek. He feels his whole body flush as he sits down.

"I didn't dare approach you at Ravenscliff," she says, retaking her seat. "I hope it was okay to leave you the note at school."

"What's going on? Is anything wrong?"

She wraps her arms around herself. "Oh, Devon. *Everything* is wrong!"

"What do you mean?"

"Ever since I got here, everyone has been so hostile." Her eyes find his. "Except for you."

"That may be changing. Cecily is going to try to be more friendly. And if Edward would just spend more time with Alexander, he'd lighten up, too. That's all it is with him. He's afraid you're taking his father away from him."

Morgana looks as if she'll cry at any moment. "Last night was a turning point for me. When Edward treated me roughly—" She can't finish. She looks away, composing herself. When she speaks again, Devon is surprised at the anger in her voice. "I don't like being treated as a piece of property."

Devon nods. "I understand. You have a reason to be angry. Edward was a real jerk."

She lifts her chin in defiance. "I'm thinking of leaving. Getting out of Misery Point, going back home— far, far away from here."

Devon looks at her intently. "Where *is* home, Morgana?"

She seems not to hear him. "I wouldn't even tell anyone. I'd just leave. Edward would just find me gone."

"I can understand your feelings, but—"

"But what, Devon?" she asks, leaning forward. "Do you not want me to go?"

"Me?" He stutters for words. "Well, I don't know what I have to do with it—"

"Because, Devon," Morgana says, her voice becoming tender, "*you're* the reason I can't bring myself to leave."

He looks at her, unable to speak.

"I know it might not be right," she says, reaching across the table to touch his hand, "but I think I've fallen in love with you, Devon."

"Here's your calamari," Andrea suddenly interrupts, placing the greasy little critters on a platter in front of him. "Your Coke's coming up."

"Um," Devon mumbles, not looking up, pushing the plate across the table. "You want some?"

Morgana has withdrawn her hand. "I shouldn't have said what I did."

"No," he says. "Probably not."

"It's ridiculous. You're a teenager."

"Yeah. A teenager."

"And I'm engaged to Edward."

"Yeah. Engaged to Edward."

Devon feels as if might faint.

"But I can't help myself," Morgana says, leaning in again. "Your kindness, your gentleness. You're so different from Edward, so different from any man I've ever known."

He gulps.

"Devon, tell me. Tell me how you feel."

"Here's your Coke," Andrea says, depositing the beverage between them. "You want anything, ma'am?"

"No," Morgana says hoarsely, looking away. "Thank you."

Devon just sits there. He can't move. He might be a Sorcerer of the noble Order of the Nightwing, but he's also a fourteen-year-old boy, who's just been told by a gorgeous twenty-two-year-old woman that she's in love with him. He can barely breathe.

He forces himself to look over at her. Her eyes—so

dark, like his. So beautiful. More beautiful than anyone in the world. He tries to speak.

"I—"

"Yes, Devon?"

"I—luh—"

"Say it, Devon."

She's gripped his hand in hers.

"I—lov—"

"Good afternoon," comes a voice, startling him. Devon knocks over his Coke. It spills across the table, getting Morgana wet. She yelps.

"Andrea! Bring a sponge!"

It's Rolfe. He's looking down at Devon with suspicious eyes.

"Rolfe," Devon mutters. "We were just—"

Andrea's suddenly on the scene, sopping up his spilled Coke. "You want another? I won't charge you."

"No," Devon says. "That's okay."

Rolfe sits down at the table with them. "You're usually much more on guard than that, Devon," the older man tells him, almost scoldingly. "I could have been anyone. Or any*thing*."

Devon feels suitably chagrined. Rolfe's right. He had lost track of himself there, stunned by what Morgana had just revealed. What if it had been a *demon* sneaking up behind him, and not Rolfe?

"Ms. Green," Rolfe says, finally acknowledging her. "What a pleasant surprise to see you again."

She smiles. "And you, Mr. Montaigne. I apologize for Edward's behavior last night. And I thank you for your gallantry."

"Are you all right?" he asks her.

"Fine, now, thank you." She smiles over at Devon. "My young friend here has been very supportive."

Young friend? Devon feels himself growing indignant. *A minute ago, she was telling me she loved me.*

"Devon," Rolfe tells him, "maybe you ought to run along. I'll pay the tab, and see Ms. Green back to her car."

"I just got here," Devon complains. "We were talking."

"It's okay, Devon," Morgana says. "We can finish our talk later."

Devon reluctantly stands. "I didn't even get to eat my calamari."

Rolfe stands, too, putting an arm around his shoulder. "Go on back to Ravenscliff," he whispers. "Use your father's ring. It may tell you something interesting that I've discovered. If it doesn't, see me tomorrow."

"What's it about, Rolfe? Why did you risk coming to the house last night?"

"It's about the gnome. Something I've discovered."

"Bjorn? Tell me, Rolfe."

"Not now. Your father's ring may tell you the same thing. Now, go."

He removes his arm and sits back down at the table, turning his attention again to Morgana. Devon's not sure what makes him angrier: Rolfe's refusal to tell him any more of what he knows about Bjorn or the fact that he's usurped Devon's place with Morgana, here in this dark corner in the back of the bistro.

"That mean old Rolfe Montaigne steal your lady love away from you?" Andrea asks as he trudges toward the door.

Devon just grunts.

"Rolfe thinks he's God's gift." Andrea laughs. "But she was too old for you, anyway, Devon. Trust me. Stick with Cecily."

He just pushes outside into the cold late-afternoon air. The sun is beginning to set. The sky is aflame with color. A few tiny snowflakes swirl around him. The wind is picking up, salty and sharp, blowing in from the sea. Devon tries his disappearing act but it doesn't work.

Great, he thinks sullenly. *Now I'll have to walk all the way up that long cliffside stairway.*

What's worse, of course, than the steep, crumbling stairway, is what it leads to at the top of the cliff: the cemetery.

* * *

THE WIND smacks him across the face as he steps off the steps into the tall, broken grass. Here in the old cemetery, where the Muir ancestors all were laid to rest, Devon first looked upon the face of the Madman. The beast was standing here, just a few feet from his grave, and the maggots were eating his face. Devon shivers remembering it.

But something disturbs him more at the moment: what Morgana had just told him. Could it be true? Could she really be in love with him? He's fourteen. She's twenty-two. He wants it to be true and at the same time prays that it isn't. As if his life isn't complicated enough as it is.

He passes the grave with the broken angel, the stone marked DEVON, and the crypt that holds the remains of Ravenscliff's founder, the great Horatio Muir. It's getting darker. He picks up his pace heading through the cemetery. He's suddenly frightened, but he's not sure why. As he passes a crooked brownstone gravestone, its inscription worn off by decades of sea wind, a seagull calls out overhead. The wind begins to howl.

And a hand pushes up from the frozen earth, seizing him by the ankle.

Devon screams.

The ground below him trembles. The hand keeps

its grip around his ankle despite Devon's best attempts to struggle free. Soon an arm is revealed and then a shoulder. Mostly bones with some rotting sinew and muscle.

"Let me go! I command you! Let me go!"

But the corpse does not surrender its grip. It sits up now, the frozen earth breaking off its hideous body like clay. Its skeletal jaw opens and closes as if to speak; its pulpy eyes burn in their sockets as it glares at Devon.

"I'm stronger than you!" Devon shouts, but still he can't break free. He stumbles, falling to the ground, landing face-to-face with the stinking dead man. He hollers out in disgust and fear.

Now, all around him, he can see hands pushing up from the dirt. The whole cemetery is coming alive! The corpse beside him moves its bony hands to Devon's neck. It begins to choke him. As Devon struggles for breath, he sees an army of zombies emerging from the earth, staggering toward him.

He hears the unmistakable laughter of Isobel the Apostate.

"I have come for you, Devon March! I will triumph! Ravenscliff will be mine!"

The corpse tightens its grip around his throat. Devon passes out. All is darkness.

* * *

HE OPENS his eyes with a start. He leaps to his feet, ready to fight.

But there's no sign of any undead corpses. The ground around him is undisturbed.

Was it only a vision? Another warning?

He spins around, just to make sure no zombie lurks in the shadows. How long has he lain here? He's cold, he realizes, chilled to his very core. It's pitch dark, and the snow has gotten heavier.

I must have been out for an hour or more, he thinks, brushing snow off his clothes.

When he gets to the house, he realizes it was even longer than that. The grandfather clock in the foyer reads eleven-thirty. It seems everyone in the house is asleep.

I could have frozen to death out there, Devon thinks, *and nobody here would ever have known.* Nor did it seem that anyone cared.

Some guardian Mrs. Crandall is. Did she even inquire about his whereabouts when he failed to show up for supper? He has a mind to report her to the state authorities for neglect. *Yeah, for what? So they could take me away from here and prevent me from ever learning the truth about what I am?*

Sometimes he thinks he'd trade ever finding that knowledge for simply having a normal life. Maybe it wouldn't be so bad to be taken away from Ravenscliff, placed with a normal family in a normal house. But the problem with that heartwarming little scenario is simple: Devon would never be a normal boy. Not so long as he has these powers. No matter where he went, his past would follow him. After all, the demons had turned his boyhood closet in Coles Junction into a Hellhole. Wouldn't that be a treat for a nice new foster family?

Devon knows there is no escape. This is his destiny. Dad told him as much. He must stay here and defend the portal at Ravenscliff, the only Nightwing left to do so.

Walking into the parlor, he stares up into the eyes of Horatio Muir. "You wouldn't have wanted your family to renounce their powers, no matter what," he speaks to the portrait. "I can't imagine you're happy with the Hellhole being left undefended."

It's up to you, Devon March.

Whether that's the Voice speaking inside his head or Horatio Muir somehow communicating with him from beyond the grave, Devon isn't sure. But he knows, whoever the speaker, the words are true. Especially after that episode in the cemetery, Devon is convinced he's facing a showdown with Isobel the Apostate. It's just a matter of time.

He's got to learn more about her. Back in his room, he does as Rolfe suggested. He tries on his father's ring.

But nothing happens. No visions. No words. Devon sighs, replacing the ring in his drawer. He tries to sleep but can't. All sorts of questions are running through his mind: *When will Isobel strike? What did Rolfe want to tell me about Bjorn? Were those zombies out in the cemetery real or a vision of what is to come?*

And of course, *Is Morgana really in love with me?*

He sits up in bed.

"The books in the basement," he whispers. He might be forbidden access to the volumes in the East Wing, but he'd stumbled upon a stash of books—children's books—once before. They're picture books about the exploits of the great Nightwing of the past. Perhaps one of them might contain some clue, some bit of useful information, about Isobel.

He finds a flashlight in his desk and hurries out into the corridor. Walking as quietly as he can through the dark house, he heads downstairs, keeping his flashlight unlit until he pulls open the cellar door. Flicking on the switch, he pierces the darkness below. He swallows, overcome with a blast of sudden fear. His heart is beginning to pound in his ears.

Stop it, he scolds himself. *Your fear makes you weak. You're strong only when you're not afraid.*

He takes the first couple of steps down into the basement. It's cold and damp down here. He descends to the cracked stone floor and swings his flashlight beam across the junk that's piled everywhere. Empty boxes and crates, old locked trunks with stickers from foreign countries plastered all over them. A dressmaker's dummy and an ancient sewing machine. And everywhere, dust and spiders' webs.

The books are piled high against the far wall. Just as it did the last time, the hair on Devon's arm suddenly stands up, attracted to the books as if by electricity. He sits on the cold damp floor and lifts the first book off the pile, reading with his flashlight. *The Adventures of Sargon the Great.* "Once upon a time," Devon reads, "many years ago, in the land of the forgotten days, lived a sorcerer named Sargon."

Having now seen the real Sargon, Devon thinks the crude illustration looks nothing like the great sorcerer. He flips ahead to Sargon's battle with a two-headed dragon. When he'd first seen this book, Devon had assumed the creature to be some childhood-fairy-tale character. Now he knows it's a demon from the Hell-hole.

He puts the book down. He's looking for one that might be set around the time of Isobel. He lifts another from the pile and glances down at the title. *The Mystical Journey of Diana.* This one is an adventure in space, with Diana speaking and breathing outside the earth's orbit. He has no idea what year it's supposed to be set in. Other books have dates, but *Brutus and the Sea*

Monster takes place too early in British history for there to be any mention of Isobel, and *Wilhelm's Magical Adventures in Old Holland* is set in a completely different country. Devon has hopes for *Vortigar and the Knights of Britain,* but there's no mention of any Apostates.

These are books for kids, he reminds himself. Stories for young Nightwing-in-training. The authors wouldn't want to give them any information on Nightwing gone bad.

Still, he looks through several others, hoping for some clue about Isobel and her times. *The Magical Spells of Tristan. Don Carlos and the Spanish Gold. The Secret of Philip of Troy. Abigail Apple and the Monster of Loch Ness.*

"Cool," Devon says to himself, reading about a kooky Scottish Nightwing who tames a demon from the Hellhole and turns it into her pet. "So that's where the Loch Ness monster comes from."

He pulls another book off the pile, enjoying their little fables and forgetting, for the moment, any pursuit of Isobel. *"The Treasure of Childebert,"* he reads, settling in for another good read.

But then he hears a sound.

Low at first, but steady. It builds, becoming louder. The *sobbing.*

Once more, it strikes Devon as the most gut-wrenching sound of grief he's ever heard in his life. Terrible, agonizing weeping—and it's coming from somewhere in the basement.

It's the same sound I once heard in the tower, Devon thinks. *This must be where Bjorn brought whoever it was.*

A woman—that much he's sure of. Could it be Isobel?

"Oh oh oh oh," the voice sobs.

The sound echoes through the darkness. Devon stands, moving his flashlight from one corner of the room to the next, searching for its source. Nothing but old boxes.

"Ohhhhhhhhh," the voice cries, reaching a new crescendo of anguish.

Devon follows the sound down a corridor that ends at a cracked plaster wall.

There's no mistaking it: The sobbing comes from behind this wall.

"Who is there?" Devon asks.

The sobbing stops.

"Who are you?" he asks. "Why do you cry?"

There's silence at first, then the voice answers through the wall.

"I know you," it says. "You have come at last!"

Devon says nothing, staring at the wall.

"Devon! It is you!" The voice is exultant. "You have found me!"

EIGHT

❦

A SUDDEN
TRANSFORMATION

HOW DO YOU know me?" Devon asks the voice. "Who are you?"

He's struck by sudden light. He turns, squinting into the glare.

"Once more, I find you talking to yourself."

It's Bjorn Forkbeard, shining his own flashlight into Devon's face.

"Who's behind this wall?" Devon demands.

"Not sure," the gnome replies. "Who'd it sound like?"

"She knows me!" Devon shouts. He bangs on the wall. "Hello? Who are you?"

But now there's only silence.

Bjorn puts his ear to the wall. "I don't hear a thing, my friend. Not a thing."

"What's behind here?" Devon feels along the wall. "How do you get in?"

"It doesn't appear you *can* get in," Bjorn says. "There's no door, and it's closed off from end to end. There's no way anyone could get behind there."

Devon spins on him. "Well, there *was* someone there. I heard her sobbing. It's the same sobbing I've heard for months."

"Sobbing." Bjorn looks up at him with wide eyes. "Ah, but then I've heard the sobbing, too. It's the ghost of Emily Muir, I'm sure of it."

"It's *not* Emily Muir," Devon says. "It's someone else."

Bjorn Forkbeard looks at him cagily. "And who do you think it might be, then?"

"This was the same voice I used to hear sobbing from the tower—the same woman who once called my name from the tower window. And I saw you take someone out of the tower. You can't deny that. You brought her down here."

Bjorn looks at him plainly. "There are many things in this house that only appear to be real. You know that, my young Nightwing friend."

"*Am* I your friend, Bjorn?"

"But of course. I owe you my life."

"Then tell me what you know of Isobel the Apostate."

The little man's face goes white. "Iso—bel—?"

"Surely you know who she is."

Bjorn nods. "But why do you ask about her?"

"Don't you know? Is it Isobel I've been hearing? Is it she who's behind that wall?"

Bjorn seems staggered by this new line of questioning. He sits down on a crate and rests his flashlight on his lap. The breath seems to have been knocked out of him.

"No wall could contain Isobel the Apostate," he says. "Why do you speak of her?"

Devon studies him. Either Bjorn is a very good actor, or this has truly unnerved him.

"I believe it's she who's been trying to get the portal opened," Devon says.

Bjorn looks at him with terrified eyes. "Then we are doomed. We have not the resources to fight her."

"Oh, yeah? Well, I've been into the Hellhole and came back out alive. If she'd just show her face, I'm itching to take her on."

Bjorn smiles weakly. "The arrogance of youth. My good friend, the spirit of Isobel the Apostate has been loose for five hundred years. She has opened more Hellholes all over the globe than any other renegade sorcerer, and each time her power has grown greater. Of all the Nightwing, dead or alive, I fear her the most."

Devon stares back at the wall in silence.

"If that was her I sensed trying to unbolt that door

in the East Wing," Bjorn says, "then it is far, far worse than I thought."

Devon looks back at him. "You could just be trying to scare me."

"But why would I do that, my boy? Why do you resist trusting me?"

"I've learned that Ravenscliff is a place where trust often gets me in big trouble. And after all, you almost delivered me right into her hands when you sent me down the Stairway Into Time."

"That was merely to show you the extent of your powers, Devon."

"Oh, yeah? So how come it just so happened to land me in Tudor England, where they were burning Isobel the Apostate?"

Bjorn seems anxious, constantly throwing the beam of the flashlight around the basement every time he hears a creak. "The Stairway takes one where one needs to go. I couldn't control it even if I wanted to. It is a brilliant manifestation of Horatio Muir's master sorcery."

Devon sighs. "I wish I could trust you, Bjorn. I need an ally in this house. Somebody with answers. But until you can tell me who's behind this wall—"

"I can't tell you what I don't know."

Devon tries willing himself behind the wall. He's

not surprised when it doesn't work. He tries seeing *through* the wall, but that proves fruitless, too.

Not yet, the Voice tells him, without any explanation. *Not yet.*

"I'm going back to bed," Devon says, frustrated.

"A good idea. You must be rested and strong, if indeed we face an enemy such as you suggest." Bjorn follows him as they head toward the basement steps. "Read all you can, learn all there is to be learned. Isobel will arrive with no warning and grant no mercy. I've seen the destruction she's left behind, villages in ruins, strong men eaten alive—"

"Okay, already," Devon gripes, annoyed by Bjorn's prattling. "You trying to give me nightmares?"

It takes Devon a long time to fall asleep. But when he does, instead of nightmares he dreams of Morgana, the most delicious dream yet that he's had of her.

"I love you, too," he tells her, and she moves in for the kiss.

A N UNEASY QUIET settles over Ravenscliff for the next several days. Bjorn makes no further mention of their encounter in the basement. Mrs. Crandall says nothing about Isobel. And Morgana keeps a cordial but safe distance, seemingly embarrassed by what she'd told him at Stormy Harbor. Devon is both grateful for and disturbed by the distance. On the one hand, he's not sure how to handle the situation either; having some space just makes it easier. But on the other, he wants so much to be with her, to talk to her, to kiss her lips the way he does in his dreams.

Once again, he wishes his father were still alive. *Why are my feelings so tangled up in knots? Here I have a great girl like Cecily who likes me, and who I really, really like, too—but Morgana just makes me melt every time I see her. What's up with that? And what if she really meant what she said—that she's in love with me? How am I supposed to deal with that?*

Dad would've known how to explain everything. Devon tries wearing his father's ring, hoping for another visitation—but nothing. He yanks it off his finger. What's the use in having all these magical powers and trinkets if they're so unreliable?

The worst thing of all, however, is that Rolfe seems to have left town without telling him. He's never at the restaurant when Devon tries to see him. The first time he stops by, Roxanne says Rolfe is in Boston on business. On subsequent fruitless visits, Devon grows agitated, telling Roxanne that Rolfe had wanted to reveal something about Bjorn. Roxanne says she's sorry, but she doesn't know what it is.

"I'm troubled," she admits to Devon. "It's not like

Rolfe to go away without letting me know more details."

With all that, Devon's mood darkens at school, and his friends notice. He feels a little guilty about not filling them in on all that's been happening. After the last time, when they fought the Madman, they made a vow to keep each other informed on things. But with D.J. and Cecily acting so weird and Marcus so worried about the pentagram, Devon has kept most of what he knows to himself. He's got to tell them, though, and plans to do so at Gio's after school.

The pizza joint is packed. They know they're an odd little clique, but no one hassles them: They all remember Devon's amazing strength at subduing that kid—who was, in truth, a demon in a teenager's clothing. They slide into a booth, D.J. and Devon on one side, Ana and Cecily and Marcus on the other.

"Can we get pineapple pizza?" Ana asks.

"Yuck," Cecily says. "Your taste in food is as bad as your taste in clothes."

"Uh, I'm not the one still wearing Capri pants, and in January, no less."

Cecily makes a face. They decide on pepperoni when Gio comes around to take their order, his stained T-shirt inching up to expose a hairy round belly.

"And put a scald on that, okay, Gio?" D.J. calls out.

"Extra crispy on the pepperoni," the pizzamaker says, jotting it down in his book.

"Listen, you guys," Devon says. "I've got to talk to you about something."

"Uh-oh," Ana says. "Please don't let it be about monsters or going to hell."

Devon smiles wanly. "Well, if you don't want to hear . . ."

"What is it, Devon?" Cecily asks. "And why haven't you shared it with me?"

"Well, for six out of the past ten days, you haven't been speaking to me."

She pouts. "I said I was sorry."

"Will you all just let him talk?" Marcus asks.

Devon settles back in the booth. "There's an evil entity trying to open the Hellhole."

"Is it Jackson Muir?" Cecily asks, suddenly terrified.

"No," Devon tells her. "It's the spirit of a Nightwing from the sixteenth century. Isobel the Apostate."

"Isobel?" Ana asks.

"A woman?" Cecily seems fascinated, almost excited by the idea. "Well, cool."

"*Cool?*" Devon leans across the table at her. "This isn't fun and games, Cecily. We're talking major destruction here."

"You can handle the situation," she says. "You did last time. I have complete confidence in you."

"Thank you most kindly. However, may I point out that Isobel has been around for five hundred years? I think she may know a few tricks I don't."

"Why do you think it's her?" D.J. asks. It's the first thing he's said since Devon brought up the topic.

"I had a vision using my father's ring. There have been other clues, too."

"But you haven't seen her?"

"Well, I did, sort of. I sensed she was in the East Wing."

"Did you check the portal?" Marcus asks.

"Yes," Devon says. "It was still bolted."

D.J. leans his head on his elbow looking up at Devon. "And no sign of this Isobel?"

Devon has to admit there wasn't. "But I *know* it's Isobel that we're dealing with. I've heard her laughter, several times."

"So what do we do?" Cecily asks.

"I'm not sure. Just be on guard for now. But I wanted to let all of you know."

Marcus lets out a long sigh. "Feels pretty frustrating knowing someone is going to try to open the Hellhole and not being able to do anything about it."

Devon nods. "As soon as Rolfe gets back, I need to talk with him. He was going to try to find someone to help. A Guardian perhaps, or maybe even another Nightwing."

"Another Nightwing?" D.J. asks, his eyes lighting up.

"Yeah." Devon smiles. "You know, maybe that's where Rolfe has disappeared to. It must be."

"Let's hope so," Ana says. "I never want to see another one of those demons as long as I live."

Gio arrives with their pizza and they devour it in less than ten minutes. D.J. gets cheese on his gold chin piercing and Cecily tells him he's gross. They complain about the unfairness of Mr. Weatherby's grading system and gossip about Jessica Milardo and her new boyfriend, Justin O'Leary, who were caught making out in the girls' room. D.J. tells them he's thinking of giving Flo a new paint job in the spring, and Ana announces she can't decide whether or not she wants to go out for cheerleading again after this year.

It's at times like this that Devon momentarily forgets about the things that have haunted him since he was six years old, forgets that he's a Sorcerer of the ancient and noble Order of the Nightwing, the one-hundredth generation from Sargon the Great. For just a few, fleeting moments, he can pretend he's just an ordinary kid, with ordinary problems like grades and teachers. But then something always happens to jog his mind back, and he remembers the truth.

There are demons out there that want to force me to do their bidding.

"Listen, man," D.J. says, as they're heading back to his car, "I've been thinking."

"Whoa," Devon says, smirking. "One never knows where *that* might lead."

D.J. laughs. "I'm serious. I think you ought to take me in to check out that portal in the East Wing."

Devon stops in his tracks. "What for?"

"Just to see if I can pick up any clues you haven't."

Devon frowns. "Deej, I'm not sure it would do any good. What could you see that I didn't?"

"Who knows?" D.J. leans into him, stopping him from following the rest of the group to the car. "Come on. How about it? Let me see the Hellhole, okay?"

"D.J., even *I* can't get in there without a key. How am I supposed to let you in?"

D.J.'s face is intense. "I want to *see* it. Come on, Devon! After all we've been through together, after all I had to deal with while Jackson Muir was on the loose, I would think you'd trust me enough—"

"It's not a matter of trust," Devon says. "I just can't get in there—"

"We can break in." D.J.'s eyes dance. "Believe me, I could do it. In junior high, I broke into more places than I'd ever own up to."

"No, D.J." Devon pushes around him to join the others at the car. "It's too dangerous. There's no reason for you to go in there."

On the way back to Misery Point, D.J. is quiet. No one notices but Devon, as D.J. is often quiet while the girls and Marcus yap on and on. But Devon detects a dark cloud hanging over his friend's head, a roiling, angry energy exuding from his body.

What is going on? Devon asks himself. *Is this a side to D.J. I've never seen, part and parcel with his crazy crush on Morgana?*

Or is it, Devon fears, something else—something far more sinister than the swing of a teenaged boy's mood?

THAT NIGHT Devon has his most intense dream yet about Morgana.

"Oh, my love," she says, covering his face with kisses. "How much I want you. Need you."

She is so breathtakingly beautiful. She wears a sheer black lace nightgown. He is aroused in a way he's never been before. He feels at the peak of some high precipice, waiting to jump into the darkness of her eyes.

"Then come away with me, Devon! Leave this place! Come with me! Come!"

"Yes—oh, yes, I will—yes—yes—yes!"

He sits up in bed with a shout. His whole body is shuddering.

"Man oh man," he mutters. "What just happened?"
Sweat drips from his brow.

"Oh, *man*," he says.

He sits there for several minutes, just panting.

Then he gets up and takes a shower.

IT'S SATURDAY morning. He's up early, not having been able to go back to sleep for the rest of the night. The house is quiet and still, draped in the blue shadows of early morning, a few highlights of pink reflecting on the walls. No one else is awake yet.

Or so Devon thinks.

"Hey," he says, starting down the stairs and spying Alexander hiding in the shadows of the foyer. "What are you doing down there?"

The boy suddenly runs to the foot of the stairs. "Devon, stop! Don't go any further!"

"Why?"

"Just wait," the boy shouts frantically. He bends down quickly over the bottom step and seems to retrieve something. "Okay, now you can walk down the rest of the way."

Devon does, coming to stand over the boy. "What did you just do, Alexander?"

"Nothing. I just thought—thought I saw something on the stairs."

"Saw something? Like what?"

"I don't know." The boy hesitates. "I thought it was a mouse, but I was wrong."

"A mouse?"

"So I was wrong!" Alexander seems anxious to move off the subject. "How come you're up so early? Usually the only one who gets up this early is Morgana."

"I've got a better question," Devon says. "What are *you* doing up so early?"

"Nothing."

"Come on, Alexander. If you're going to lie to me, you can do better than that."

"I'm not lying." The boy folds his chubby arms over his chest. "So are you staying down here or going back up to your room?"

Devon eyes the boy slyly. "You don't *want* me down here, do you, Alexander? What are you up to?"

"I told you. *Nothing.*"

"Yeah, whatever. I'm going into the kitchen to get some cereal. Want to join me?"

Alexander shakes his head. "No. I'm gonna—I'm gonna go back upstairs."

Devon smirks. "Good idea."

He watches as the boy starts slowly up the stairs. Devon has no idea what the boy is up to, but he's got that old malicious look in his eyes, the look of mischief that Devon had become so wary of in his first days in this house.

Is everyone freaking out around here? Alexander? D.J.?

Me?

In the kitchen, he pours some milk over a bowl of Frosted Flakes and settles down at the table. He's glad no one else is up yet. He's still really disturbed by his dream. Dad had told him his hormones would start kicking in around now, as they do for all boys, and that they can make you think and act crazy at times. That's all it is: He has a stupid crush on an older woman who—

Who said she loved me.

Devon puts his spoon down. Suddenly his throat is tight and he can't swallow his Frosted Flakes.

That's when he hears the crash from the foyer and someone shout out in pain.

He dashes out there as quickly as he can. He finds Morgana sprawled face-first on the floor at the bottom of the stairs. Alexander is scampering down from the landing.

"She fell, Devon!" the boy shouts. "She might be dead!"

Devon is at Morgana's side. "She's not dead," he says. "Don't be ridiculous."

But her face *is* banged up, and her lip is bleeding.

She seems to be in shock as Devon helps her to her feet.

"Morgana," he says. "Are you okay?"

"I—I think so," she says.

He escorts her into the parlor and helps her sit on the couch. "Stay here. Let me go get some ice."

Alexander is in the doorway. "Is she going to be scarred for life?"

Devon grabs the boy's ear. "You come with me."

"Ow, you're hurting me."

He leads the boy into the kitchen. While popping ice cubes out of the tray into a dishcloth, Devon grills Alexander. "Did you push her? Don't lie to me, Alexander. I'll know if you're lying. You were up to something when I saw you."

"I did *not* push her," Alexander insists, folding his chubby arms over his chest.

Devon moves past him and hurries back to the parlor. "Here," he says, pressing the ice gently against Morgana's cheek. "Hold this so we can keep down the swelling."

"Oh, Devon, you're so kind."

"Are you okay otherwise? Looks like you have a scrape on your elbow. Any pain anywhere?"

She manages a smile. "I think I'm going to be fine. I was more in shock than in pain."

Devon sighs, looking down at her. "Did you lose your footing? Is that how you fell?"

She looks at him deliberately. "It felt as if I tripped over something."

Devon turns around to glare again at Alexander, who looks up at him with angelically innocent eyes.

"I suppose I should go find Edward, and let him know what's happened," Devon says.

"No," Alexander says quickly. "She's okay. Why do you have to go get my father?"

"Yes, Devon," Morgana says. "I'd appreciate it if you did go find Edward. Bring him here."

Devon nods. He hates getting his little friend in trouble, but he's convinced Alexander had something to do with Morgana's accident. And seeing her in pain has made Devon angry. He shakes his head at the young boy as he walks past him and hurries up the stairs.

Edward Muir is not in his room. Devon can't find him anywhere, and concludes he must either be out or in his mother's room, where Devon's forbidden to enter unless invited. So he just heads back down to the parlor, concerned that Morgana's injuries might have gotten worse while he was away from her.

He's on the landing overlooking the foyer when he hears her voice. And Alexander's, too.

"I hate you!" the boy is saying. "I'm going to tell my

father not to marry you! I'm going to tell him I'll run away if he does!"

Devon pauses on the stairs, listening.

"You little skunk," Morgana says, her voice low and mean. "You tried to kill me, and I won't forget that."

"I hate you! I hate you! I hate you!"

"I hate you, too, you little skunk!"

Devon figures he'd best get in there. He hurries back into the parlor and seems to surprise both of them. Morgana, still sitting on the couch, looks away. Alexander runs to Devon and throws his arms around his waist. "She put a curse on me! She's a witch!"

"Stop that, Alexander," Devon says, though he has to admit he is taken somewhat aback by the ferocity he heard in Morgana's voice. He looks at her. "Edward's not in his room."

She smiles. She's her soft, gentle self again. "I'm fine now, Devon." Her eyes find his. "Thanks to you."

He manages a small smile in return.

"Edward must be with his mother," Morgana says, standing. "I'll go upstairs."

"Are you okay to walk?"

She nods. "I'm fine, Devon. Really. Your concern means the world to me." She kisses him on the cheek on her way out.

"Ewww," Alexander says. "Wipe your cheek."

"Why do you hate her so much?"

"She put a curse on me. You should've heard her yelling at me."

"I did." Devon looks down at the boy. "Empty your pockets. Let me see what you have in there."

Whether it's the Voice telling him to look or it's merely a hunch of his own—and maybe, after all, there isn't much difference between the two—Devon feels the boy's pockets will produce something interesting. Alexander resists at first, but Devon tells him he'll look himself if he has to. Finally the boy reaches down inside and pulls out a length of fishing line. Clear, strong, and nearly invisible.

Devon snatches it from his hand. "You strung this across the step, didn't you? That's what you removed when you saw me coming downstairs. Then you put it back so Morgana would trip."

"Okay, so I did. And go ahead—tell my father! She's a witch! And if I don't stop her, nobody will!"

The boy rushes out of the room. Devon just stands there, staring down at the fishing line.

CECILY WANTS him to go shopping with her at the mall near Newport, but he's in no frame of mind to put up with trekking through The Gap and Abercrombie & Fitch. So she calls Marcus and Ana instead, knowing full well D.J. would refuse, and gets Bjorn to drive them. "Try to stall any demon invasion until we get back, okay?" she asks. "I don't want to miss out on any action."

"You're taking this far too lightly," he tells her.

"If I walked around here so serious all the time the way you do, I'd go crazy. So we live in a haunted house. Deal with it." She hurries outside as Bjorn honks the Cadillac's horn.

Devon wishes he could pretend to be light and carefree the way Cecily does. But ever since the encounter with Alexander this morning, he's felt the temperature rising in the house and the pressure starting to close in from the walls. *Something's happening,* he thinks. *Whether it has to do with Isobel or whoever it is that's locked in the basement, I don't know. Maybe it's all part of the same thing. Whatever it is, I've got to talk with Rolfe.*

He's getting dressed to head over there when he hears a sound. But it's not a sound from anywhere nearby. Devon listens intently. Scratching, banging— and it's coming from the tower. Just as before, his ears have suddenly become superattuned to noises from great distances, even through brick walls. He looks quickly out of his window. It's shaping up to be a beautiful day, with a sharp, crisp blue sky. But the sunlight reveals no sign of any motion in the tower windows. Still, Devon's certain: The sounds he hears are coming from somewhere inside that crenellated structure.

It's the first time he's heard or seen anything suspicious in the tower since Bjorn took whoever had been living there down into the basement. Devon tenses: The tower is where he first heard the mocking laughter of Isobel the Apostate. Might this be it? His showdown with her over the Hellhole?

As he concentrates, he begins to make out an image of something far less formidable.

"D.J.," he whispers, and he wills himself to disappear.

He reappears in a thicket of evergreen bushes surrounding the base of the tower. D.J. is jostling a window, trying to break in.

"Uh, excuse me," Devon says, tapping his friend on the shoulder.

D.J. gasps and spins around. "Dude! You scared the smoke right outta my nostrils!"

"What are you doing?"

"Devon, you wouldn't help me. I had to try. I have to get into the East Wing!"

"Why?"

D.J. grips him by his shoulders. His eyes are wide, the pupils dilated. "I've got to see the Hellhole!"

"What is wrong with you?"

"Devon, we've got to check the Hellhole! I've got to see it!"

"I told you, *no*, D.J.!"

"Let me inside!" The teenager's voice is low and raspy, nothing like his own. "I've got to get in there!"

"No!"

D.J. shouts out suddenly as if in pain. He grips Devon around the throat.

"Let—me—go!"

D.J.'s eyes glaze over as he throttles Devon.

"I'm sorry to do this to you, buddy," Devon says, choking for breath, "but you really give me no choice."

All at once D.J. is yanked away from Devon, as if pulled by some gigantic magnet, and flung across the yard into a row of hedges.

Devon walks over to him and helps him to his feet. "You okay?"

D.J. stands, shaken but unhurt. "What came over me, man?"

"I don't know." Devon looks at his friend. "Go home, D.J. I promise I'll get to the bottom of this and defeat whatever's got hold of your mind."

"Thanks, man," D.J. says, grimacing as he brushes leaves and twigs off his body. "Sorry for the freak-out back there."

"No problem."

"It just got into my head. I don't know why—"

"Go home, D.J. It's not safe for you here." He looks up at the dark mansion. "I don't think it's safe for anyone."

* * *

ALL THE STRANGE *behavior people have been exhibiting in this house—it's got to be because of Isobel,* Devon thinks. *D.J., Alexander, Bjorn—Isobel's using them, making them act in ways contrary to their own natures.*

But why? He sees no purpose in what she's doing. Why send D.J. to break into the East Wing when she knows only Devon can open the Hellhole? Why make Alexander try to kill Morgana? And what did Rolfe want to tell him about Bjorn? And where in the world is Rolfe?

Once Devon is sure that D.J. has driven off in his Camaro, he returns to the house for his coat. Sorcerer he might be, but that doesn't ward off the cold on brisk January mornings. He wonders if Horatio Muir or Sargon the Great could withstand the elements. He suspects there must be ways; in fact, he has a sense that he's only begun to tap the potential of his powers. New ones—like his superhearing and invisibility—keep popping up all the time.

How leisurely it would be to simply read the books and use the crystals to learn all about his Nightwing heritage, without having to worry about Apostates like Jackson Muir or Isobel. Would he ever have that freedom? How awesome it must be for Nightwing kids whose pasts aren't kept from them: They get to grow up with a proud Nightwing childhood, trained by their Guardian in the use of their powers, encouraged to learn about their history from their parents and family. For Devon, everything is difficult.

"Why can't it ever just be easy?" he mumbles to himself, as he closes his eyes and wills himself across town. Opening them to see that he's standing out on the precipice near Rolfe's house, he laughs. "Well, I guess some things *are* pretty easy."

He prays that Rolfe is home. He's gladdened by the fact that he spots the Porsche in the garage. Where could Rolfe have been all this time? There's so much they need to discuss.

Remembering how he interrupted Rolfe and Roxanne last time in the midst of a rather intimate moment, he chooses to disappear and reappear in Rolfe's kitchen, where a spiral staircase leads down to his study. He can hear Rolfe below.

"Oh, my darling, how beautiful you are," Rolfe is saying.

Great. Just great. Devon sighs. *Once again my timing is exactly wrong. He and Roxanne are making out again.*

But as he peers over the railing to look down at the room below, he sees not the mysterious golden-eyed Roxanne on the couch with Rolfe, but rather—

Morgana.

Devon backs away and covers his mouth to suppress a sound.

Morgana—in Rolfe's arms!

Part of Devon wants to leap down there and punch Rolfe in the gut. Part of him is so angry and so jealous that he doesn't care suddenly whether Isobel the Apostate is back at Ravenscliff at this very minute, opening the Hellhole. *Morgana told me she loved me! But now she's with him! This is why she's been so distant! This is what has been occupying Rolfe's time!*

They've been together!

Another part of Devon strains for some logic. *Something is wrong here,* he thinks. *Something is very wrong.*

"Devon!"

He jumps.

Alexander's voice, inside his head.

"Help me, Devon!"

He hears the boy as if he were in the next room. But Devon knows Alexander is at Ravenscliff.

And he's in danger.

"Devon!!!"

He gateways to the foyer at Ravenscliff. Cecily is just then heading up the stairs, loaded down with packages from the mall. She lets out a yelp when Devon suddenly appears.

"You've got to quit that, Devon!" she shouts. "Scared me half to death!"

"We've got to get up to Alexander's room. Something's wrong!"

It's clear she recognizes the urgency in his voice. She sets her bags down and quickly follows Devon up the stairs and across the landing into the upstairs corridor. "Alexander!" Devon is shouting. "Where are you?"

He throws open the door to the boy's room. It is quiet. Empty.

"Alexander?"

Cecily looks around. "He's not here."

"We've got to search the house."

Cecily looks at him with concern. "What's happened now? Tell me, Devon."

"I don't know. I just know that he's in danger. I heard him call—"

They're suddenly distracted by movement under Alexander's bed. The blankets draped over the side rise and fall, as if something were behind them, under the bed.

Cecily grips Devon's arm. Devon takes hold of the blankets in his right hand.

"Be careful," Cecily whispers.

He whisks the blankets away.

From under the bed dodders an enormous skunk, its black-and-white tail held high in the air.

NINE

THE ASSAULT

CECILY SCREAMS.

"Get it, Devon! Before it sprays!"

Devon can only stand there, staring at the animal.

"What's the matter?" Cecily shrieks. "Zap it away with your powers or something."

"I—I can't do that."

She clutches his arm tightly. "And why *not*?" she asks through gritted teeth.

"Because—" Devon gulps. "Because I think it's Alexander."

She looks at him as if he's gone completely insane on her. Then she moves her eyes back to the skunk, now busily nosing through Alexander's dirty laundry on the floor. It lifts a pair of his undershorts on its snout.

"Alexander?" Cecily asks quietly.

The skunk goes about its business, sniffing around Alexander's bureau.

"How is it possible?" Cecily asks Devon. "How do you know? Are you sure?"

Devon's head is spinning. *Yes,* the Voice confirms for him. *Trust your instincts.*

"I'm certain," he tells her.

"But how? Who did this to him? And why?"

Devon hesitates. "I—I can't say for sure."

Cecily looks up at him with wide, frightened eyes. "But you'll be able to change him back, right?"

Devon swallows. "I hope so. For now, we need to put the skunk somewhere and keep it safe."

Cecily is squatting now, beckoning the skunk toward her. "I have to admit," she says, suppressing a small smile, "it *does* kind of look like the little monster."

Devon looks around the room. "What can we put him in?"

"We have a dog crate in the basement. I had a fox terrier once before Mother made me give him away. She complained he barked too much and kept her up at night." She scowls. "As if we didn't already have enough *ghosts* doing the same thing."

"You had barking ghosts?"

She smirks. "How am I supposed to take you

seriously about this skunk being my little cousin if you start cracking jokes?"

"Sorry." He smiles. "Go fetch the dog crate for me."

In truth, finding humor in the situation merely belies the true terror Devon feels. Once Cecily is gone, he looks down at the skunk still scuttering through the mess of Alexander's room. Morgana had called him a little skunk. She'd threatened him.

And Alexander had said she put a curse on him.

"No," Devon says, not wanting to believe the idea that's suddenly forcing its way through his consciousness. "Morgana has no powers—she wouldn't do anything evil—"

He closes his eyes and Morgana is kissing him again, coming to him in the night as she has all these many nights, telling him she loves him—

"Here's the crate," Cecily announces, startling him back to reality.

"Okay," Devon says, collecting himself. "Put him in there."

She recoils. "Why do *I* have to do it?"

"He's your cousin."

Cecily frowns. "If I get sprayed, buddy, you're in big trouble. You'd better know some spell to counteract skunk stink."

But the fat little fellow simply totters obediently into the crate when Cecily opens the door, tapping her fingers and calling, "Here, Alexander! Here, you little skunk!" Once she latches the door behind the animal, she looks up at Devon and grins. "First time I ever got to call Alexander a skunk without him finding some way of getting back at me."

Precisely at that moment, the skunk lets out its stink.

They run yelping from the room, Cecily screaming about a bath in tomato soup, the only supposed cure. For Devon's part, he seems to have avoided a direct hit, and after changing his clothes, he's fine.

Except, of course, he's not.

Morgana.

What is happening to people in this house? Is Isobel the Apostate behind all of this?

Devon hates to admit it, especially with his little friend turned into a skunk and locked up in a dog crate. But the worst part of it all is knowing Morgana is with Rolfe instead of him.

THE DAY PASSES in a quiet funk. The calm before the storm, Devon suspects. Edward and Mrs. Crandall have been out of the house all morning and by midafternoon are still not back. Devon sits alone in the library, reading through the official texts on the Muir family history, hoping to find something—*anything*—

to help Alexander. He's been through these many times before, and once again they prove to be of no help. Just the same old story of Horatio Muir founding the house in 1902 and the wonder felt by the villagers when all the ravens took up roost here to live. There's nothing about Apostates or Hellholes or counteracting magic spells. Devon slams the book shut in his lap.

He's tried, of course, to will the skunk into changing back into Alexander, but nothing has worked. He even sought out Bjorn, deciding to trust the caretaker enough to inquire if any of those powders in his bag of tricks might help the poor kid. But Bjorn, too, is nowhere to be found. Devon feels lost. It rips a hole in his gut that he can't go to Rolfe about this—Rolfe, his mentor, the man who was supposed to help him understand his powers and make sense of all the sorcery. Rolfe—who's got Morgana in his arms. *Morgana, who should belong to me—*

Stop it, that's crazy, Devon scolds himself. *I've got to shake off these stupid feelings for her! They're not letting me think straight!*

He stands, shaking his head in frustration and confusion. What connection might there be between Morgana and Isobel the Apostate? Might Isobel have placed Morgana under her power the way she did D.J.? Devon feels like tearing the hair out of his head. He can't stay here in the house any longer. He has to *do* something.

He's got to confront Rolfe—*and* Morgana. He's got to go back over there.

But—wouldn't you know it—his transporting power fails him.

Consider your state of mind, the Voice tells him. *You are frustrated. Frightened.*

"Well, yeah, maybe I am." He's angry, too. "Like Sargon-I'm-So-Great was never scared in his whole entire life?"

Devon grabs his coat and hurries outside.

So I'll walk. I don't care. I still have legs like any other kid. I'll walk—even if Rolfe's house *is* several miles away and it's getting dark and beginning to snow.

Devon pulls the collar of his coat more tightly around his neck.

". . . beseech the elemental gods . . ."

Devon listens. There are voices in the swirling snow.

". . . unleash your power . . ."

From the edge of the cliffs a thin curl of blue smoke rises among the falling white snowflakes.

Devon makes out a figure at Devil's Rock. A small figure. As he approaches, he sees it's Bjorn.

"I call upon the power of the old Knowledge," the gnome is chanting.

He's stirring a big black cauldron with a broken tree branch, and the smoke is rising from whatever brew he's concocted. It's just like a cheesy Halloween cartoon, with a witch boiling bat wings.

"What is this?" Devon asks, startling the gnome. "If it's tonight's dinner, I think I'll pick up Burger King."

"Come no further, my young Nightwing friend," Bjorn says. "Do not pass through the smoke of my enchantment."

"I thought you had no powers."

"I myself do not. But I know spells and potions that may protect us from the Evil One you suspect draws near."

Devon folds his arms across his chest. "I don't believe you, Bjorn. I think you're in league with Isobel. You and Mrs. Crandall are keeping her down in the basement, for whatever reason. I've *heard* her. I know the truth!"

"Back away, boy!"

"No," Devon says, and with a wave of his hand levitates the bubbling cauldron and tips it over the cliff. Its steaming blue soup empties into the waves hundreds of feet below.

"Foolish one!" Bjorn shouts, his face turning red with anger. He shakes his little fist at Devon in a rage. "You will be sorry you did that!"

"I've had enough of threats and lies," Devon tells him.

Just then he spots headlights swinging up the long

driveway. It's Mrs. Crandall's Jaguar. The automatic garage door opens and the car glides inside.

"And it's time I started demanding the truth," Devon says, turning on his heel and running across the estate, leaving the gnome to fret over his inverted cauldron. Devon reaches the garage and flings open its back door.

"Devon!" Mrs. Crandall cries, startled. She has just gotten out of the car. Her brother is emerging from the passenger's side door.

Devon strides up to her and looks Mrs. Crandall straight in the eye. "My father sent me here because he hoped you'd protect me. He hoped you'd teach me, guide me."

She makes a face. "What ever *are* you talking about?"

"I'm talking about the danger I find around every corner in this house. A danger you refuse to admit, or let me try to defeat."

Edward slams his car door shut. "You're not starting that again, are you?"

Devon ignores him. "Who's in the basement, Mrs. Crandall?"

She draws herself up, chin in the air. "I have no idea what you're going on about."

"Is it Isobel the Apostate?"

She looks at him with contempt. "This is all too absurd. I'm going in the house." She brushes past him toward the corridor that leads into Ravenscliff.

Devon follows. "I've heard her down there. And in the tower, too."

Edward Muir is behind him. "You can be very irritating, you know that, Devon?"

Devon spins on him. "By the way, if you go looking for your son—not that it's something you do very often—you might want to be careful."

Edward lifts an eyebrow at him. "Careful?"

"Yeah. You wouldn't want to get sprayed like Cecily did."

Mrs. Crandall stops as they enter the kitchen of the great house. "*Sprayed?*"

Devon faces them both. "Alexander has been turned into a skunk."

"*What?*" Edward shouts.

"Oh, Devon, *really*," Mrs. Crandall says, turning away.

Devon nods. "Oh, yes. And guess who I suspect did it?"

"Isobel the Apostate," Edward says, rolling his eyes.

"No." Devon allows for a dramatic pause. "Your fiancée."

He watches both of their faces. Edward reacts as Devon expected: with outrage. But Mrs. Crandall's face goes white.

"How *dare* you?" Edward charges. "You stop this nonsense right now—"

"Listen to me," Devon says. "We face a real danger. Isobel the Apostate wants to open the Hellhole, and she's manipulating people here. I believe she may be using Morgana in the same way she used D.J."

"Edward," Mrs. Crandall says, her voice suddenly serious. "Go upstairs and check on Alexander."

Her brother flusters a bit but does what she says. When he's gone, Mrs. Crandall looks Devon carefully in the eye. For all her obstinence, she is a smart woman. She survived the cataclysm that killed her father and remembers the days when sorcery was practiced openly at Ravenscliff.

"Are you saying," Mrs. Crandall asks, "that you suspect Morgana is in league with Isobel the Apostate?"

"Not wittingly." Devon still can't believe that Morgana would do anything evil of her own accord. "But how else can I explain what she did to Alexander?"

"The boy . . . he was really changed into a . . . a . . . ?"

"*Skunk,* Mrs. Crandall. Alexander is a skunk. And this whole house is going to be destroyed if we don't act to save ourselves."

"Isobel the Apostate . . . can it be so?"

"I want the truth," Devon says to her, seeing the change in her eyes. "I know you hired Bjorn to watch over the woman in the tower, and now he's transported her into the basement. I don't know if I can trust Bjorn or not, but I want to trust *you*, Mrs. Crandall. My father sent me to you. I have to believe that *he* trusted you."

She says nothing, but Devon can see she's considering his words.

He presses on. "If you're keeping Isobel prisoner somehow, perhaps in hopes that you'll contain her power, you need to understand that she's free. She's found a way out."

Mrs. Crandall closes her eyes. "You don't know what you're talking about, Devon."

"Don't lie to me anymore!"

"I'm not lying to you!" She's angry now. "If you say we face a threat from Isobel the Apostate, I believe you."

Edward Muir has rejoined them. "Okay," he says, clearly annoyed. "So there's a skunk in a crate in the boy's room. That doesn't prove anything."

Mrs. Crandall eyes him coldly. "Will you always forfeit responsibility, Edward? Will you never face up to what you must do?"

He's taken aback by her change in tone. He says nothing in response.

Mrs. Crandall turns back to Devon. "I will take care of this. I assure you of that."

"You always say that. What can you possibly do without powers?"

"Please, Devon. Trust me. Go stay with Cecily."

Edward glares down at him. "Where's Morgana?"

Devon smiles, only too glad to tell him. "Let's see. Last time I saw her, she was with Rolfe Montaigne. In his arms, actually. Looking quite cozy."

Edward looks as if he'll have a coronary. His face turns purple, the veins in his forehead pop out and pulsate wildly. "How *dare* he—?"

"Edward!" Mrs. Crandall takes hold of her brother's arm. "There's no time for that. We need to go upstairs and check on Mother."

WHAT DO *they* do *up there?* Devon wonders. Whenever there's a crisis, they run to Mother—a senile, bedridden old lady. Every time Mrs. Crandall has vowed she'll take care of things, she heads up there to check on Mother. What does she really do? What goes on in the old lady's room?

Whatever it is, Devon puts no faith in it. Mrs. Crandall's efforts did little against the Madman; Devon holds out no hope for a better result this time.

I've got to go back to my original plan. I've got to confront Rolfe and Morgana.

This time, his transporting power works just fine.

No longer caring whether he interrupts a lovers' nest, he pops into view right in front of them, as they sit together in each other's arms in front of a blazing fireplace.

"Devon!" Rolfe shouts, clearly startled.

"We need to talk," the boy tells him.

"I'm—I'm busy right now."

"Yeah." Devon glares at him. "I can see that." He moves his eyes over to Morgana, who peers up at him sheepishly from under her lashes. "Hello, Morgana."

"Hello, Devon," she says quietly.

Rolfe stands and approaches the boy. "You need to leave. I can't have you just popping in here without any notice whenever you feel like it—"

"I *needed* to, Rolfe! Things are happening! I just caught Bjorn conjuring up some spell on Devil's Rock. Tell me what you found out about him!"

Rolfe's eyes are empty. "It's nothing important. It doesn't matter now."

"Doesn't *matter*? We're in the midst of a crisis here!"

Rolfe looks at him coldly. "You'll have to deal with it on your own."

His words nearly topple Devon over. "On my own? Rolfe, what's happened to you?"

Rolfe moves his eyes away from Devon, gazing back at Morgana. He's like all the others, Devon realizes, like

Devon himself—completely spellbound by her. This is not Devon's mentor, the one person he's come to rely on, the only hope he's had for ever understanding his past. Devon feels as if he's been punched in the stomach. He watches as Rolfe turns away from him and sits back down with Morgana, pulling her close.

He can't bear to watch. He closes his eyes. When he opens them he's outside Rolfe's house. The snow is heavier now and the wind whips angrily up from the sea, slashing against his face. He feels ridiculous, but he can't help shedding a couple of tears.

"It's just the wind, that's all," he says, wiping his face.

He looks up to see Roxanne walking toward him. She seems to emerge from the snowy air, wearing no coat.

"Hello, Devon March."

"Roxanne." He composes himself. "Listen, you can't go inside right now."

She smiles at him sadly. "I know what I would find. Rolfe with Morgana."

"You know?"

Roxanne nods.

"I don't know what's come over him," Devon says, surprised by how thick with emotion his voice sounds. "He's changed. He's not himself. I think a strike by

Isobel the Apostate is going to happen any minute, and Rolfe doesn't seem to care."

"No, he doesn't care. You're right, Devon. Something has come over him. Something that has made him cold and distant and consumed by only one thing." Roxanne looks off toward the house. "That's what happens when one is seduced by a succubus."

"A—a *what*?"

"A succubus. A demon in the form of a woman." Roxanne sighs. "She comes in the night, seducing mortal men, taking control of them."

Devon is stunned. "But it can't be. Morgana—she's no demon."

Roxanne says nothing, just holds his gaze.

He won't believe it. "Look, here's what I think. She's being manipulated by Isobel the Apostate—"

"She is a *succubus*, Devon." Roxanne places her hands on Devon's shoulders. "And she's very dangerous. She will get inside your mind, cloud your thoughts, your reason." She looks with concern over toward the house. "As she has done with Rolfe."

Devon tries to resist the idea, but it makes sense. *Everything* suddenly makes sense: Rolfe's behavior, D.J.'s infatuation, his own erotic dreams . . .

"What are we going to do?" Devon asks. "We need to help Rolfe."

"Yes. I have come to do what I can." She frowns. "But she is powerful, Devon."

"I'll help you," he promises.

Roxanne shakes her head. "Your powers will not work against her. The hold she has over you is too great. Only those who find no allure in her sensual charms can defeat her."

Devon realizes she's right. "But Isobel the Apostate is going to try to make me open the Hellhole. Today! I can feel it. I *need* Rolfe. I can't have him here, trapped by some—some *succubus.*"

"Go back to Ravenscliff, then. I will do what I can here. But remember this, Devon March." She looks at him intently. "Your fear will cripple your power. Be not afraid, and you will be strong."

H E TRIES keeping her words in his head, but they do little good: He remains frightened, so frightened that he cannot make his powers work, and he has to hitchhike a ride back into town and, from there, climb the steep cliffside staircase to Ravenscliff.

When he staggers inside, shivering from the cold, he's surprised to see Marcus and Ana sitting in the parlor with Cecily.

"What's going on?" he asks, hanging up his coat.

"I asked them to come over," Cecily says. "I called

D.J. too, but he hasn't shown up yet. I was getting worried about you. Bjorn said you'd gone a little mad."

"Bjorn's the one who's mad," Devon says, walking into the parlor. "I found him trying to conjure up the spirit of Isobel the Apostate. I'm sure of it."

Cecily embraces him quickly, then looks into his eyes. "Mother said you told her it was *Morgana* who turned Alexander into a skunk."

Devon looks around. "Where's your mother now? And Edward?"

"With Grandmama."

He shakes his head. "Still up there, huh? What do they *do* up there?"

"Devon," Marcus asks, "why do you think it was Morgana who did that to Alexander?"

"I heard her call him a skunk this morning."

"That doesn't mean she has any supernatural powers."

Devon feels something twist down in his gut. "Well, she does. I've just talked with Roxanne. Morgana's got Rolfe under some kind of spell now. She's a—" Devon can barely speak the word. "She's a succubus."

"A *what*?" Cecily asks.

"Nasty," Ana says. "Whatever it is, it sounds nasty."

"It's a demon in the form of a woman," Devon says.

Cecily snorts. "And this is news? Maybe next time

you'll listen to me, Devon. I might not have powers or Voices in my head, but I know a few things."

Marcus is nodding. "It makes sense. Since our last go-round at the Hellhole, I've been reading up on demonology at the library. A succubus takes the form of a woman, an incubus the shape of a man. That way they divide and conquer. But see, a succubus has no power over women. In fact, women can have an instinctive distrust."

"That explains our feelings toward her," Ana says.

Marcus laughs. "Well, she didn't count on one thing. See, I've been having these dreams about her, ever since I met her. Morgana would come into my room and try to seduce me."

"Yeah," Devon admits, not looking at Cecily. "Me, too."

"But I'm *gay*, Devon," Marcus says. "She didn't know that, of course, so she was trying to get me under her spell just like she had you, D.J., Edward, and now Rolfe. But with me she *failed*." Marcus seems rather pleased with himself. "My lack of response was making her *angry*. Night after night, my dreams of her got worse. I started seeing her vent her frustration. I saw the *evil* behind those gentle eyes."

The front doorbell chimes. They all jump. Cecily peers through the window and announces D.J. has arrived. She opens the door and their pierced, wiry friend shambles into the foyer, looking as if he's had no sleep for days.

Devon approaches him. "You okay, buddy?"

"My butt's a little sore from where I came down hard in those hedges," he says.

They all head into the parlor to sit in front of the fireplace and make some plans. No one has any great ideas, truth be told, and Devon's getting edgier by the minute. The heat and the pressure are building at a rapid rate now, and the Voice keeps telling him over and over, like that dumb old *Lost in Space* robot, *Danger! Danger! Danger!*

"Okay," Devon says, trying to get a grip on his fear, "here's the situation we're facing. Rolfe is out of commission. He can't help us. Alexander has been turned into a skunk, and I'm not sure how we're going to turn him back. Mrs. Crandall and her brother are upstairs with their mother, doing God knows what. I believe Bjorn is working in league with Isobel the Apostate. That leaves us here, by ourselves, to defend the Hellhole."

"I think I hear my mother calling," Ana says in a small voice.

Devon looks at her. "You *should* go now. All of you. There's no reason for you all to be put in danger, not again."

"We're in this together, man," Marcus tells him. "Right, D.J.?"

D.J. hesitates, then nods.

Cecily is near tears. "I'm so sorry my crazy family has such awful skeletons in its closet."

"Look," Devon says. "Before you all decide anything definite, I need to tell you about a vision I had. My father showed it to me when I used his ring."

They all look at Devon with wide eyes.

"In the vision, I opened the Hellhole. I was forced into it somehow. And the demons took over this house, destroying it." His voice cracks. "And they killed all of you."

"*All* of us?" Ana asks.

Devon nods. "I saw you all. Dead."

The friends are quiet. D.J. stands and walks over to the window, looking out onto the cliffs below. They can hear the surf from where they are, crashing and violent.

"I wouldn't blame any of you for leaving," Devon says.

Marcus looks at him intently, his eyes aglow. "I'm not leaving you, Devon."

Ana is trembling. Cecily puts her arm around her.

D.J. turns to them. He's crying. Devon is stunned. D.J. Stoic, cynical D.J., shedding tears?

"I'm sorry," D.J. says. "I didn't want to do it. But she was inside my head. She made me do it."

Devon stands, walking over to him. "Made you do what, D.J.? And who? Who are you talking about?"

"Dude, I'm so sorry." D.J. grabs ahold of Devon's hands. "Please forgive me! I love all you guys. I'd never want to do anything to hurt you—"

"Tell me what you did, D.J.!" Devon shouts.

"I led them here! Led them here and now it's too late!"

All at once the windows blow inward, raining shards of glass all over the room. The five friends dive for cover behind couches and chairs but none of them escapes some injury. The shattering of the glass is followed by a horrible screech, loud enough to topple the suit of armor standing in the corner.

Then the worst terror of all: An enormous purple demon, with the head of a dragon and a wingspan of at least ten feet, flies into the room, its giant claws clutching for anything it can grasp.

"Remember!" Devon shouts. "You share my powers! Don't be afraid! Fight as you've done before! Just trust your body to know what to do!"

The screeching demon is followed by dozens of ravens, tiny and insignificant compared with its monstrous size. But the dark-wing protectors of the great house are fearless, flying at the beast, their little beaks pecking at its hard, reptilian skin, even if most of them are swatted away like so many flies.

The demon lands on its two feet, folding in its terrible wings. It twists its hideous neck this way and that, its gigantic glassy eyes searching the room for prey.

And it spots him.

"It's me you want," Devon shouts. "Not the others!"

The thing screeches.

"Come on, ugly," Devon says. "I've taken on far worse than you. Come on!"

Just then the doors to the parlor swing open behind him. Ana screams. There stand two more demons, identical to each other, skeletal humanoids rubbing their rotting hands eagerly together.

"Fight!" Devon commands.

And his friends obey. Marcus is first, springing at the winged demon as if he had rockets in his shoes, landing a hefty elbow punch right in the thing's eye. The beast screams, extending its wings, knocking dozens of books from the shelves and sending them scattering to the floor.

Devon meanwhile lunges at the two creatures behind him, landing a powerful double blow across both of their chins, sending them staggering backward. Cecily moves in to assist, disappearing and then rematerializing behind the demons, where she lands a swift roundhouse kick to the backbone of the first one. It falls to the ground but its mate, enraged, charges at her.

"Prepare to meet your doom," the demon rasps, raising its arms.

Cecily smirks at the thing. "Excuse me a minute while I pat down my goose bumps, okay?" Then she lashes out with one—two—*three* swift karate chops, leaving the demon in a clump on the floor.

"See?" she says. "I knew I'd be a natural at this Nightwing stuff."

The winged demon, its eye gouged out and dripping red pus onto the floor, is emitting a horrible shrill call. Ana cripples one of its legs with a cheerleading kick that suddenly takes on superhuman force. The beast is furious, raging in pain around the room, knocking aside everything in its path.

One of the humanoids has recovered enough to come back at Devon. But it's knocked down before Devon even has a chance to defend himself—by D.J., leaping through the air and slamming both feet against the beast's chest. The thing goes down, sliding across the floor through the foyer to come to a crashing stop against the front doors.

"Thanks," Devon tells him.

"This is only the beginning, Devon. There are more, lots more. We've got to be strong."

The wounded demon in the center of the room is

still making that terrible sound. "It's a distress call," Devon realizes. "Get ready!"

At that moment, dozens of the beasts fly through the window—so many that it's hard to make them all out. The room reeks with their filthy odor. Bug-eyed flying things that look like huge, hideous insects. Scaly snakelike things that come slithering over the broken glass of the window. Hairy piglike creatures with mouths full of fangs. Lizards that walk like men. Humanoids with glassy eyes and bones sticking through their flesh.

"There are too many!" Ana cries out.

Devon's in the foyer, so he can't see her. But he hears her scream—a scream that's quickly silenced.

"She's down!" he hears Marcus cry in panic. "Ana is down!"

"That's my best friend you just hit," Cecily screams. Devon watches as she leaps in Ana's defense toward some hulking, hairy thing. "You big brute! Haven't you ever heard it's not good form to hit a lady?"

"Cecily!" he calls out. "Be careful!"

She lands a solid blow against the demon's head, but now Devon feels tentacles wrap around him from behind, squeezing the breath out of him. He breaks free, but his heart is pounding high in his chest.

Don't be afraid, he tells himself. *Your fear is your downfall. You can't be afraid.*

But it's my vision—it's coming true. The destruction of the house, my friends being killed—

No! It can't happen!

He sees D.J. bravely throw himself against a reptilian demon three times his size, only to be batted away, slammed against the wall.

"You see? It is happening."

Devon spins around.

A cloaked and hooded figure stands behind him.

"Open the portal, Devon," it tells him. "Open the portal or watch your friends die, one by one."

"No!"

The figure draws closer. He can't see its face. He can't tell who—or what—it is. A demon—or something else?

"Open the portal, Devon. It is your destiny. Your path to true power. Ultimate power. Beyond anything that's been promised you so far."

Why does this figure terrify him so?

"Who—who are you?" he asks.

"You know who I am, Devon."

The voice. He's heard it before.

"Isobel?" he asks in a tiny voice.

He hears Marcus scream. He turns but can't find him in the midst of all the screeching, flying demons.

"Your friends are falling," the cloaked figure tells him. "Come with me, Devon. Open the portal!"

"Don't do it, Devon!" It's Cecily. He sees her on the stairs, battling a beast with six arms. She stands in the exact spot where his vision showed him she will die, in a pool of blood at the foot of the stairs.

"We can still win, Devon!" Cecily tells him. "Don't open the Hellhole! No matter what happens, don't open the Hellhole!"

She's going to die! Devon thinks, his greatest fear coming true. *The vision was right! This is how it will end!*

The cloaked figure is nearly upon him. "Open the portal, Devon! *Now!*"

The grandfather clock chimes nine o'clock.

"No!" Devon shouts, and turns, running down the corridor toward the library, away from the door to the East Wing.

I'll draw them away from Cecily and the others! It's me they want!

Indeed the beasts follow, and Devon's fear mounts.

There's no way out! Ana and Marcus may already be dead. D.J., too. And Cecily—

He hears her scream.

A beast is upon him, sharp talons gouging into his throat. He struggles to fight it off, but he can't. It's too strong—or he's suddenly too weak. He grabs onto the nearest thing he can find to steady himself—the doorknob of a linen closet. The door swings open under his grip.

He gasps, the talons slicing into his throat. He sees that the door reveals not a linen closet, but a staircase, leading down.

Devon stumbles onto the stairs as he finally shakes the demon from his back. He begins to run down the steps as the thing pursues him, snarling and spitting at his neck.

Only then does Devon fully understand that he is descending the Stairway Into Time.

TEN

◆━━◆

THE DARK TUNNEL

"HERE, DEVON! This way!"

A man is taking hold of his arm, trying to pull him from the stairs. With the demon breathing down his back, Devon's not fully aware of who this guy is, and the sounds around him make no sense at first. There's light—bright, eye-squinting light. It occurs to Devon that, just like his last trip down this staircase, he finds himself no longer inside, but outdoors. Bright sunlight dapples the last few remaining steps of the Staircase Into Time, which ends at a dusty cobblestone road.

The demon lunges again. Its talons grip Devon around the waist. He swings back with a fierce elbow thrust and the beast howls in pain.

"Send it away, Devon," the man is shouting. "You can do it!"

Devon throws the brute off his back, spinning

around to face it. The thing gnashes its yellow teeth, dripping great gobs of green saliva all over the cobblestones.

"You have the power," the man tells him. "You are Nightwing!"

For the first time Devon realizes who this observer is: the same man in the brown hooded robe and long white beard he saw on his first, aborted trip down the Staircase.

"Banish it, Devon!" the man is urging him. "Before it attacks again!"

Devon turns his attention back to the demon. It is about to spring, its hideous yellow eyes flashing.

You have the power, Devon. You are Nightwing!

"Back to where you came," Devon calls out. "I command you! Go back to hell!"

The thing screams, its ugly face lifted to the sky. Then it is sucked up into the air, rocketed away into nothingness.

"You did it!" the bearded man exclaims.

Devon leans against a building for support, breathing heavily. His eyes scan his surroundings. A small crowd has gathered to watch the battle. Devon sees he is standing in a village square, and more people are gazing down at him from second-floor windows. From the architecture of the buildings—half-timbered black-and-white houses, flattened arches, checkerboard chimney stacks clustered in groups—Devon realizes he's in Tudor England.

I've gone back in time, he says to himself, awed. *Back to the time of Isobel the Apostate.*

"The boy must be a sorcerer to do what he did," one man shouts from the crowd. "He must be in league with the witch!"

"You are fools to think such," the bearded man tells them. "You witnessed what he did here. He sent the filthy demon back to hell—the same kind of demon that has been plaguing your homes and families lo these many months. He can help you! He can stop the witch!"

The crowd murmurs to itself, still looking at Devon with disbelief.

"I—I need to go," Devon manages to say.

"Yes, you have important business to attend to," the man says, taking his arm. "My good people, what you witnessed here today marks the end of your suffering. From all over the world the great Nightwing are arriving in England, and they will be told of the devilry of the Witch of York."

Devon looks up at the man. He's seen him before, not just in his earlier trip down the stairs. Somewhere else, too . . .

But there's no time to figure it out. "Look," Devon tells the man, "what I meant was that I've got to *go.*

Back up the staircase. Back to my own time. My friends are in danger."

"But you have come to defeat the witch, have you not?"

Devon manages a small smile. "I'm doing my best to accomplish that in my own time. Really, I've got to go."

The man releases his grip on Devon's arm. The boy takes a deep breath and starts across the square, heading back to the staircase. It's just a series of stone steps leading up the side of a building to a wooden door.

"Please!" an old woman cries, rushing out of the crowd. She is dressed in rags and her face is dirty. She grabs Devon by the hand. "Do not leave us! She has killed my whole family! Save us from the witch!"

"Save us!" someone else calls out.

Devon looks back at them uncomfortably. "Um, look, I'm really sorry and all—"

"Burn the witch!" the crowd begins to chant. "You must burn the witch!"

"I—I don't have time," Devon protests, feeling ridiculously guilty. But then he remembers his friends: Cecily, D.J., Marcus, and Ana may all be dead already. Every second he delays makes it more likely. "Look," Devon says, "I can tell you this much. She *will* burn. I know. I'm from the future. I read all about it. She'll burn and you'll all be safe."

He turns quickly, not wanting to see their dazed, pitiful faces anymore. He hurries up the stairs but pauses outside the door to look back.

"This is the door to the future," he shouts down to them. "Please believe me that everything is going to work out all right for you."

The crowd remains silent, looking up at him with bewilderment.

He opens the door.

A woman screams.

"Help!" she calls. "Thomas, help me!"

She is taking a bath.

Devon gulps, looking around the room. This isn't Ravenscliff. This is a sixteenth-century inn, and a middle-aged woman sits in a round wooden tub filled with water. Thomas—Devon quickly pegs him as the woman's husband—comes barging through another door, his eyes bugging out of his head.

"My mistake!" Devon shouts. "I'm sorry!"

He rushes back out the door, slamming it shut behind him.

The crowd below is laughing at him.

"The door to the future?" one man shouts out. "The door to Mistress Bessie's inn, I do think."

Devon feels his cheeks burn in embarrassment. The crowd is dispersing, the people laughing, shaking their heads, their belief in him gone.

"Hey," Devon calls after them. "I still managed to kick that demon butt back to hell for you."

"And they are grateful for it," the bearded man tells him from the foot of the stairs. "But they are looking for a savior. Not a boy who bungles his way into a lady's bath."

"But these *are* the stairs, aren't they? The ones I came down when I came from the future?"

"They are indeed," the man says as Devon descends, scratching his head. "But the Staircase Into Time appears and disappears of its own accord. Who knows where it may appear next—if anywhere at all."

"But it's *got* to," Devon says, desperate now. "I've *got* to get back. I've got to save my friends. They're *this close* to getting killed."

The bearded man in the hooded robe looks down at him with wise old eyes. "My boy, your friends are in no danger."

"How can you say that? I just left them—the demons are loose and I know Ana and D.J. are already down. Cecily was near to being taken out, too."

The man laughs. "My boy, it is the year fifteen hundred and twenty-two, year thirteen of our great lord King Henry. Your friends are in no danger. They will not even be *born* for close to another five hundred years."

Devon looks into the man's deep blue eyes. "Now I

remember where I've seen you," he says at last. "In my visions, when I've read *The Book of Enlightenment*. Except then you were always wearing a purple robe with stars on it."

"Ah, yes, my ceremonial garb. Which I will don tomorrow, for the opening day of Witenagemot." He smiles. "Allow me to introduce myself. I am Wiglaf, a teacher at the great school of the Nightwing in the southwest of England. I am a Guardian, and I have been waiting for you, Devon March."

Devon considers him a little suspiciously. "How do you know who I am?"

"I was asked to meet you here at this spot. I was given specific instructions, and details about your situation. I was told you'd probably be a bit disoriented."

"Who asked you to meet me?"

"There's time for talk later," Wiglaf tells him, dropping his arm around the boy's shoulder. "First we need to get you into proper clothing." The Guardian shudders. "Is this the costume to which we must look forward, half a millennium hence?"

"Hey, these sneaks cost me eighty bucks."

Wiglaf is reading Devon's sweatshirt. "And what does Abercrombie and Fitch mean? Are they sorcerers in your time?"

Devon laughs. "Only to teenage consumers."

The Guardian clearly has no clue what he's talking

about. "Come with me. I have arranged for a proper doublet and a pair of boots for you. If you are going to attend the Witenagemot, you must not arrive in—" He hesitates, trying to remember the distasteful name. *"Sneaks."*

THEY TRAVEL about half a mile along the dusty cobblestone road. The gutters of the street stink with rotting pig and chicken flesh, mixed with moldy human waste. Rats swarm everywhere. A woman dumps a bucket of brown slop from an upper window as they pass. It splashes into the gutter, causing Devon to jump back.

"Sewers haven't been invented yet, I guess," Devon says, holding his nose.

"Sewers?" Wiglaf asks. "What are sewers?"

"Oh, believe me. You'll appreciate them." He shudders. "I'll never take them for granted again."

"They must be very wondrous indeed."

"That's not the word usually used in connection with sewers, but you've got a point." They head down a narrow alleyway. "So tell me about Witenagemot."

"No," Wiglaf whispers. "Too many ears everywhere. And already news of your little exhibition earlier is spreading like wildfire throughout the town."

The Voice is telling Devon that he can trust Wiglaf.

But as fascinating as he finds the prospect of attending a Witenagemot, he remains uneasy about slipping out in the middle of a fight, leaving Cecily and the others on their own. And poor Alexander is still a skunk, trapped in a dog crate.

But Alexander isn't born yet, Devon reminds himself. *Neither is Cecily, or any of them. So how can they be in danger?* It boggles his mind.

He follows Wiglaf through a small door of a wooden house at the end of the alleyway. Blackened oak timbers support whitewashed plaster walls, with the second story of the house projecting out over the first. They climb steep, narrow steps and emerge into a small room, unfurnished except for a wooden table and two chairs near the window overlooking the street. There's also an ornately carved wooden chest in the center of the room. Devon makes out the engraving to be a sorcerer battling a dragon.

"Sargon?" he asks Wiglaf. "Looks like pictures I've seen of him."

"Yes, indeed. The chest depicts the great Sargon slaying the dragon."

"None of the pictures of him resemble what he really looked like." Devon smiles, a little smugly. "I *know.* I've met him in person."

"You're his hundredth-generation descendant," Wiglaf says as he opens the lid of the chest. "I'm sure he found a way of meeting you. Tell me, was he impressed?"

Devon just grunts and looks away. When he looks back at Wiglaf, the Guardian is smiling. He seems to know all about Devon's less-than-satisfactory encounter with his famous ancestor.

"How do you know so much about me?" Devon asks. "How'd you even know I'm hundredth-generation?"

"Never mind that now. Put these on."

He hands Devon a pair of padded breeches, a tight-fitting doublet of satin brocade trimmed in fur, and a hat made out of fur, too.

He looks down at the clothes with a pained expression. "I'm supposed to *wear* this stuff?"

"Well, you're not supposed to *eat* it." Wiglaf folds his arms across his chest. "Please, Devon. Don't tarry. Just put them on."

Devon obliges. "I look like Little Lord Fauntleroy," he gripes, placing the mink hat on his head at a jaunty angle. "Cecily would *so* hate that this is real fur. She's big into animal rights and all that."

"You look like a proper English squire, and that's precisely what is necessary for you to move about with ease."

"So why am I here? I thought I just blundered my

way down the Staircase Into Time. But you were expecting me."

"Yes, I was." Wiglaf motions for him to sit with him at the table. They look out onto the street below. "You see, Devon, it grows dark. Look at the fear on the faces of the villagers. Watch how they pull their shutters inward, bolt them against the witch."

"Isobel the Apostate," Devon says.

"Yes. I have been told that is how she will be remembered in the Nightwing history. But now she is known simply as Lady Isobel Plantagenet, the Witch of York."

"She claims royal blood," Devon says. "She's trying to overthrow Henry the Eighth."

Wiglaf nods. "And there are many, both here and on the Continent, who would like nothing more than to see the king usurped. She has made allies. Important allies who protect her. Meanwhile, she ravages the villages and the countryside, building her own army with the aid of her creatures from hell."

"So what am I supposed to do about it?"

"That much I do not know. I was simply told that you would be arriving on this particular day from the future, and that you had a destiny with the witch." Wiglaf smiles. "For a moment earlier today I thought my instructions might have been wrong. For you appeared but turned around and went back up the stairs, disappearing back to your own time."

Devon laughs. "That wasn't today. That was *weeks* ago."

Again Wiglaf smiles. "My boy, you need to surrender your concepts of time. Once one begins to travel through it, time is no longer linear. What was to you weeks ago was naught but a few hours for me."

"It's freaky."

"I assume you mean that it is bewildering. Yes, it is. I had a difficult time grasping the concept myself at first. But, of course, I had the advantage of having it explained to me by one of the great Nightwing masters of time." Wiglaf pauses. "The very man, in fact, who instructed me, some two hundred years ago, to wait for you today."

"Who, Wiglaf? Who told you to meet me?"

"His name is Horatio Muir."

Devon's stunned. "Horatio Muir? But that's impossible! Horatio Muir isn't even born yet. Just like my friends!"

"What did I just explain to you? Horatio Muir *built* the Staircase Into Time. He has traveled both far into the past and well into the future."

"But I've never met him. He died long before I came to Ravenscliff."

Wiglaf gently knocks his fist against the side of

Devon's head. "Is your head made of wood, boy? Have you been absorbing anything I've said? Time is not the orderly progression you have always assumed it to be. You *will* meet Horatio Muir at some point. It hasn't happened yet along your own particular time continuum, but it has along his. When he made his journey to the year 1304—when I was just a young lad of ninety-nine years old—he had already met you, and he knew of the battle you would wage against Isobel the Apostate in the early part of the third millennium. He also knew that you would arrive here in the year 1522—on today's exact date—and he asked me to wait for you." Wiglaf grins. "He knew you would be a little confused."

"Confused doesn't begin to cut it," Devon says, rubbing his temples. "This is wigging me out, Wiglaf."

"Just keep your mind on the present. That's all there is."

"But Cecily—"

He isn't able to finish, because they're distracted by a loud noise on the street below. A man is shouting, pointing up at the sky. An enormous demon drops into view—an apelike creature with reptilian wings on its back. Devon can't help but think of the winged monkeys from *The Wizard of Oz.*

"It would appear that your services are needed below," Wiglaf says dryly.

"Superman to the rescue," Devon says, a little wearily. He snaps his fingers and he's outside on the street. The flying monkey has attached itself to the window of a second story and the man is throwing stones at it.

"It's going to take my children!" the man shouts in terror.

"Hey, man, take it easy," Devon says. "I can handle this."

The demon turns and hisses, spotting Devon in the street. It leaps from the building at him. Devon braces himself for the impact.

It doesn't come. The demon stops in midair, a look of surprise on its ugly face. Something has caught him from behind. Devon watches as the beast is suddenly swung around by its wings—by a girl who looks exactly like Cecily!

"To your stinking netherworld!" the girl cries, and with one fling of her arm sends the creature hurtling through the sky over the rooftops of the village.

"The Nightwing have arrived!" the man in the window is shouting. "The Nightwing have come to save us!"

The girl smiles at Devon. "You must be quick, my friend. You mustn't tarry so long as you did. It gives them too much opportunity. Take them from behind, when they are unawares."

"Cecily?" he stammers.

"My name is Gisele." She approaches Devon, smiling. He can't speak momentarily, stunned by the resemblance. She is the *exact image* of Cecily: red hair, green eyes, the same saucy lift to her chin. "I hail from Zeeland and the court of the Count of Flanders. I am here for Witenagemot. And you?"

It's clear she recognizes him as a fellow Nightwing. Devon tries to stammer out a reply. "I am—Devon March."

"A curious name. Is it English?"

He considers how much to reveal, and decides on caution. "Uh, yes. Yes, it is." He considers her accent. It's different from the old English that Wiglaf speaks. "But you're not from here, are you?"

"I am from Flanders. My father is Arnulf, my mother Sybilla of Ghent, and we hail from the line of Wilhelm of Holland, the great Nightwing artist." She smiles, evidently proud of her lineage. "And from what line do you descend, Devon March?"

"Uh, I'm—um—well, I descend from Sargon the Great."

Gisele raises her eyebrows. "But we all do. Who is your father?"

"I don't know." Devon swallows. "I'm Nightwing. That's all I know."

She gives him a bemused look. "A captivating tale, I

would think. You have no knowledge, none at all, of your parentage?"

"None at all." This is a new voice. Devon turns. It is Wiglaf. "The boy is under my guardianship for the moment, Gisele."

"Wiglaf!" The girl hurries to him, embracing him warmly. "I was *so* looking forward to seeing you."

"You know each other?" Devon asks.

Gisele turns to him. "Wiglaf was my teacher for several years when I attended the school in the southwest of England. Did you not attend there as well, Devon March? I thought all Nightwing children were trained there."

"Not for this young master, I regret to say," Wiglaf tells her. "Devon was not told of his heritage until very recently."

"Yeah," Devon admits. "I have a lot of catching up to do."

Gisele seems puzzled. "But you are here for Witenagemot, just as my parents and I are?"

Devon shrugs. "So Wiglaf tells me."

"It's my first," Gisele says, batting her lashes a bit and smiling at him. "I should enjoy being with someone for whom it will also be the first time."

Devon blushes. Is she flirting with him? She looks so much like Cecily that he definitely feels drawn to her. It's weird: He feels both a little guilty *and* completely natural when he smiles back at her.

"My father says there is to be a secret meeting tomorrow, before the official ceremony begins," Gisele tells Wiglaf.

"You must be quiet about that," Wiglaf chastises her. "You must say nothing too loudly, for the witch has ears everywhere."

Devon draws close to them. "The secret meeting. It's about Isobel, right?"

Wiglaf nods. "The Nightwing have determined something must be done. She is to be officially named an Apostate."

Gisele shivers. "I've heard of Apostates before. So *she* is the one who sent the demon I vanquished."

"Lady Isobel has set many demons free upon this land," Wiglaf explains. "She must be destroyed."

"But how?" Gisele asks.

"That is for the Nightwing to decide, not me." Wiglaf sighs. "I am just a Guardian." He puts his arms around the shoulders of both young people. "Now take us to your parents, Gisele. I suspect my young ward would enjoy meeting them."

THAT HE certainly does. To Devon's astonishment, Gisele's mother looks exactly like Mrs. Crandall—

except that Sybilla of Ghent is warm and inviting, offering him a cup of hot broth as he sits in front of the fire. For the moment, Gisele's father is not in their suite of rooms at Kelvedon House, loaned to them by an English Nightwing for the duration of Witenagemot. Devon wonders if Arnulf will look like Cecily's father. Of course, Devon would have no way of judging, as he's never seen Peter Crandall. Not even a picture.

But when Gisele's father walks through the door, Devon is stunned. Arnulf of Zeeland is the spitting image of Rolfe Montaigne!

"Devon March, this is my father," Gisele says.

Arnulf stands tall over him, looking down with Rolfe's piercing green eyes. "Welcome to you, my young friend. Wiglaf tells me you know not your father. It is a pitiful thing, and a condition I hope you can remedy."

"I intend to," Devon tells him. "I am determined to discover the truth of who I am."

It's uncanny, watching these people. Devon could swear they're Rolfe, Cecily, and Mrs. Crandall dressed up for some costume party. But the warm embrace exchanged between Arnulf and Sybilla, husband and wife, convinces Devon these are very different people from the two foes of the twenty-first century. Yet it gives Devon a little glimpse into the affection once shared between Amanda Muir Crandall and Rolfe

Montaigne, a love that has now turned into hatred and resentment.

Now turned into? Sipping his ale at the long wooden table, Devon reminds himself yet again that time is no longer what it was. There is no "now" but the present—and the present is 1522. Not only have Rolfe and Mrs. Crandall yet to begin their feud, they have yet to be *born*. Their grandparents, their great-grandparents—even their great-great-great-great-great-grandparents—have yet to be born!

But he's just got to find a way to return to his own time. What if he's trapped here? What if that had been Isobel's plan all along? To send him back here so she could have free rein at Ravenscliff in the future. Maybe she knew she'd defeat him here and, armed with that knowledge, dispatched him from the twenty-first century to meet his destiny here. It suddenly all starts to make sickening sense to him.

"More ale, my young friend?" Arnulf asks him.

"Sure," Devon says. Back home, he isn't old enough to drink beer. But here in the sixteenth century, he's already a man. Fourteen-year-olds get married, own property, march off to war. He'd learned that in Mr. Weatherby's class—or, rather, he *will* learn that, four and a half centuries from now.

He can't help grinning wryly to himself. *I'll be the first person in history to have the dates on my tombstone in reverse. My birth year will be later than my death year.*

"Devon March," Gisele says, coming around to the end of the table where Devon sits, "care you to walk with me outside? There is a full moon."

The ale has made him a little heady. "Sure," he says. He notices Wiglaf give him a small smile as he gets up to leave. Then the Guardian returns to the discussion he is having with Arnulf and Sybilla about the secret Nightwing convocation to be held the next day.

Outdoors the village is quiet, seemingly deserted. "They are all afraid," Gisele says. "This witch—she has control of a very large portal, I would assume."

Devon looks at her. "You ever been down a Hell-hole?"

Her eyes widen. "Of course not. Have you?"

"Yeah," he says nonchalantly. "I went down there to rescue a kid. Didn't take all that long."

Gisele seems stunned. "You went into a Hellhole to rescue a *goat*?"

Devon laughs. "No, a human kid. A child. A little boy."

Her eyes dance in wonder. "And you made it out *alive*? Oh, Devon March, how brave of you."

He smiles. He likes impressing her, especially after she beat him to the punch in defeating that demon earlier.

"You know," he says, "it must be pretty awesome growing up with Nightwing parents, going to a Nightwing school. All my life I've just had to wonder what my powers were, why I could do things other kids—other children—could not."

"I expect that would have been very difficult for you." Gisele smiles up at him, the moonlight reflecting off her face. "Tell me, Devon March. Are you betrothed?"

"Betrothed? You mean, like, engaged to be married?"

She nods.

"Well, where I come from fourteen is a little young to be thinking about that. But I do have a girlfriend." He grins. "You remind me an awful lot of her."

Gisele seems to consider the word. "Are you planning on going back to this place where you come from? To this *girl-friend*?"

He sighs. "I hope so. But I'm not sure I know how."

Gisele takes his hand in hers. "Perhaps you will come back to my country with me. It is beautiful this time of year. The tulips are growing. There are boats we can take, on the canals . . ."

Devon begins to flush a bit and tries to change the subject. "So, what did they teach in Nightwing school? Did you learn about—?"

But his eyes catch something moving across the

street. Something small, lurking in the shadows. A patch of moonlight suddenly reveals what it is—or, rather, *who*.

It is Bjorn Forkbeard.

D EVON!" Gisele cries. "It is just a gnome!"

But he's pursued the little man down the street. Despite Devon's cries to stop, Bjorn continues on his way, scurrying through the shadows.

Gisele catches up with Devon. "What do you want from him?"

"I *know* him," Devon tells her.

At first glance, Devon had been inclined to chalk it up to yet another extraordinary resemblance. After all, everyone else from Ravenscliff seems to have a double in this time. Why not Bjorn?

Until Devon remembered that Bjorn is six hundred and sixty-two years old in the twenty-first century. Meaning that he would be alive *now*, in 1522. The gnome Devon saw wasn't Bjorn's double: It was Bjorn himself.

"I have reason to suspect he's allied with Isobel," Devon tells Gisele. "I've seen him calling on the spirits, stirring a witch's cauldron. He's in league with her. I know it."

"Then we should tell my parents, and the other

Nightwing," Gisele suggests, pulling on Devon's doublet to make him stop.

He leans in close to her. "What's the matter? You can swing flying monkeys around by their wings but you're afraid of a little gnome?"

Gisele huffs. "I am *not* afraid, Devon March."

"Then come with me."

"I shall."

"Good."

They resume their pursuit. Devon suspects that seeing Bjorn here was no mere coincidence: He was *meant* to discover him here and his connection to Isobel. In *fact*, Devon is starting to believe, Bjorn is probably the one who brought Isobel to Ravenscliff, just as Simon had once done with the Madman. Bjorn wants power in the same desperate way Simon wanted it, the kind of power he can only get by assisting an Apostate in opening the Hellhole.

"He's gone in there," Gisele says. "That door behind the tavern."

Devon saw him, too. He strains to pull open the heavy oaken door that Bjorn had just so effortlessly moved through. "They're strong, these little guys," Devon tells Gisele. "But we have sorcery. Gnomes don't. Stand back, please."

He waves his hand majestically, willing the door to open. It doesn't budge. *The powers don't work merely to impress,* the Voice reminds him. Devon realizes he's still smarting a little over the fact that Gisele showed him up in the battle with the demon, and he was hoping to dazzle her a bit with his own sorcery.

"Shall I try?" she asks.

"No," he grunts, managing to yank the door open with his own muscle power. "There are some things better done without any magic." It creaks open and they slip into the darkened room.

"How cold it is," Gisele says, shivering.

Devon tries to look around. "Wish I had a flash-light."

"You need light?" Gisele asks. "So be it."

She snaps her fingers and the room is suddenly filled with a hundred candles, each offering flickering golden light.

Devon looks back at her. "So how come you can just do that? My powers aren't nearly so reliable."

"You must practice, Devon March. Now be vigi-lant."

The candlelight reveals only wooden kegs of ale. Only the one door leads into the room, so Bjorn couldn't have gone out another way.

"He's a crafty one," Devon says. "I wouldn't be sur-prised if he was hiding in one of these kegs."

"He'd emerge quite drunk if he were," Gisele says.

Devon concentrates. Maybe it's easy for Gisele to

just snap her fingers and suddenly bring forth light, but there's more to being a Nightwing than magic tricks. There's what Dad used to call *sensitivity.* You get ideas, thoughts, impulses. *Yes,* the Voice tells him. *See with your mind, not just your eyes.*

"Under there," Devon says suddenly, pointing to a couple of overturned kegs. "Roll them away."

Gisele obeys. On the earthen floor behind the kegs is revealed a small wooden trapdoor with a bronze ring attached.

"A *portal,*" Gisele breathes.

"But I feel no heat, no pressure," Devon says. "It can't be a Hellhole."

"Then what might it be?"

"Only one way to find out," Devon says.

He curls several fingers through the bronze ring and yanks at the door. Once again it's very heavy. He dares not try his powers again just in case they fail, so Gisele leans in to help him. Together they manage to lift it, revealing a dark hole, a tunnel, below.

"Did the gnome go down there?"

"Yes," Devon tells her, the Voice confirming it for him. "And I've got to follow."

"Not alone you won't."

"Gisele, I don't know what's down there. I have nothing to lose. I'm not from this place. I don't belong here. But you do—you have parents, friends, a whole life here."

She stiffens. "I am a Sorcerer of the Order of the Nightwing."

Devon can't hold back a smile. "Yes, you are." She's just like Cecily. Exactly. And it reminds Devon that, powers or not, Cecily descends from Nightwing stock, too.

He starts down the tunnel. It bores through the earth at a gentle angle, nothing too steep, but they are definitely going down. It is narrow at first but grows wider as they travel. Not wanting to signal Bjorn of their approach, they remain in the dark.

"If this isn't a Hellhole," Gisele whispers, "how was it created? What could possibly cut through the earth in this way?"

"A gnome could. Look." He indicates the rough surface of the tunnel's sides, which are covered with little ridges and valleys the size of fingers. "Have you never seen a gnome's fingernails? Harder than stone. They built mines like this all through northern Europe with their bare hands."

Gisele shivers. "Gnomes give me the oopalas," she says.

"The what?"

She laughs. "The Voice in my head says to tell you 'the creeps.' "

Devon smirks. "Look how well we're communicating and we've barely known each other a day."

Gisele starts to say something back but is distracted. "There!" she whispers, pointing past him. "Up ahead."

Devon sees a small, flickering light. It must be Bjorn. The gnome has paused in a larger hollowed-out area of the tunnel. Devon waits until they're only a few feet behind him before calling out.

"Bjorn Forkbeard!"

The gnome nearly drops his candle in surprise, but he recovers in enough time to turn around and hold the flame up to their faces. In the backglow his little eyes peer at them in terror.

Devon realizes Bjorn doesn't know him. Of course not—they haven't met yet. That day will come nearly five hundred years from now. But it dawns on Devon that on that fateful day on the icy driveway of Ravenscliff, the gnome will know exactly who Devon is, because they had met here, in the past.

"We are Nightwing," Devon says to him, "and we command you to tell us your business. Why did you not stop when I called to you on the street?"

"Noble sir, great lady, I ask your pardon. But I was so consumed by my purpose this night—surely you understand."

Devon looks at Gisele, then back at Bjorn. "What are you talking about?"

Just then they hear a sound. A squeaking sound— the sound of a bat somewhere off down the tunnel ahead of them.

"No!" Bjorn says. "She comes!"

"Who comes?" Devon asks.

Bjorn's eyes are filled with fear. "The witch!"

"Isobel?"

Bjorn nods.

"Then you *are* in league with her!"

"No, good sir. Of course not. I was instructed by the great Clydog ap Gruffydd to meet her here. Surely you know that?"

"Who's Clydog ap Gruffydd?" Devon whispers to Gisele.

"A very important Nightwing, of course," she tells him.

He grunts. "Hey, I didn't go to your exclusive Nightwing academy, remember? My high school back home doesn't offer Sorcery 101."

Bjorn is fretting. "Oh, why have you come? If she sees you, all is lost."

Devon turns to Gisele. "Can you make yourself invisible?"

"Of course I can. It's one of the first things Wiglaf ever taught me."

"Then do it."

Both of them promptly fade from sight.

Just in time, too: Bjorn turns from them in terror, watching as the bat flies into view from the tunnel.

Devon watches as well, his eyes riveted. The bat slowly transforms into a woman. Isobel the Apostate, wrapped in a swirling cape of green and gold.

At long last, Devon looks upon her face. Her dark hair, her dark eyes, her extraordinary beauty.

And he sees what he has known perhaps all along but has never been able to admit.

Isobel is Morgana.

ELEVEN

THE WITCH'S CASTLE

THERE IS A presence here, gnome," Isobel says, her black eyes flashing. "Perhaps more than one!"

"No, no, milady, it is only me."

She sniffs the air. Devon and Gisele freeze, desperately trying not to make a sound.

"Don't lie to me, you little cretin. I am a Nightwing. I can sense—"

"Milady," Bjorn interrupts. "I have brought you vital information."

The sorceress glares down at him. "What sort of information?"

"About the Witenagemot. There is a plot against you, to seize you."

"Just as I suspected. My foolish weak-kneed Nightwing brethren. Using their mighty powers only in the pursuit of good. Where has that ever gotten them?"

"They will strike at midnight when you enter the convocation. You will be surrounded by three hundred Nightwing. There will be no escape!"

She throws her head back and laughs. It is the same horrible, mocking sound that Devon remembers so well. He feels Gisele shudder beside him.

"May I go, then, milady?" Bjorn asks. "I have told you all I know."

"No!" she snarls, grabbing the terrified gnome by the collar of his shirt. "You have served your purpose for me. But I have hungry demons back at my castle. They'd like nothing better than roasted gnome for their dinner!"

"No, milady, no!"

Her hold on the gnome tightens. She transforms herself once more into an enormous bat, its black claws gripping Bjorn's flesh and lifting him, carrying him kicking and screaming down the tunnel. All the while her hideous laughter continues to fill the space, so loud and so evil that it threatens to suck the air right out of Devon's lungs.

I S IT safe now?"

"Yes," Devon says, and they both rematerialize.

"So he *was* in league with the witch," Gisele says, "if he told her the Nightwing plan to defeat her."

"Then why didn't he reveal *us*? He *protected* us. Why would he do that if he were truly helping her?"

They hurry back down the tunnel, anxious to get back to Kelvedon House. There, they relate what they have seen to Gisele's parents and Wiglaf. Arnulf is angry; he slams his fist on the wooden table, upsetting a goblet of wine.

"You took great risk following the gnome," Arnulf says. His wrath is the same that Devon has seen in Rolfe's eyes. He cannot shake the feeling that it is Rolfe standing there, scolding them. "Had Bjorn not distracted the witch, she would have discovered you, and then all our plans would have been destroyed."

"But Bjorn *revealed* those plans to her, Father," Gisele tells him. "He told her that the Nightwing would take her at midnight at the Witenagemot."

"That's what he was *ordered* to tell her, by none other than Clydog ap Gruffydd!"

Wiglaf leans in toward Devon. "Clydog is a great Welsh sorcerer, one of the most respected Nightwing in all of Europe."

Sybilla of Ghent has come forward to stroke her daughter's titian hair. "Why did you suspect Bjorn Forkbeard? You know the gnomes have always been devoted servants of the Nightwing."

"Devon said he'd seen him, stirring a witch's cauldron, calling on spirits—"

"But of course," Wiglaf chimes in. "That is what gnomes do. They have no powers of their own, save their tremendous strength. But they *are* masters of potions, brews, and spells of nature."

"Wait a minute," Devon says. "Just so I understand. This Clydog guy was using Bjorn to pass fake information to Isobel?"

"You comprehend our meaning at last, Devon March," Arnulf says, turning away in frustration to stand over the fire, warming his hands.

"So when I saw him in the future, he really *was* trying to ward off Isobel." Devon sighs, cursing his own impetuousness. "And I dumped his cauldron into the sea."

"If I may be so bold as to explain the Nightwing plan," Wiglaf says, "the intention is to seize Isobel in advance of Witenagemot, not at the convocation as she was told. That way, she can be taken unawares."

"Is there a plan to storm her castle or something?" Devon asks.

Arnulf laughs as he gazes down into the fire, but he says nothing.

"No, my boy," Wiglaf says. "Nothing so obvious as that."

Sybilla smiles at Devon. "Do you understand her powers fully?"

"I know she's a Nightwing. She has powers like any

of us. So it makes sense that a bunch of us together could overpower her."

"Not just any 'bunch of us,' as you put it," Sybilla tells him. "You see, Isobel has learned certain skills from her liaisons with the demons. She has acquired a very specific power that she can use over certain Nightwing." She pauses, looking back at her husband. "The *male* Nightwing."

Arnulf just grunts.

"You've seen her," Wiglaf says to Devon. "She is very beautiful, is she not?"

"She's a succubus," Devon says. "Isn't she?"

Sybilla nods. "That she is. A Nightwing succubus. Any of our men who would attempt to capture her would be vulnerable to her lethal charms. She has seduced many men of the villages away from their wives. Simply being Nightwing does not make our men any more immune."

"We are men first," Arnulf grumbles, still looking into the fire. "Human in every way but our powers. All *too* human."

Devon can fully relate to that. "But she *will* be defeated," he insists. "Look, I don't just come from another place. I come from another *time*. The *future*. And the history of the Nightwing reveals that Isobel will be burned at the stake—and that it will be the female Nightwing who will overpower her."

"You come from the *future*?" Gisele asks. "So that is where this *girl-friend* lives."

Her father seems to take some heart from Devon's announcement. "Then we will be successful," Arnulf says, brightening. "We needn't fear, then, what we must do."

"The boy did not come here to instill complacency," Wiglaf warns. "He came to engender confidence. You can still fail, Arnulf, and then the whole course of history will be altered. You must each play your part as destiny has written it."

THEY DECIDE to rest for what is to come. Devon is given a bale of straw to spill out in front of the fireplace. He settles down, inhaling the pungency of the straw, trying to find a comfortable position. Wiglaf is already snoring in his chair; Gisele and her parents have disappeared into another part of the house.

What if I'm trapped here? Devon thinks again. *What if this is my destiny? To bring confidence to those who would defeat Isobel in this time?*

He supposes it's not such a bad fate. Sure, he'd have to make do without television, cars, computers, movies, ice cream, and pizza—but he'd have knights and castles and sorcerers' conventions and free-flowing ale to take their place. Sure, he'd have to get used to raw sewage in the street and a lack of indoor plumbing, but he'd get to grow up with a clan of Nightwing, maybe even attend the Nightwing school where Wiglaf teaches. It had to be better than dealing with sweaty old Mr. Weatherby.

And, in truth, he already felt comfortable with these people, with their remarkable resemblances to Cecily, Rolfe, and Mrs. Crandall. Hey, there's even Bjorn—if he can be rescued from Isobel, that is. And Devon knows he will be, because he's going to be alive and well five hundred years from now.

But if Devon stays here, who will vanquish Isobel in the twenty-first century? Who will save Ravenscliff from her assault? Will the vision his father showed him come true? Even if he isn't there to physically open the Hellhole, he'll bear culpability for it if he isn't around to prevent Isobel from doing so. Will Cecily and the rest of his friends lie dead in a pool of blood? Will Alexander live out his days scuttling around as a skunk? And what about Rolfe? Will Roxanne be able to save him from Isobel's spell, or will he become her slave forever as the Apostate rules first over Ravenscliff and then the world?

"Restless, Devon March?"

He looks up. Gisele stands over him in her nightdress, holding a candle aloft.

"Well, it's sure not like my bed at Ravenscliff."

She sits down beside him. "Tell me about it. About the future, I mean."

He sighs. "Well, there's a lot of reasons to recommend it. You can get around a lot faster. We have cars and airplanes—"

"Airplanes?"

"Yeah. Like boats, only they fly through the sky."

"Is this Nightwing sorcery?"

"No, just regular old mortal technology."

"Technology?"

"Know-how."

She nods, seeming to grasp his meaning. "And what about women in the future?"

"Oh, you'd *really* like that. There's like total equality. Or nearly anyway. Women can do whatever they want, be whoever they want to be."

Gisele smiles. "Well, that *is* good. I pity ordinary women today. They are subjects of their fathers and husbands in all things. Nightwing women are different, of course, but in our daily activities with normal folk we must pretend to be obedient, lesser creatures." She makes a face. "It offends me to do so."

"I can understand."

She looks at him with affectionate eyes, the glow of her candle lighting her face. Devon looks at her and sees Cecily.

"As wonderful as the future is, Devon March," Gisele pleads, "do not leave us to go back there."

He gives her a small, sad smile. "I'm not sure I'll even be able to."

"You'll come to accept that this is your time now. You will be a great sorcerer here. I know this."

She reaches over and kisses him lightly on the cheek before heading back to her room. Devon stretches out again on the straw. He can barely sleep all night. The witch is in his dreams still, with all her cunning, all her powers of seduction. "I will resist you," he says, but she just laughs at him. Cold fear overwhelms him. More than the witch, he dreads his own fear. *That's what will defeat you,* the Voice tells him, even in his dreams.

I N THE MORNING, the plan goes into action. Devon follows Arnulf and Sybilla through the streets, avoiding the eyes of townsfolk who might remember him from the day before. "Where is the secret meeting to be held?" Devon asks Wiglaf.

"Now, if I knew, would it be secret?"

"Well, Arnulf must know."

"We stop here," Arnulf says suddenly.

They are standing in a field of goldenrod at the end of the village. It is a sea of glimmering yellow stretching to the horizon. It reminds Devon again of how unlinear time has become. When he left the twenty-first century, it was frigid winter. Here it is late summer, muggy and hot.

He can't understand, however, why they've simply stopped in the middle of a field. "The gathering is to be held outside?" Devon asks. "How smart is that?"

"This is where we were told to meet," Arnulf explains.

Devon notices other people wandering into the field now. He presumes them to be other Nightwing. But as he watches, one by one they seem to become obliterated by the sunlight reflecting off the fierce glow of the goldenrod. Then he realizes he himself is glowing, and so are his companions.

"What's happening?"

There is no chance for anyone to answer him, for in the next moment Devon sees they are no longer standing in a field but instead are assembled inside a stone structure. They stand upon a marble floor and look up at a great mosaic of red and blue stars that form a majestic dome over their heads. The place is filled with Nightwing—hundreds of them. Devon knows they are Nightwing because the hair on his arms stands up, just as it did when he approached those books in the basement of Ravenscliff. He is suddenly flushed and breathless, surrounded at last by others like him.

"Is this where Witenagemot will be held?" he asks.

"Yes, boy," Wiglaf tells him, "though the official gathering does not begin until midnight tonight. We come together now for one purpose only: the defeat of the witch."

"I call this assembly to order," a giant old man is saying in a deep, booming voice, banging a gavel at a lectern in the front of the hall.

"That's Clydog ap Gruffydd, the most powerful sorcerer in Britain," Wiglaf tells Devon.

Clydog looks fierce enough: long white hair, deep-set black eyes, a hooked nose, and monstrous hands that grip the lectern as if to break it in two. He stands nearly seven feet tall, with a shoulder span of some four feet. "Sure glad he's a good guy," Devon says.

"Aye," Wiglaf says. "Very good. But very formidable."

The Nightwing file into pews. Men, women, children, all speaking their own languages: English, French, Dutch, German, Finnish, Swedish, Russian, Polish, Greek, Italian, Spanish, Turkish, Chinese. The colors of their skin reflect the far-flung diaspora of the Nightwing, from pale white to deep, shining ebony. Devon slides into a pew beside Gisele, his neck twisting around to soak up as much of the sights as he can.

"We are honored to have with us today an emissary from His Majesty King Henry," Clydog ap Gruffydd is telling them. "The Duke of Suffolk."

"That's the king's brother-in-law," Devon whispers to Gisele, pleased that he's remembered something else from Mr. Weatherby's class.

The duke is a large man, though standing beside Clydog he seems puny. He wears a fur hat not unlike Devon's own, but his doublet is studded with rubies and emeralds. "Long have we heard the whispers of the great Nightwing in our midst," the duke addresses the crowd, "but not until now did I truly believe."

He seems awed by the assemblage in front of him. Devon can understand: After all, he'd just witnessed hundreds of people simply materialize in the hall.

The duke gathers his wits. "His Majesty turns to you for help in ridding this kingdom of a scourge—a woman who would usurp his throne, and use the power of England for the glory of the devil!"

The Nightwing murmur their assent.

"But how can we do this, when a very look from her reduces a man—even one of you—into a puddle of fear and lust?"

There is a ripple of laughter through the crowd. Devon is startled when Sybilla stands. "My lord, nearly half of this assembly is immune to the witch's sorcery. The strategy to defeat her should be obvious."

"But you are mere women," the duke says.

Again, laughter. "As is she, the scourge that you and

your king fear so greatly," Sybilla says, and sits back down.

Clydog ap Gruffydd has moved back to the lectern. "Sybilla of Ghent is right. We must rely on our Nightwing sisters to overcome the witch."

Now it's Wiglaf's turn to stand. "Great Clydog, if I may be permitted a word?"

"Of course, Wiglaf. You are the greatest of our Guardians. What have you to add?"

Wiglaf nudges Devon to stand. "If I may, noble Nightwing, introduce a young visitor to our time—"

"Wiglaf, what are you *doing*?" Devon blushes fiercely, whispering through gritted teeth. "Why are you—"

"His name is Devon March," Wiglaf continues, ignoring him, "and he comes with the blessing of Horatio Muir."

Devon feels as if he'll melt right there in the pew. The faces of three hundred Nightwing have turned to look at him. *Him!* Only a few months out of Coles Junction, New York. As if he had any of their knowledge, their experience, their understanding of Nightwing history and tradition—

You plunged into a Hellhole and emerged alive, the Voice reminds him.

"Ah," Clydog is saying, "Horatio Muir. Our time-traveling descendant from the future. Tell us what news you bring, Devon March."

Devon stands, hoping no one—especially Gisele—will notice his knees shaking. "Well, um—" Devon stammers, looking over at Wiglaf.

"Tell the assembly about seeing the witch," his Guardian explains.

"Well, yeah, I did see her. Isobel. The witch." He looks down at Gisele. "We—Gisele and I—followed the gnome, Bjorn Forkbeard—"

"You did what?" Clydog booms. His face is contorted suddenly in dark anger. A murmur of outrage jogs through the crowd. "He was sent on a mission! How dare you jeopardize—?"

"Hey, don't get all worked up, okay?" Devon takes a breath. "She didn't see us." He looks down at Wiglaf. "Did you do that deliberately to get me in trouble?" he says under his breath.

"There are consequences for every foolhardy action," Wiglaf whispers, a mischievous little wiggle to his ears.

"Be that as it may, Devon March," Clydog intones from his lectern, "you put our mission at risk. As did you, Gisele of Zeeland."

Devon feels bad that Gisele's been dragged into it. "It was totally my idea," he tells Clydog. "Please don't blame her."

He glances down at her. She gives him a small smile.

"But the other thing is," Devon adds, looking around at the group, feeling suddenly more confident, more a part of them, "I know from studying Nightwing history in the future that you will win against her. Isobel will be burned at the stake. I know that from reading history—"

"Then history must be changed!"

The entire congregation is stunned by the sudden voice—a shrill, high-pitched utterance that seems to emanate from every corner of the room. Within seconds, Devon feels claws gripping his shoulders—invisible claws—and he is lifted from his place into the air. The crowd gasps.

The claws holding Devon by his shoulders materialize. Above him grins one of those hideous flying monkeys, its reptilian wings flapping furiously in the air.

But far more terrifying is the image that suddenly appears at the front of the hall, hovering over Clydog. Its laughter tells Devon who it is even before he sees her face.

Isobel the Apostate.

And she is descending on Clydog, who simply falls to his knees.

"Shall I reduce him to nothing, right here before

you all?" Isobel shrills. "Turn him into a quivering, drooling creature—your great leader, the mighty Clydog?"

"Please," Clydog begs, covering his face.

"Tell them how much you desire me, Clydog. How you dream of me, night after night—"

The great warrior cowers before her.

"Your little gnome messenger was so easy to bend to my will," Isobel tells the crowd. "I learned all of your schemes from him. I knew last night not to trust him when I sensed the presence of these two children. Think not that you can defeat me!"

Devon struggles to break free of the demon's grip, but he finds he cannot—not while he hears Isobel's voice. Or rather, *Morgana's* voice—

I think I've fallen in love with you, Devon.

Try as he might, he can't deny the feeling he has for her, even now, even as she threatens to destroy them all . . .

But maybe he won't have to. Several of the female Nightwing have leaped from their seats in an attempt to take her, including Gisele. Devon watches Isobel's flashing black eyes. She has something up her sleeve— literally. Just as the Nightwing approach her, Isobel hurls something out into the air—something shiny— something gold—

It is a golden chain, and it magically wraps itself

around Gisele, the smallest of the army that surges forward.

"Gaze upon her!" Isobel commands, as Gisele struggles in the air, bound by the chain. "She is under my power now. Your gnome proved very useful, revealing many secrets. Including the special gold mines in the Arctic whose enchantment is so great they can even contain Nightwing!" She laughs hysterically.

The women stop in midair, concerned about what might happen to Gisele if they continue.

"Such will be the fate of all who oppose me," Isobel says, her shrieking voice echoing throughout the room. "And now, my Nightwing brothers and sisters, I bid you a fond farewell. I'm sorry that I shall not be able to join you at Witenagemot. May you enjoy your last gathering—for when I have achieved my victory, you will all be banished into my Hellholes!"

"Seize her!" Clydog shouts from the floor.

"Oh, and I must not forget," Isobel says, laughing once more, "a couple of young hostages for safe-keeping."

Her eyes lock onto Devon's. The beast gripping him by the shoulders begins to flap its wings. It flies over the crowd and heads straight for an enormous stained-glass window. Saint George slaying the dragon, just like the one at Ravenscliff, Devon realizes as he protects his face with his hands. The last sound he hears is the smashing of glass. Then all is dark and quiet.

HE AWAKES in a dungeon.

It looks like every dungeon he has ever seen in movies or books. On the far wall, two men hang from chains on their wrists. Rats crawl over filthy, stinking, moldy straw. The only light comes from slivers of windows far up the stone walls.

Devon groans. His shoulder kills—the monkey demon had ripped open the same spot where he'd been wounded before. *Or will be wounded,* Devon thinks. *Whatever.*

"Here, my young Nightwing," comes a voice near him in the dark. "Let me assist you."

It is Bjorn Forkbeard.

"Here, in the pocket of my breeches, I have a powder," the gnome tells him, extracting a vial. "It will aid in your healing."

"Thanks," Devon says, remembering how the powder worked the last time. He pulls down his bloodied doublet to reveal his shoulder. Bjorn shakes the powder onto the wound; instantly the pain is relieved.

"It is all my fault," Bjorn says, tears dropping down his cheeks. "She forced it out of me—the place where the Nightwing were meeting—and she made me forge that golden chain."

"I want to trust you," Devon says. "I want to believe you didn't squeal of your own choice."

"On King Henry's name, I vow I did not! She has ways—she gets into a man's heart, his thoughts, his very soul!"

Devon sighs. That much he knows to be true. Who could resist Isobel when she turns on the charm? Even Devon himself hasn't been able to do it.

"But there *is* something I can do," Devon says, standing. "I can free these men."

With a wave of his hand the men chained to the wall suddenly find themselves free, sliding down the stones to stand on the floor of the dungeon, weak in their knees but standing nonetheless.

"You are a great sorcerer," one of them says in awe, looking at Devon. "You must defeat the witch!"

"Yes," the other man adds. "The witch imprisoned us after taking our homes and all of our land. She must be stopped!"

"Yeah, I'm with you on that," Devon says. "But just how to go about doing that I'm not sure."

He tries willing open the door to the dungeon but it doesn't budge. He feels Isobel's power behind it: It's as if as he tries to push it open, she's on the other side, holding it shut. Nightwing power, head-to-head, and Isobel is stronger.

"I've got to help Gisele," Devon says. "What was that golden chain you made, Bjorn?"

"It is forged out of gold from the Nightwing's own mines in the north of Finland. It has the power to contain a sorcerer, to prevent him from using his power."

"Or hers," Devon grumbles. "Gisele is powerless against Isobel, then."

"I am afraid so."

The men Devon has freed are stretching their legs and exercising their stiff arms. "When the guard comes," one man whispers, "we will retreat to the shadows and overpower him."

"And then what?" Devon asks. "I'll run smack up against Isobel and who knows what will happen then. I need a better plan. Let me think."

He tries to reassure himself that he knows how this all will end—Isobel burning at the stake, her hands bound by the same golden chain that now keeps Gisele a prisoner. But can history be changed? Has Devon's very presence in this time altered history enough so that Isobel might win? If so, what consequences would that have on his own time? Might Cecily and his friends truly die at the Apostate's hands?

Or—the thought nearly knocks Devon over— might they never even be *born*?

He realizes that it's not just his current dilemma over which he must triumph. It's also something far greater: In his hands he holds Cecily's very *existence*—and maybe even his own! If Isobel is able to win here in the sixteenth century, then the very course of Nightwing history will be changed. Horatio Muir may never even come to be born. So Cecily—and Mrs. Crandall and Edward and Alexander—will never exist!

And Devon's parents, whoever they are, may too fade from the pages of history.

What happens then? Devon shudders. *I'll just disappear,* he thinks in terror. *I'll cease to exist. Maybe that was Isobel's plan all along. Send me back in time and thus change the course of history, allowing her to win in 1522!*

"The guard comes," one of the men says. "I hear his footfall. Be ready!"

Devon has no choice but to act. The guard is a misshapen creature, with a hunchback and one empty eye socket. He unlocks the door to the dungeon and lumbers in awkwardly, carrying a bowl of foul-smelling liquid and a goblet of dirty water. The two prisoners easily overpower him, allowing Devon and Bjorn to escape.

"Defeat her!" one of the men cries after them. "Save us from the witch!"

Devon doesn't respond. He is growing more frightened by the moment, convinced he is merely playing the patsy in Isobel's grand plan. He wishes he could talk to Rolfe—or Wiglaf.

Your fear is your downfall, the Voice reminds him. *You must believe you can win.*

"Believe I can win," Devon mumbles to himself as he hurries up the damp cold steps into the witch's castle.

"Of course you will win, good sir," Bjorn says beside him. "I believe in you."

Devon looks down at the little man. Is he friend or foe? He wishes the Voice would tell him for sure . . .

Trust your gut, the Voice says. *You need no assurance other than that.*

They've emerged into the great hall of the castle. Devon gasps at what he sees ahead of them. At the far end of the hall an empty throne is set up upon a pedestal. A throne fit for a king—or queen. Banners with the royal arms hang over the throne, and beside it are hunched two demons, sleepy-eyed beasts with faces like apes.

"Stay back," Devon whispers to Bjorn as they crouch in the shadows. Devon surveys the room. It is empty except for the throne at one end and a banquet table in the middle of the room. But then he hears a sound. The clanking of a chain. He looks up.

There, in what looks like a silver birdcage attached to the rafters, is Gisele.

She has spotted them. Their eyes hold without saying a word. Devon feels confident he can free her from the cage, but he'd still be powerless to remove the chain from her wrists. Only a non-Nightwing could do that . . .

He looks down at Bjorn.

It's as if the gnome has read his mind. "Bring her down," Bjorn says, "and I will break the chain. I am strong enough!"

Turn around, the Voice suddenly commands him. *Quickly!*

Devon spins back toward the demons. One sleepy eye has opened wide, and it is trained right on him.

"We've been spotted," Devon whispers. "Now!"

He concentrates. The door to Gisele's cage swings open. With his mind, Devon brings her down safely to the ground. But the demons have now launched themselves across the hall, shrieking out hideous monkey calls that bring more of their filthy kin flapping in as backup.

"Free Gisele!" Devon barks to Bjorn as he fights off the first demon, landing a punch on its jaw and sending it sprawling back across the hall. But another is on him then, and then another—

"Let him go!"

The voice is Isobel's. The foul-smelling beasts have knocked Devon to the floor but roll off him obediently when their mistress commands it. Isobel's shadow suddenly falls over Devon as she approaches, standing over him to stare down with her bewitching black eyes.

"Who are you, my little time traveler?"

Their eyes lock. It is Morgana—how well Devon knows those eyes. His heart leaps.

I think I've fallen in love with you, Devon.

"Who are your parents, boy?" the witch demands.

Devon says nothing. Isobel doesn't know him. She has no idea that they will meet five hundred years from now—or does she?

She is studying him. "I could suck your lifeblood into nothingness," she tells him. "But you intrigue me. I want to know who you are."

Still Devon says nothing. In his peripheral vision he can see Bjorn being restrained by the demons. Gisele remains shackled, unable to help him.

Isobel smiles. "You have great spirit," she tells him. "I could enjoy having you at my court. For only those Nightwing who join me will be spared."

"I'll never join you," Devon tells her. "I've come back in time to stop you!"

She throws her head back and laughs. Devon recoils from the sound. It is the same cruel, manic sound he heard that day in the tower.

"You cannot defy me, boy. You saw what I did to the great Clydog. I will soon have the king's throne—and I will rule all of Europe by year's end! In another year, I'll have the world!"

She laughs again, a hideous cackle pealing throughout the hall. Her merriment offers Devon just enough time to act. With her eyes turned away from him, he finds the strength to pull his legs up and back, landing a powerhouse kick right on her shins. It sends her flying back across the room.

He's quickly on his feet. "My father always told me to never hit a lady, but in your case, he'd make an exception."

The demons are enraged, dive-bombing at Devon, but he's so pumped by his success in taking Isobel by surprise that he confidently swats them away like so many flies. Isobel has regained her feet, her eyes blazing in fury.

"You will pay for that!" she howls. "You will burn!"

"No, I think that dance card is reserved for you," Devon says, leaping through the air toward her.

She parries him with a simple wave of her arm. Without even touching him, she sends him crashing into the far wall. Devon is dazed for a moment, but regains his senses just in time to find Isobel in his face, bearing down at him.

"You don't want to fight me, Devon March," she purrs, her voice dripping with honey. He tries to avoid her eyes but he cannot. They overtake him, fill up his vision. "You'd rather *kiss* me, wouldn't you, my love?"

"No," he groans.

But his strength is ebbing. He smells her—Morgana—lilacs. She touches his hair.

"You will fight me no longer, will you, Devon March?"

He looks into her eyes. She is so beautiful—the most beautiful woman who has ever lived—

She smiles. "I think I've fallen in love with you, Devon."

The room goes black. Devon feels horribly light-headed as everything begins to spin. Then he feels himself falling, falling, falling . . .

She's won, he thinks, his last thought before losing consciousness. *And I no longer exist . . .*

———◆———

WITENAGEMOT

REE THE GNOME.
  It is the Voice.
  You're still here, Devon.
 Free the gnome!

Wherever he is, Devon realizes that his spirit still exists. He still has some link to the world. He wills himself to visualize Bjorn being held down by the demons. He sees the little man kicking and twisting.

Get off him, Devon commands. *You have no power over him!*

In his mind's eye he watches as the demons suddenly fall backward off their prisoner. The gnome springs to his little feet.

And suddenly there is light again. Devon opens his eyes and realizes he is back in the great hall. In the rafters, to be exact—looking down as Bjorn rushes over to Gisele as Isobel approaches her ominously.

"Hey, Izzy," Devon shouts. "Up here!"

Isobel the Apostate looks up in shock.

"You've lost your charm, I'm afraid," he tells her, dropping down to land both feet on her back, sending her crashing into the floor.

It gives Bjorn enough time to rush to Gisele's side and snap off her chain. The demons are now attacking from all sides, and Gisele knocks the first few easily aside. But there are dozens of them—and more keep arriving, their talons scratching at the stone floors, their wings flapping up windstorms.

"There's too many of them!" Gisele shouts.

She's right, Devon realizes. It's the scene at Ravenscliff all over again. Devon does his best to fight the creatures off, but they keep coming, one after another. Bjorn cowers under the banquet table. The demons are not concerned with him; they care only about defeating the two young Nightwing who have so humiliated their mistress.

Isobel is back on her feet. "They can't best you all!" she shrieks to her minions. "They cannot defeat the power of Isobel!"

A green-eyed feathered thing with an enormous beak has landed on Devon, trying to peck out his eyes. He thrusts it off him, but his strength is fading.

Don't give in to your fear, he reminds himself. *Do not be afraid!*

"You can still live, Devon March!" Isobel calls to him. "You can still join me!"

The beast with the feathers is back on him, squawking in his ear. He fights it but falls to his knees.

"Don't surrender, Devon!" he hears Gisele call from somewhere in the mayhem. "You are a great sorcerer!"

"Yes," he tells himself. "I am the one-hundredth generation from Sargon the Great!"

With that, he easily tosses the demon off of him, sending it shrieking through the air, disappearing into its Hellhole.

He is on his feet facing Isobel again.

"One-hundredth generation," she is saying, looking at him in wonder.

"Yeah," he says. "Thought that might impress you."

"Who are you? From what line do you come?"

He smiles. "Your guess is as good as mine on that one. But I know I'm Nightwing. Exactly one hundred down from Sargon."

"You still cannot overcome my power," she seethes.

"Maybe not, but I'm sure going to give it a try."

Just then the floor seems to explode. The trapdoor to Bjorn's tunnel, leading from the village to the witch's castle, has sprung open. And through it fly dozens of Nightwing—female Nightwing!

Suddenly their odds improve greatly. Devon watches as the Nightwing overpower the demons. The beasts are booted, punched, kicked back to hell. Sybilla of Ghent comes to the aid of her daughter, sending a hairy creature thudding into the wall.

Devon is assaulted again by something he can't see. Talons grip him from behind, closing around his throat. He elbows the thing in the ribs, knocking it off him, and watches as another Nightwing lands a punch to the beast's gut, sending it screeching through the air.

But it's not a female Nightwing as Devon expects. It is a young man—and as Devon looks at him, he sees he is the spitting image of Marcus.

Devon smiles.

"Not all of the Nightwing men are so easily ensnared by the witch's charms," the young Nightwing tells Devon.

Isobel is standing below, screaming in fury as she watches her demons defeated. "No! No! No!"

"Actually," Devon tells her, landing in front of her, "I think that's a *yes*."

Gisele is suddenly in front of him, lashing the golden chain around the wrists of the witch.

As soon as Isobel is bound, the last few remaining demons disappear, sucked back down their Hellholes.

"Until we meet again," Devon tells Isobel, as the Nightwing gather around her in victory.

The Apostate says nothing, just fixes on Devon with her great black eyes.

* * *

AND SO Devon watches her burn. She is condemned that very day, and the king's court makes haste to attend her execution. The villagers celebrate, dancing in the streets. There are musicians and jesters and vendors with their little spider monkeys. Standing beside Wiglaf, Devon watches as Isobel the Apostate is led to the pyre. Her eyes remain locked onto his. He sees such hatred there, such desire for revenge. Then the green wood and peat around the stake is lit, and the flames consume her.

Devon was given the great honor of being the sole Nightwing witness to the witch's death. Better to not inflame the superstitions of the populace more by a gathering of sorcerers. Let history record only that the traitor to the king was executed. Let there be no mention of sorcery in the official accounts. Mr. Weatherby's history books will never tell the whole story.

Isobel's eyes defy her captors. Even before Devon sees her rise from the flames, her arms outspread like the wings of an ascending bird, he knows she is not defeated.

She'll be back—five hundred years from now.

Devon coughs, spitting soot from his mouth. He has to sit against the side of a brick building, away from the smoke.

"Are you all right, my young friend?" Wiglaf asks.

"I suppose so." Devon can't get the taste of burning flesh off his tongue. "It's just that watching somebody get burned alive at the stake isn't something you do every day."

"The eyes of a Nightwing must become accustomed to such horrors."

Devon makes a face. "You don't have to tell me that, Wiglaf. I've seen rotting corpses come out of their graves. I've had slimy beasties from hell gnawing on my bones. So believe me, I'm accustomed."

Wiglaf gives him a sympathetic smile. "It is not an easy path, the road of the sorcerer."

Devon covers his face with his hands. "I just want to know why me. All of this craziness—and still I don't know where I come from. Who my parents were. Why it's me, just a kid from Coles Junction, stuck here in the sixteenth century battling witches and demons."

Wiglaf places a hand on his shoulder. "Tonight, at Witenagemot, there will be many wise Nightwing. Perhaps some of them can help you."

"Look, Wiglaf, as much as I'd like to see it, I can't stick around. I need to try to get back to my own time. Now that I've helped defeat Isobel here, maybe I'll be strong enough to defeat her in the future."

"Not yet, my friend. You must first give your report to the council."

"But Cecily may already be dead—" Devon stops.

"Okay, I forgot. She's in no danger because she hasn't been born yet."

"Precisely. So you must attend Witenagemot. You were the only Nightwing to witness the destruction of the Apostate. You must relay the story of how you saw her rise from the flames."

They head back to Kelvedon House to rest. Devon sleeps on the straw and dreams of his father. Even for all of Ted March's advanced years—he was some three hundred years old when he died in the early twenty-first century—he still has yet to be born in this time. Devon awakes feeling more alone than he ever has.

WITENAGEMOT is held at midnight in the great hall of Hampton Court. So grateful is the king for the Nightwing's assistance in ridding him of Isobel that he has allowed them use of Cardinal Wolsey's exquisite palace outside London. It's many miles away from York, of course, requiring several days' journey for normal folk on horseback, but that is no issue for sorcerers such as these. They disappear en masse from the environs of York to reassemble outside the red brick of Hampton Court.

Devon is completely awed. They file into the great hall, a large room with a hammer-beam roof ornately decorated with pendants that Devon recognizes from

Mr. Weatherby's class as influences from the Italian Renaissance. He lifts his eyes along the room's main supports, elaborately carved with foliage patterns and studded with the pomegranate badges of the queen, Catherine of Aragon. Devon smiles, knowing that those badges will be replaced and then replaced again as King Henry keeps changing his wives.

At the far end of the hall a fan-vaulted bay window sheds moonlight upon the dais, where the Nightwing leaders are gathering, talking joyfully among themselves, clapping one another on the back. If the splendor of the room entrances Devon, he is even more awestruck by the sorcerers themselves, dressed in their ceremonial purple robes with sashes of bright yellow. They wear chains of rubies and diamonds; the women have emeralds in their hair. Many sweep into the room wearing capes and feathered hats. Wiglaf and other Guardians have shed their drab brown robes for garments embroidered with stars and moons.

"The tapestries are Flemish," Gisele tells Devon, indicating the rich fabrics hanging from the walls, depicting the story of Abraham. "A gift from my people."

He smiles. The room is abuzz with chatter and good cheer. The wine and ale flow freely, even among the young. Devon smiles, remembering how Andrea at Stormy Harbor was always so vigilant checking customers' IDs when they tried to order a beer. Here youths as young as eight imbibe freely, wiping the froth from their chins with the backs of their hands.

Devon spots the young Nightwing who looks so much like Marcus, who saved him from the demon in Isobel's castle. "Hey, man," Devon calls. "What's up?"

"What is up?" the boy echoes. "The moon, presently."

Devon laughs. "Just a phrase from where I come from. Thought I'd say thanks for helping me out earlier today." He extends his hand. "I'm Devon March."

"I am Thierry of Paris," he says. "From the line of Louis of Chaumois. My father is Artois and my mother Berengaria of Navarre. And you?"

Devon realizes it's standard for Nightwing to introduce themselves by offering a genealogy. It had been the same when he'd met Gisele. She pipes up now, offering her own descent from Wilhelm of Holland. Thierry of Paris shakes her hand warmly, then turns his eyes in anticipation to Devon.

He sighs. "I'm afraid I don't know what line I come from," Devon admits. "All I know is that somehow, from somewhere, I'm Nightwing."

"And a powerful Nightwing at that," Thierry says, "if your battle against the witch is any indication of your powers."

Devon shrugs. "Well, yeah, I guess."

They are distracted by the thunderous bang of a

gavel from the dais. Clydog ap Gruffydd is calling the Witenagemot to order. Long benches magically appear throughout the room, and the sorcerers take their seats.

"Let a joyful noise be spread throughout this land and beyond the seas," Clydog says. "The Apostate has been defeated."

Wiglaf stands, telling the body that Devon has his own report to make. The Nightwing all turn in fascination as Devon stands. Their eyes regard him proudly, with deep respect.

"Look," he says, "I hate to throw water on your parade or anything like that. But she's not gone. Not really."

The crowd mutters.

"Oh, you guys are okay. I don't think she's coming back to this time. I just know I saw her rise from the flames—and that she'll turn up in my own time, some five hundred years from now."

"Then her unrepentant spirit still burns with the desire for revenge," Clydog says.

"So, look," Devon tells the group. "I need help in getting back to my own time so I can try to stop her there. She's trying to do the same thing in the twenty-first century that she did here."

The great Clydog looks at him with some compassion. "We have not learned the secret of time travel, my young friend," he says. "That will be left to our descendant, Horatio Muir, who has graced us often with his presence."

Devon feels desperate. "So he never told you how he does it? How he gets the Staircase Into Time to materialize?"

"No, Devon March. Such would go against the rules of time. It is not knowledge we are destined to have for several centuries."

Devon sighs. "But what good is defeating Isobel here if she's able to come back and start up again in the future?"

"We shall look into that, my friend. Perhaps we will learn how to stop her spirit from ever returning."

"But I've got to go back. We've got to do it *now*!"

There is a small ripple of sympathetic laughter in the hall. "We have five hundred years to study the problem, Devon March," Clydog tells him.

Devon sits back down. *Five hundred years,* but Devon will be long dead by then. Is that it, then? Is this his destiny—to live out his days here, in the sixteenth century? He'll never know how the future unfolds, what happens after he disappears from Ravenscliff in the midst of battling the demons. Will his friends die? Will the house be destroyed? Will Isobel the Apostate gain control of the Ravenscliff Hellhole? And then what?

Maybe Roxanne will snap Rolfe out of Morgana's

spell. Maybe he'll be successful in finding other Nightwing to defeat Isobel. Maybe they'll all be okay, maybe they'll manage to defeat her on their own.

But they'll always wonder where Devon went—and why he abandoned them when they needed him most.

A SENSE OF gloom settles over Devon. He can't concentrate on the proceedings. He doesn't really understand them, either, with all sorts of words and phrases being bandied about that mean nothing to him. Finally Devon slips out to the fountain courtyard. The moon is high and very bright. He sits beside the cascading water and closes his eyes.

"I would think a novice sorcerer would be inside, absorbing as much as he can."

Devon opens his eyes. It's Wiglaf.

"I just can't concentrate," Devon says. "My heart's not in it."

"You have much you need to learn, Devon March."

"Tell me about it."

Wiglaf sits beside him on the cold stone bench. "You must try to forget your friends' peril. It is not part of your reality anymore. It is not happening now."

"But it *will* happen."

Wiglaf sighs. "Yes. It will happen."

An idea suddenly hits Devon. "Horatio Muir knows

how to transcend time. When do you think he'll be back here?"

"I know not. When last I saw him, which was more than two centuries ago, he gave no indication that he would return. Perhaps he will never, at least not in my lifetime."

"But you said I will meet him, and I haven't yet."

Wiglaf nods. "That is so. But consider, Devon March, that Horatio Muir might not return for many years. You may be an old man."

Devon is flabbergasted. "But I can't return to my own time as an old man! That would be just too weird!"

"And by then you might not *want* to, my friend. You might have come to consider *this* as your own time."

Devon sighs. "But maybe I can change history. Maybe Horatio can send me back in time to stop Isobel from ever appearing in our time. I can prevent Edward from ever meeting her and so she'll never be brought to Ravenscliff."

"But then there would be no reason for you to travel back to this time, would there? You see the paradox you create, Devon. You can do nothing but trust in your fate. I offer you one important lesson. *Where you are is always where you are meant to be.*" Wiglaf smiles. "It is one of the first things I teach my students."

Devon looks up at the moon. He doesn't know what to think.

"Do you understand, my young friend?" Wiglaf asks. "You played a part in Isobel's defeat here. If you had never come back, she might have triumphed, and the whole history of the world might be different. You are inextricably a part of this time, Devon. You always have been and always will be."

Devon gives him a little laugh. "Then I got gypped, because the history books make no mention of how I saved the King of England."

"No. His Majesty has decreed that no chronicler will write the story of Isobel the Apostate."

"But, Wiglaf, if I stay here, I'll never find out who I am."

The Guardian considers this. "Do not be so certain of that, my good friend." He grasps an amulet that hangs from a silver chain around his neck. He unclasps it from the chain and hands it to Devon. "Do you know what this is?"

Devon holds the amulet in his hands. Imbedded in its middle is a crystal.

"It's your crystal of knowledge," Devon says. "All Guardians have one."

Wiglaf nods. "See what it tells you, my boy. Hold it tightly."

Devon obeys. Might it reveal some truth to him? Might it explain who he is?

Might it even return him to where he belongs?

"MY BABY."

It is a woman's voice. A voice he thinks he's heard before . . .

Devon keeps his eyes squeezed shut. He concentrates on seeing what the crystal has to show him, but everything is blurred. He makes out only shapes moving against a dimly lit background. The only sound is the woman's voice.

"My baby. Don't take my baby away."

Where am I? The place looks familiar . . .

Suddenly he knows.

It's the tower at Ravenscliff.

"My baby! My baby! My baby!"

The woman's voice rises higher and higher in despair. He sees hands clawing the air. He hears footsteps running down stairs. Lightning flashes. A baby cries.

"My baby! My baby! My baby!"

But now the woman's cries are mixed with laughter—a wicked cackle he knows all too well.

Isobel.

"You think I am gone? You think you have defeated me so easily?"

He smells the fire again. The taste of burning flesh collects at the back of his throat. Devon gags.

"It is not I who will burn this time, Devon March! It is you!"

Suddenly the flames roar around him. He feels the heat and the pain as they begin licking his skin. He screams out.

And tosses Wiglaf's amulet away from him as far as he can.

WHEN HE opens his eyes all he sees is sky. An umbrella of deep violet studded with stars.

Let me be home, he thinks, sitting up. *Let me be home.*

Yet although the face hovering above him is Cecily's, her dress tells him she is in fact Gisele.

"I'm still here," he says, scrunching up his face.

Gisele takes his hand, sitting beside him on the grass. "Is it so horrible, this place?"

He looks at her. "I just want to go home."

Her eyes glisten with tears. "It is this *girl-friend* of yours. She is the reason."

Devon says nothing. Wiglaf has retrieved his amulet and now stands looking down at Devon.

"I was concerned when you left the hall," Gisele says. "And I come out to find you sprawled here on the ground. Please, Devon March. Try no more to return to your own time. It is too dangerous."

"What did the crystal show you?" Wiglaf asks.

Devon sits up on one elbow, running his other hand through his hair. "I'm not sure. It may have been a clue as to who I am. There was a woman, crying over a baby . . . but then there was Isobel, telling me she wasn't gone for good."

Wiglaf shakes his head. "I know not what to make of it."

Devon looks up at him suddenly. "Isobel had a child, didn't she?"

"Yes," Wiglaf says. "A son by Sir Henry Apple, the husband poisoned by the witch."

"But the son? Isobel's child?"

"Good Queen Catherine has agreed to raise him far from the scene of his mother's evil. When the time comes he will be trained at my school. Fear not for him. The children of Apostates are not doomed to repeat their parent's folly."

"Then maybe what I saw was Isobel crying over her son. But I'm certain the woman in the vision was from my own time. She was in the tower at Ravenscliff. What connection is there?"

"What is Ravenscliff?" Gisele asks.

He looks at her. "It's my home."

Even with all the horrors he's had to face since coming there, Ravenscliff has indeed become his home. With his father gone, Ravenscliff and Misery Point and the people who live there—Cecily, Alexander, Rolfe, his friends—have become his only family. He's homesick thinking about them, people who don't even exist yet.

"Stay here with us, Devon," Gisele says. "You are among your own kind here. You can come back with me to my country. You will like it there, Devon. I promise you."

"The assembly adjourns for the moment," Wiglaf announces. "Even Nightwing need time to heed the call of nature." He smiles. "Why don't you walk among them, Devon? Clear your thoughts."

"That's a good idea."

"We reconvene in an hour," the Guardian tells him. "I will look for you inside the hall."

Devon agrees, bidding the two farewell for now. He wanders off through the garden into the small village of houses surrounding Hampton Court. Nightwing are everywhere, their capes snapping in the breeze, their rubies and emeralds flickering in the moonlight.

Stay here, Devon. You are among your own kind.

My own kind.

It's true, Devon realizes. Back home he was isolated and alone, stumbling through life not fully understanding his Nightwing powers or heritage. In his own time, it's a game of chance, hoping Rolfe can find some answers in his father's books or that Mrs. Crandall might be forced into revealing some of what she knows. Here, he can attend a Nightwing school, grow up with other Nightwing, become a great sorcerer . . .

But forget about watching television. Or getting his driver's license. Or playing basketball. Or exploring the Internet.

Or ever seeing Cecily again.

But there's Gisele, Cecily's double—and in this time, Cecily has the same powers as he does. How cool would that be, back at home? There he can only share his powers with his friends in times of crisis. Here he and Gisele are equals.

She looks just like Cecily. And her father looks like Rolfe. He's met Marcus's double and he suspects he'll meet doubles for D.J. and Ana and Alexander, too, and maybe other people in his life. It would be like having all his friends with him.

Except it's not.

"What'll it be, man?"

Devon looks up. Without even being aware of it, he's wandered into a tavern. Many Nightwing are filling their mugs with ale, laughing heartily among themselves. A few spot Devon and nod graciously to him.

"An ale for you, too, young sir?" the man behind the bar asks again.

"Um, sure," Devon says.

"Here you go." The bartender, a portly, bearded man with muttonchop sideburns, slides over a mug to Devon. "You're the young Nightwing that battled the witch, are you not?"

Devon nods, leaning against the bar. "Yeah. I had help, though."

"Well, of course you did, lad. If not for the ladies, we'd all be sliding down those infernal holes with the devils and the hobgoblins."

Devon nods. The ale is bitter. He sets it down, figuring he'd rather keep a clear head. He looks around the room. It could be a bar anytime, anywhere. It could be Stormy Harbor. The men drinking beer, carrying on, getting a little too loud.

"Everything but a jukebox, eh?" the bartender says, leaning in over the counter at him.

"Yeah. Everything but—" Devon spins around. "Hey! How do you know about jukeboxes?"

The bartender taps his head. "I can see things sometimes. I saw what you were thinking. You were thinking about another time."

Devon nods. "Yeah. My own time. Where I want to return."

The bartender chuckles. "Well, I'm not sure why,

young sir. You're a hero here in the sixteenth century. You could have quite the glorious future ahead of you."

Devon laughs. "I don't care about that."

"Really? Why, every sorcerer dreams of being a great and glorious hero, does he not?"

"You're obviously not Nightwing. That's not what it's about. If that's what you're after, you're never going to become very powerful." He sighs. "All power comes from good, and must be used in pursuit of good."

"Your Guardian teaches you well," the bartender says, clearly impressed.

"Yeah. I guess I'm getting the hang of it."

"You will have many friends here, sir. I am certain of it."

Devon nods. "I already do. I suppose it wouldn't be so bad. It could be a lot worse." His voice chokes. "But I can't just keep jumping from place to place. My dad died not so long ago, and well, I finally found a place where I felt at home. Where I finally found friends. Even a family. A family that somewhere, in some corner of another time, is in danger. And I want to help them. Not because I want to be a hero, but because I love them."

The bartender smiles sympathetically. For the first time Devon thinks he's seen him before, but can't quite place his face.

"Then you truly *are* getting the hang of being a

Nightwing, good sir," the bartender tells him. He gestures to Devon's mug of ale. "Too bitter for you?"

"Uh, yeah. But it's okay."

"No, I've got another keg in the antechamber across the room. Would you be a good lad and fetch it for me?"

"Really, you don't need to on my account," Devon tells him.

"It would be a grand favor to me if you'd do it."

"Okay." Devon looks at the wooden door toward which the bartender is pointing. "Through there?"

"Aye, good sir. Many thanks."

Devon crosses the room, shouldering past Nightwing who seem to be growing louder and more tipsy with each ale they consume. They call after him heartily, clapping him on the back. Devon smiles, reaching the door and pulling the iron ring to open it. He peers inside. The room is dark. He looks back at the bartender, who smiles and nods.

"Go on ahead, young sir. Inside."

Where have I seen him? Devon thinks, trying to remember. *His face—I've seen his face . . .*

Devon moves into the room, only to realize it's a set of stairs leading down into a root cellar. The pungent stench of moist earth reaches his nostrils as he starts down the steps. At the foot of the stairs is another door.

This is strange, Devon says. *He said the keg was in an antechamber, not in the cellar.*

He pushes open the door.

At once he is struck by light. Bright, electrical light.

He's not in any cellar.

He realizes—looking around—that he is back at Ravenscliff, in his own time.

And he realizes one thing more: Morgana—Isobel the Apostate—is coming at him!

THIRTEEN

◆━━◆

A REVELATION

S O," SHE SAYS. "We meet again."

She throws back her hood to reveal her face. She was the cloaked figure he'd seen right before he went down the Staircase Into Time. Her bewitching eyes ensnare him anew.

"No," Devon says, turning from them.

As he does so, he realizes he is in the upstairs corridor of Ravenscliff. How much time has passed since he's been gone? Is it too late to save Cecily and the others?

"They are all dead," Isobel says calmly, almost sympathetically. "There is no point in your fighting any longer. If you learned anything from your little visit to the past it's that I don't give up easily. Even burning at the stake couldn't stop me."

He guesses she's lying. He's able to glance into his room, grateful he'd left the door ajar. The digital clock at the side of his bed glows the time: 9:02. The clock had chimed nine o'clock just before he made his time-slip. While nearly two days had elapsed during his time in the past, he's returned just a couple of minutes after he left.

"You still need me to open the Hellhole," he says, keeping his eyes averted. "If my friends are dead, you have nothing to bargain with. You may as well kill me, too, because I'm not opening that portal."

"Perhaps I no longer need you to help me," Isobel says. "Perhaps I have discovered someone else who can. Another Nightwing!"

"I sealed that portal," Devon says. "Only I can open it."

"You silly child. I've had five hundred years to observe history." Her black eyes seem to pulse with fire. A smile drawn with malice stretches across her face. "You told me you weren't sure from which line you sprang. But *I* know, Devon. I've discovered who you are. I watched it all unfold from the world beyond. Do you hear me, Devon March? *I know who you are!*"

Without intending to, his eyes shift back to Isobel's face.

"Yes, Devon. Don't you want to know?"

He gulps. He tries to look away but cannot.

"Don't you want to know from which line you

come? From which line of Nightwing you can claim descent?"

He says nothing as she approaches. Her laughter, low and mocking, starts deep in her throat.

"You come from *my* line, Devon March. *Mine!* In your blood runs my blood! *We are the same, you and I!*"

"No!" he shouts, just as she closes in, arms outstretched.

He disappears from her grasp, leaving her hands clenching only air.

H E REAPPEARS downstairs, just in time to slug a demon in the face that's looming over Cecily, ready to bite off her head.

"Back to your Hellhole!" he commands, and the thing is gone.

He's furious, outraged.

It can't be true! I am not like her!

"Back to your Hellholes! All of you!"

He realizes suddenly that he's growing—bigger, taller. He's a giant, ten feet or more, and his voice reverberates like deep thunder. He lords over the beasts, who suddenly cower in awe. The lights in the house dim as a great wind spirals through the house. The marauding demons shout in pain and surprise, and within seconds all of them are gone.

Devon returns to his normal size. He rushes to Cecily, who's slumped at the foot of the stairs covering her head. "You okay?"

She nods, realizing it's safe to look up. "I think so." She squints at him. "Why are you dressed like that?"

He realizes he's still in sixteenth-century clothes. "Never mind now," he tells her, hurrying into the parlor. The place is a shambles, books strewn all over the floor, the suit of armor smashed. Shards of glass from the window crunch underfoot as Devon makes his way to check on his friends. D.J. and Marcus, scratched and with their clothes torn, are helping Ana to the couch.

"Is she okay?" Devon asks.

"Not sure," D.J. says. "She took a pretty bad hit." He makes a face at Devon. "Dude, what's with those clothes?"

"Never mind that for now," Devon says. "Where are you hurt, Ana?"

"I think I broke my ankle," she says. "Got carried away with my kicks, I guess."

"An ankle can be fixed," Devon says.

"Yes, it can." They look around. Bjorn has come into the room carrying his purple sack. "May I look at it?"

Ana nods. She winces as the little man removes her

shoe and examines her ankle. Bjorn fumbles through his bag and produces a salve. He rubs it over the swollen area, then binds the ankle with a green bandage. "Give it an hour or so," he tells her. "Don't put any pressure on it until then."

"An hour?" Ana asks. "Shouldn't I go down to the clinic and get a cast or something?"

The gnome shrugs, standing. "If you prefer."

"Trust him, Ana," Devon tells her.

Bjorn looks up at him. "If only you thought the same."

"I'm sorry, Bjorn. I really am. I should've trusted you."

The gnome eyes him with interest. "Your clothes suggest you have made the timeslip and returned."

"I've been to the past, if that's what you mean."

Bjorn grins. "I was wondering when it would happen. I never got the chance to thank you, my friend, for rescuing me that day in the witch's castle. It seems you've made a habit of saving me. I am truly grateful."

"And I to you." Devon smiles. "Is that why you came here to Ravenscliff? Because you knew me in the past?"

"No, 'twas but a happy coincidence. I recognized you that first day, knew you were a great Nightwing. But it was clear you had not yet lived our first meeting, that your own time continuum had yet to catch up with mine. After you told me you feared Isobel the

Apostate was coming, I suspected it would be soon that you would make your timeslip. And I hoped that when you returned, you might trust me finally."

"I do." Devon looks around. "Now we have to work together to stop her. She's in the house, and she'll attack again soon."

"You have humiliated her once more by overpowering her demons," Bjorn says. "She will lick her wounds for a bit now, so we have a bit of time to prepare. But not much."

Devon is confused about something. "How did you know I'd return to this time, Bjorn? You had no way of being sure I'd make it back here."

"True enough. I wasn't positive. But I suspected you would. For you became quite the legend in the sixteenth century—the young Nightwing hero who disappeared forever from Witenagemot, never heard nor seen from again."

"Really? Awesome."

"Wiglaf said he felt certain you'd gone back to your own time. I only had to wait five hundred years to find out for sure."

Devon smiles. "It's so weird. For me, it's been only a matter of minutes."

"How did you do it?" Marcus asks.

Devon's friends have gathered around him, looking at his clothes and listening to his story. "I'm not quite sure how I got back here," Devon admits. "There was this guy, at a pub, and he led me to Horatio's Staircase—"

He stops suddenly, glancing up at the portrait that hangs over the mantel. Somehow, even with all the commotion caused by the demons, the portrait of Horatio Muir remains intact. It hangs there still, its eyes glaring into Devon's soul.

"It was him!" Devon shouts. "It was Horatio Muir!"

"Ah," Bjorn says, nodding. "The great Master of Time himself."

"Wait a minute," Cecily says. "You actually went back into the *past*, Devon? How is that possible? When did you have the time? One minute you were over there in the corridor and the next you were on the stairs, wearing those silly clothes, helping me." She eyes the trim of his doublet disapprovingly. "And is that real fur?"

"I spent two days in the past, but only missed minutes here."

"Two days?" Marcus asks. "That's impossible!"

"No, it's not," Devon assures him. "And it gave me plenty of time to learn about Isobel." He glances up toward the stairs. "We have no time to talk. She's *here*. She's still determined to open that Hellhole."

"But you've showed her you're stronger than she is,"

D.J. says. "Look at how, when you got mad enough, you just sent all those nasties right back to their Hellholes."

Devon sighs. "That might not matter now. She says she's found another Nightwing to help her."

He notices Bjorn shudder.

"You know who she means, don't you?" he asks the gnome.

"I—I can't—"

Devon grabs him by the front of his shirt and lifts him a couple inches off the ground. "Yes, you can! We're equal now, Bjorn! Our time continuums or whatever they are have caught up to each other! I suggest you tell me what you know. Finally!"

"I suggest you put him down," comes a voice from the landing at the top of the stairs.

Looking up, they all gasp.

"Grandmama!" Cecily shouts.

Old Mrs. Muir, fully poised and sane, begins descending the stairs.

W HAT A MESS," says Greta Muir, looking around the parlor. With a wave of her hand, she fixes everything: the shattered windows, the broken chandeliers, the scattered books, the smashed suit of armor. In an instant the room looks as if nothing had ever happened.

No one can manage to utter a word.

"Really, Mother," Mrs. Crandall says, following her now into the room with Edward coming up behind. "Such ostentatious displays of power—"

"Oh, hush, Amanda," the old woman tells her impatiently. "You know I can't *think* with such clutter."

"But there are *others* present."

Mrs. Muir eyes D.J. and Ana and Marcus, then turns her gaze upon Devon.

"They are not *others*, Amanda," she says. "They are the comrades of a sorcerer."

Devon is staggered. "How—I mean—you were—"

The old woman smiles. "Before I married my husband, I was an actress. Did you know that? They were small parts, mostly B-pictures, but the reviewers said I had 'spunk.' " She laughs. "It would seem that I still have a gift. I could have won an Oscar for that crazy old lady routine, eh, Edward?"

"Yes, Mother," her son obediently agrees.

"You were *acting*?" Devon is stunned. "You were never—crazy?"

"There were reasons for the deception, Devon," Mrs. Crandall insists.

He looks over at her. "Yeah, there always are. How about if you start *telling* some of them to me?"

"You are an able sorcerer, Devon, but still an impudent youth." Mrs. Muir frowns. "Sit down and you'll receive the facts in due course."

The teenagers all follow her with wide eyes.

"Grandmama," Cecily says, a little whine in her voice, "why did you have to pretend with *me*, too?"

"Sorry, sweetness. But we thought it best." She looks around the room. "If you think what happened here tonight was terrible, it's only because you didn't live through the cataclysm that happened here before you were born. That was the night the Madman took your grandfather—my husband—into the Hellhole. We heard his screams echoing throughout the house for *weeks*."

"That's when the family renounced their sorcery," Devon says. "But you still have your powers, Mrs. Muir."

"Did you think we'd really be so foolish as to give up *all* our sorcery? We knew the Madman might return—and he did, as you know very well, Devon."

"So it *was* you!" Devon says. "It *was* you who saved me on the roof of the tower from Simon!"

"Yes. But it was important that the Madman believe I was a helpless old crone, gone crazy in my upstairs room. He had to believe that I had no sorcery left in my being, so that I could take him by surprise, if need be."

Devon's nodding, finally understanding. "That's

why you would always head up to your mother's room when things happened," he says, turning to Mrs. Crandall. "So she could use her powers."

The mistress of Ravenscliff merely sighs.

"I did my best," Greta Muir says. "But this time—"

"Isobel found out about you," Devon finishes.

The old woman glances out the window at the crashing sea below. "Yes. And she will try to force me to do what you have refused so far to do, Devon. Open the Hellhole."

Devon's on his feet, approaching her. "But you can fight her! She doesn't have the same hold over you that she has over me."

Their eyes meet. "That is true. But I am an old lady. I am still human, Devon, and these bones are old. Isobel, on the other hand, is an undead spirit. It matters not what condition her bones are in."

"We can do it," Devon assures her. "I know we can. Together, we can do it."

She smiles kindly. "I admire your courage, Devon. I always have."

He looks up at her. *She knows who I am,* he thinks. *She knows about my past. She can tell me what I need to know.*

"Isobel said I was of her line. That her blood runs in my veins."

Mrs. Muir nods solemnly. "It runs in ours, too.

Many Nightwing were descended from Isobel's son. But he grew up a proud and noble sorcerer. The evil of the Apostate need not taint the blood of her descendants."

So that much at least Devon can relax about. He figures there's a lot more that Mrs. Muir can tell him, but now is obviously not the time to start bombarding her with questions. They have an undead sorceress to defeat, and who knows when she's going to strike next?

THEY DON'T have to wait long to find out.

"Devon! Devon!" Alexander comes crying, running down the stairs.

"Oh, yes," Greta Muir says. "I forgot to mention. First thing I did was remedy Alexander's rather, er, distasteful condition."

"I couldn't do it when I tried," Devon says.

The old woman smiles. "I have a few years on you, Devon. You'll get the knack."

Alexander nearly flies into Devon's arms, completely bypassing his father. Devon notices Edward Muir look away.

"I was in a cage!" the boy cries. "Cecily put me in a cage!"

"You were a *skunk*!" Cecily protests. "What was I *supposed* to do?"

Devon smiles. "It was for your own good, buddy. Everything's okay now."

"No, it's not," Alexander says. "I just saw her. Morgana! Protect me, Devon! She's going to change me back into a skunk!"

"Where did you see her?" Devon asks.

"Upstairs. In the corridor. She walked right past me, like she didn't even see me." The boy's eyes are round and terrified. "She was heading into the East Wing."

"Time to get it on," D.J. mumbles under his breath.

Devon turns to Mrs. Muir. "I suppose we need to head to the East Wing ourselves."

"Yes," the old woman says. "But you stay well behind me, Devon. Don't look into her eyes."

"Mother, no," Mrs. Crandall says, suddenly rushing forward and gripping her arm. "You mustn't. Let's all just go away. Leave Ravenscliff."

"That's exactly what I've been advocating all these years," Edward grouses.

"Mother, please!" Mrs. Crandall is near tears, desperate. "I couldn't bear it if—" Her words break off. She's overcome.

Devon has never seen her like this. Her usual steely composure shattered, Mrs. Crandall looks like a little girl, holding on to her mother after a bad dream.

And why shouldn't she look like a child? She lost

her father to the demons of the Hellhole. Now she risks losing her mother as well. Despite her stubbornness, despite all her opposition, Devon can't help but feel a sting of compassion for Mrs. Crandall.

"We have no choice, Amanda, and you know that," Greta Muir says, gently extricating herself from her daughter's grip. "Come, Devon, there's not a moment to spare."

"These kids ought to go home," Edward says, obviously unsettled. "In fact, we all ought to leave the house. Who knows what will happen up there?"

"We didn't leave the last time," D.J. says, "and we're not leaving now."

"My ankle is completely healed," Ana says, standing up. "If you need any help up there, Devon, let me know."

He smiles. Marcus gives him a little salute. Cecily hugs him, then embraces her grandmother.

"Please be careful," she says.

"We can do this," Devon tells them all, projecting confidence.

But inside the fear is mounting, and he knows he can't let it win.

If it does, he loses.

TAKING THE old woman's hand, Devon feels himself dematerialize. It's a feeling he doesn't think he'll ever get used to, a tingling sense of disconnection, of existing only in his mind and not his body. They reappear in the upstairs parlor of the East Wing, surrounded by furniture shrouded in sheets and covered in layers of dust and cobwebs. The only light comes from a few slivers of moonglow seeping through the slats of the shuttered windows.

Greta Muir looks around at the place sadly. "I remember poor, sweet Emily here," she muses. "It was my first day at Ravenscliff. How lovely she was. How grand this room." She shakes her head. "How different things were then, before the Madman changed all our lives forever."

Devon feels the heat pulsing from the inner chamber.

"Um, with all due respect, this is no time for nostalgia," he says.

The old woman nods. "She's inside. She is at the Hellhole."

"Do we have a plan?" Devon asks.

"Yes," the old woman says simply. "We plan on defeating her."

She takes a few steps toward the door. All at once a figure moves out from the shadows, blocking their way.

"Who is there?" Mrs. Muir cries.

The figure makes no answer. It is tall, Devon observes. A man.

"Who is there?" Greta Muir calls out again.

The man passes through a slender ray of moonlight. Devon makes out his face.

"Rolfe!"

"I will not let you enter," Rolfe says, and before either of them is aware of it, he has thrown a chain around the hands of Mrs. Muir.

A golden chain.

"You foolish man!" the old woman cries. "I always thought you were stronger than that! My husband loved you like a son!"

She tries breaking free of the chain but cannot, and Devon knows why. "You can't break it," he tells her. "It's been forged from the mines of the gnomes!"

Still the old woman struggles to free herself. Rolfe has moved over to the door to the inner room and opens it. A pale green light falls out from within. Rolfe crooks his finger at Devon.

"She waits," Rolfe tells the boy. "It is your destiny, Devon. Even your father's vision predicted that you would open the Hellhole."

"Break free of her, Rolfe!" Devon shouts. "You can do it. You're strong! You've taught me to be strong! Think of your father, Rolfe. He was a great Guardian! He would never help an Apostate."

Rolfe says nothing. He steps aside so that Devon

can peer into the room filled with the strange green light. There is a figure standing in the doorway.

It is Isobel.

"Come, Devon," she says, her voice warm and entreating. "Come discover your destiny to rule beside me, with the greatest power any sorcerer has ever known."

She reaches out her hand to him. He is transfixed looking at her. He cannot think—cannot remember any of her evil, any of her treachery, any of her dark plans.

All he remembers is that she said she loved him.

"Come, Devon," Isobel calls.

He can see the Hellhole now, the source of the green light. It pulses ferociously, the creatures behind the locked door frantic with the anticipation of freedom.

"Come to me," Isobel says, and extends her hand.

"Yes," Devon murmurs, and reaches out to her.

All at once there is a flurry of motion, a rush of wind. Devon staggers backward, falling to the ground, as a force pushes past him, assaulting Isobel. It knocks her to the ground. The Apostate begins to scream.

"What? What happened?" Devon shouts.

He is being helped to his feet by Rolfe. He sees the golden chain on the floor.

He realizes that the force that has overtaken Isobel is Greta Muir.

But not Greta Muir the old woman. Instead she is

like a bird—a raven—a giant bird with enormous, powerful claws.

And Isobel—she is a rat, a hissing, snarling rat, with sharp pointed teeth and a long, greasy tail that whips back and forth in terror and rage.

The raven's beak slams down into the eye of the rat. A howl of pain shrieks from the creature's mouth, and the entire house begins to shudder with the force of an earthquake. Devon staggers, holding on to the wall to keep from falling, all the while watching the Hellhole which pulses with green light, the demons screaming and throwing themselves against the portal.

The battling creatures have resumed their human forms. Isobel, regaining her strength, rises to stand over the fallen Greta, a broken old woman who can do nothing more than lift her right hand.

Suddenly a white light overwhelms them all. Devon and Rolfe both recoil from its glare. The demons cease their noise behind the door. Through the blinding light Devon manages to glimpse Greta Muir rise up— not the old woman he's come to know, but a young, vibrant, powerful sorceress, the way she must have been many years ago, before her husband had been killed. Her hair is as red as Cecily's, her eyes blazing with fire.

"Your power here is ended," Greta shouts as she pins Isobel down on the ground. "The power of good will always triumph over the darkness!"

"No!" Isobel shrieks, trying to break free. "It mustn't end this way! It mustn't!"

With one last blast of power, she throws Mrs. Muir off of her. Greta sails across the room and crashes into a sheet-covered table. Isobel tries to stand but discovers she cannot. Her opponent has indeed bested her. She collapses back to the floor.

"No!" Isobel the Apostate screams.

The Hellhole pulses in one last burst of light, then fades into darkness. The heat dissipates. The green glow is gone.

Isobel twists and convulses, then disappears in a funnel of gray smoke. All that is left in her place is a pile of ashes—the stinking, smoldering remains of a witch burned at the stake.

Rolfe rushes to Greta Muir's side. "Are you hurt badly?" he asks.

She is old once more and badly bruised, but she manages a smile. "My husband would be proud of you, Rolfe."

He turns to Devon. "Help me with her. We've got to carry her downstairs."

"IT WAS the element of surprise that was necessary," Rolfe explains as they gather in the parlor. Mrs. Muir has been put into bed in her room, and Bjorn is with her now. The family doctor has been called as well.

"So you were just *pretending* to go along with her?" Devon asks.

Rolfe nods. "I knew the moment would come when I'd be able to turn the tables on her, so long as she never suspected."

"But, dude, how'd you break free of her power?" D.J. asks. "I *tried*, believe me, but I just couldn't do it."

"I admit I had help." Rolfe looks at Devon. "I don't think Isobel expected to run into someone like Roxanne when she came to Misery Point."

"What kind of powers does Roxanne *have* exactly, Rolfe?" Devon asks. "Is she a sorceress, too?"

"Let's leave that story for another time," Rolfe says, just as Mrs. Crandall and Edward walk into the room.

"Bjorn can't do anything for her," Mrs. Crandall says emotionlessly. "None of his potions or powders have helped."

Edward Muir scoffs. "I never believed in his hocus-pocus anyway."

"Well, it worked for me," Ana says, standing up on her ankle. "See?"

"A real doctor is on his way," Edward says, ignoring her. "And I think it's time all you children ran along home. It's late. I'm sure your parents must be wondering where you are."

"But *first*, Devon," Mrs. Crandall says, "I want you to take away their memories of everything that has happened here. It wouldn't do to have them telling tales of sorcery and witches in the village."

"Take away my memories?" Marcus says, outraged. "I think not."

The others echo his sentiments.

"I'm sorry," Mrs. Crandall insists. "It is for your own good, as well as ours."

"I won't do it," Devon tells her, crossing his arms over his chest.

Mrs. Crandall is adamant. "I am your guardian. You will do what I say."

"No," Rolfe says, walking up behind Devon to drop his arm around his shoulder. He faces Mrs. Crandall. "*I* am Devon's Guardian. Capital *G*. And you know full well that using his powers in such a way would be a terrible misuse of them. I doubt he could even do so if he tried."

"You stay out of this, Montaigne," Edward Muir snaps. "The boy's father sent him to live with Amanda, not you."

"Uncle Edward," Cecily says, getting up in front of him. "Rolfe just helped save us all from Isobel the Apostate. Don't you think you owe him some thanks?"

"*Thanks?*" Edward Muir looks as if he wants to spit. "For what? For nearly killing my mother? If he'd have just let her handle it her own way, she might not be up there right now fighting for her life. He threw that golden chain on her, remember. He admits that."

"He *had* to do it, Edward," Devon says. "It was the only way to trick Isobel, to take her by surprise. I was there. You weren't."

Rolfe has turned away in disgust. "That's all right, Devon. Let them remain consumed by their hatred of me." He glares over at Edward suddenly, then back at Mrs. Crandall. "But you can no longer keep me from Devon. The boy has a right to learn about his Nightwing heritage."

"Get out," Mrs. Crandall says. "All of you. I want to be alone."

"I'm telling you, Amanda. I will train Devon in his powers."

"I will determine what's best for him! Now I said get out!"

Rolfe shakes his head. He tells Devon he'll be in touch tomorrow. Devon has so much he wants to tell him—starting with his adventure in 1522—but he knows they'd best not push Mrs. Crandall much further. He says good night, and Rolfe heads out the door.

"I'll talk with you guys, too, tomorrow," Devon says to his friends, just as the doctor arrives. Edward and Mrs. Crandall accompany him upstairs.

"I hope she'll be okay," Ana says, hugging Cecily. "She seemed pretty cool, your grandmother."

"Yeah. Who knew?"

They pledge to keep everything to themselves. It's a vow they've taken before, and they've kept it. Not even their parents know about the supernatural adventures they've had at Ravenscliff.

"You think this is the last of the weirdos from hell dropping by this house?" D.J. asks Devon as he heads out the door.

Devon doubts it. Not with that portal in the East Wing, and the power that lies beyond it.

I SUGGEST at this point that you just try to keep her comfortable," the doctor announces, giving his verdict outside Greta Muir's room. Devon sees Mrs. Crandall's eyes burn with repressed tears. "I'm sorry, but there's nothing more I can do."

The family sits up with her through the night. Devon changes out of his sixteenth-century breeches and slips into a pair of sweatpants. He sits in the hallway outside Mrs. Muir's room, leaning against the wall.

"She's asking for you, Devon," Cecily says, sometime around one in the morning, coming out of her grandmother's room.

"Me?"

Cecily nods. "I'm not sure Mother is planning on telling you. But Grandmama keeps saying your name, over and over."

"Should I just go in, then?"

"I would if I were you."

"Your mother will be angry."

Cecily smirks. "You just fought an undead Nightwing witch, and you're afraid of my *mother*?"

Devon admits she has a point. He tiptoes into the old woman's room. She sees him approach.

"Devon," she whispers.

Mrs. Crandall is sitting beside her bed. "Mother," she says. "Just try to sleep."

"I must talk to Devon," Greta Muir insists weakly.

"You mustn't—"

"I—must—"

Devon stands over her bed. "What is it, Mrs. Muir? Why have you been asking for me?"

"No, Mother," Mrs. Crandall urges, standing now, trying to block Devon from the old woman's view.

"He has a right," Mrs. Muir rasps, her voice weak. "He should know his past."

"Mother, you are talking nonsense." Mrs. Crandall looks over at him. "Devon, really, she is truly mad now. This is no deception. She is confused, incoherent—"

"Let me—speak—Amanda!"

Devon leans in close to Mrs. Muir. The old woman

is clearly fading. It's not so much any bruises or broken bones, but her very spirit has been sapped by the encounter with the Apostate. She seems spent and broken, a pale shell of the feisty old woman he'd met just hours ago in the parlor.

"Do you know my past, Mrs. Muir?" Devon asks. "Do you know who my parents were?"

"Mother, please, don't—" Mrs. Crandall cries.

The old woman grips Devon's hand tightly with her knobby, spotted fingers. "You—must—know—"

"Know what, Mrs. Muir?"

"That you—you are one of us—"

"Yes, Mrs. Muir, I know I am Nightwing. But who were my real parents? Why did my father send me here to Ravenscliff?"

"You—you—are—"

"Mother!"

The old woman's hand falls away from Devon's. Her eyes remain open, but Devon knows she is dead.

Mrs. Crandall kneels beside her mother and cries. Devon isn't sure if they are tears of grief or tears of gratitude—that the old woman died before she could reveal whatever it was she knew about Devon's past.

FOURTEEN

◆━━◆

THE HELLHOLE

GRETA THORNE MUIR is buried beside her husband out in the old windswept cemetery at the edge of the cliff. It is a simple ceremony, with only the minister and immediate family present: Greta's two children and two grandchildren, and Devon March.

Devon stays behind after the rest have gone back to the house, watching Bjorn shovel the earth back into the grave.

"Good thing we've had this January thaw," the gnome says, the soil making a sickening thud against the treated wood of Mrs. Muir's coffin.

"Oh, come on," Devon says, smiling a little. "As if a little frozen earth could stop you. I saw that tunnel you made leading from the village to Isobel's castle. All with your fingernails, huh?"

"Yes, that is how I did it," Bjorn says, pausing in his

work and leaning on his shovel. He looks at his nails. "My father tunneled all the way from the Arctic Circle to Copenhagen. It was the largest gnome mine ever constructed."

"Is it still there?"

Bjorn shrugs, getting back to shoveling. "Haven't been back in a while."

"So what have you been doing for the last five centuries?"

"Oh, this and that." Bjorn laughs. "Do you want a year-by-year account? We'd be here all week!"

Devon looks up at the sky. It's clear and blue.

"Tell me what happened to all of them, Bjorn," he says softly. "Wiglaf. Arnulf and Sybilla. Gisele."

"I'm not sure about the others, but Wiglaf finally died in the seventeenth century, around the time of the Civil War in England. Of course, he was heartbroken when his school was destroyed. It happened not too long after you left. He never quite got over it."

"The Nightwing school was destroyed? How?"

"Oh, I'm fuzzy on the details. It must be in one of the history books."

Devon nods. *So much to learn still . . .*

"There," Bjorn says, finished with his task, patting the earth with the shovel. "May you rest in peace, great lady."

Devon looks down at the grave. "She took the secret of my past with her."

Bjorn eyes him craftily. "I told you the day we met that you have the power to find out what you need to know."

Devon smirks. "Are you suggesting I try to use the Staircase Into Time again? Because if you are, I'm not sure I'd make it back this time."

"I don't mean just the Staircase, Devon. You are a Sorcerer of the Nightwing. You are the only one left in this house now who has such power. They can't hide the truth from you forever."

Devon narrows his eyes at him. "So tell me who the woman you took from the tower was. I thought it might have been Isobel. But now that idea seems pretty crazy."

"Has it ever occurred to you, Devon, that I might not know the answer to that question? I cannot tell you what I do not know."

"So you're admitting you took someone from the tower and brought her to the basement? You just don't know who she is."

The gnome sighs. "You have powers, Devon. Use them." He flings the shovel over his shoulder. "Come on back to the house. I've got to set out dinner."

Devon laughs. "You're a man of many talents,

Bjorn. Tunnel-maker, magical chain welder, grave-digger, chef . . ."

"You could name them all, but they'd still not be as many talents as you have, my boy." They start off back through the field toward Ravenscliff. "No, sirree. Not as many as you."

WHEN SHE comes to him, it takes him by surprise. He is walking down a long corridor in some medieval castle. Torches burn along the walls, and in their glow he can see blood, glistening in the firelight as it drips to the floor. Devon hears her laughter moments before he rounds a corner and sees her standing there.

Isobel the Apostate.

"Blood of my blood, flesh of my life," she says, her arms outstretched. "I knew you would not abandon me."

Her eyes are black and as beguiling as ever. He falls into her arms and feels her mouth, like a vampire's, upon his throat . . .

"No!"

He sits up in bed. The dream has left him in a cold sweat.

She's gone! So why is she still in my dreams?

Devon swings his feet out of bed and places them

against the cold hardwood floor. His heart is thudding in his chest. Outside his window he can see it is snowing lightly.

I can just have plain old ordinary nightmares, can't I? That's all it was. It's not Isobel. She's gone. Mrs. Muir defeated her. I saw her ashes in the East Wing.

A gust of wind rattles the windows. Devon knows he can't get back to sleep now. He looks over at his clock. 3:15. He lets out a long sigh.

What was Mrs. Muir going to tell him right before she died? Had she really known the truth of his past? Why was Mrs. Crandall so desperate to keep her from talking?

He has a right. He should know his past.

That's when Devon hears it: the sobbing.

He sits in rapt silence. The horrible sound comes from far away, creeping around corners and up through floorboards. It is the same sound as ever, coming from that hidden room in the basement.

Who is it? If not Isobel, if not Mrs. Muir—who is it?

The ghost of someone who once lived here? Emily Muir?

But whoever—*whatever*—is being kept in that basement knows Devon's name.

He can't stand it anymore. He pulls on his robe and heads out into the corridor. At the landing he sees a light in the foyer. He peers over the railing. Edward

Muir is down there in his coat, wrapping a scarf around his neck.

Devon comes halfway down the stairs.

"Ah, Devon," Edward says. "I should've suspected you'd be prowling about."

"Are you going somewhere?"

"Yes. That's exactly my destination. Somewhere. Anywhere but here."

Devon notices there's a suitcase at his feet.

"I have a flight to London out of Boston at six-thirty," Edward Muir tells him. "From there I'll head on to Amsterdam. Then down to Greece, I think, where I can charter a boat to take me out into the Aegean. All I want to do is sleep in the sun and forget this wind, this cold, this—"

"Sobbing?" Devon asks. "You can hear it, can't you?"

"Of course I can hear it. I've heard it all my life."

"Who is it, Edward?"

"You have so many questions, and I suppose I can't blame you for asking them. But I can only give you one answer, Devon." Edward pauses. "As soon as you're old enough, get out of this house. Go as far away as you can."

Devon sighs. "Does Mrs. Crandall know you're leaving?"

Edward chuckles. "I've learned it's never prudent to

clue Amanda in ahead of time about anything. She'll just try to stop you. Remember that, too, Devon." He grins. "Bid my dear sister good-bye for me, will you?"

From outside a car honks.

Edward sighs. "Do you know what I had to promise to pay to get a cabbie up here to Ravenscliff in the middle of the night? Stupid villagers." He smirks, pulling on his gloves. "They think the place is haunted."

"But what about Alexander? You can't just leave without saying good-bye—"

"Really, Devon, it's for the best." Edward lifts his suitcase and heads toward the door. "The boy always makes such a scene when I leave."

Devon watches him go. He thinks of the little boy asleep upstairs, the little boy who will once again be disappointed by an uncaring father. Once again Devon considers how fortunate he was to have grown up with Ted March as his dad, who gave him everything Edward Muir has never given Alexander. Maybe Devon never got the kinds of expensive gifts Alexander receives from all over the world—and in the next few days he's certain the boy will find some outrageous toy in the mailbox from wherever his father lands. But Devon got things like support, constancy, and love from Ted March. Alexander's never going to get that from his father, especially not now, humiliated by

Morgana, browbeaten by his sister, and once again bested by Rolfe Montaigne.

"No," Devon whispers to himself. "Alexander is never going to get what he needs from his father." He pauses. "He's going to have to get it from me."

The sobbing has stopped. Devon no longer has the heart for exploring anyway, so he just heads back to his room, where he lies awake in bed until it's time to get up for school.

AND YOU will see here in these illustrations of Hampton Court the extravagance of the Tudor period," Mr. Weatherby is saying, clicking his remote from the back of the room as a series of slides flash upon a screen. "It was an extravagance intended to give a message of royal authority and security, especially after the king had vanquished the last of the claimants to his throne."

Devon watches with fascination. The paradoxes of time continue to boggle his mind. In this life he's never left the United States, but five hundred years ago he was in England.

As he watches Mr. Weatherby's slide show, he realizes not all of the illustrations of Hampton Court are accurate. In the fountain court, for example, there's an enormous clock, which must have been constructed at some point after Devon left. The village surrounding the court also resembles nothing of what Devon remembers.

But the great hall—the scene of Witenagemot—is rendered perfectly.

"You will note the high vaulted ceiling," Mr. Weatherby is saying. "And the tapestries of French design."

Devon raises his hand.

"Mr. March?"

"Actually, the tapestries are Flemish," Devon says, remembering Gisele.

"Flemish?"

Devon nods. "Yeah. They came from Flanders."

Mr. Weatherby grumbles to himself, looking down at his notes. "Ah, yes, so they did," he says. He gives Devon a face. "Thank you, Mr. March."

Devon tips an invisible hat at him. "Anytime."

SO YOU were really in the year 1522," Marcus says later as they pack into a booth at Gio's. "You've never told us the whole story."

"Yeah," Cecily says. "With Grandmama's funeral and all, you've never told me all about this girl who was a double of me."

"I met doubles of both you and Marcus, as well as Rolfe and your mother," Devon tells her.

"What about *me*?" Ana whines. "Didn't you see a double of me?"

"No, but I'm sure you were there." Devon sits between Ana and Cecily looking across the table at D.J. and Marcus. "You too, Deej. See, I have this theory that we have doubles all throughout time. I'm sure if I'd stuck around longer I would've seen doubles of everybody I know. Maybe even a double of myself."

Gio comes by for their order. "Pepperoni with a scald?" he asks.

"You got it, my man," D.J. says, nodding and licking his lips. "And would you throw some pineapple on that, too?"

"Eeew, I hate pineapple pizza," Cecily says, shuddering. "It has got to be the sickest invention of all time."

"I can think of a few sicker," Marcus says, laughing.

Devon looks over at him. There it is again: the pentagram hovering over Marcus's face. What does it *mean*? One more mystery still unsolved.

"Back to your story, Devon," Cecily is saying. "My double was a Nightwing, right? With powers."

"Oh, yeah. And she was really good, too."

Cecily grits her teeth in determination. "I want my Nightwing heritage restored. My mother had no right to renounce my powers without my consent. Isn't there some kind of ritual I can do to get them back?"

"Oh, like your mother would sit back and allow that," D.J. says.

"It's my birthright!"

"Be careful what you wish for, Cess. It hasn't always been so great, you know, growing up with things climbing out of my closet trying to drag me down to hell."

"As if that hasn't been happening to *me* of late, too." Cecily sulks. "It would just be nice to have my own powers instead of having to rely on you to *lend* me some for a couple hours. I'm not the kind of girl who likes depending on a man for everything."

"I am," Ana says. "I totally am."

Cecily makes a face. Marcus laughs. "Even still," he says to Ana, "you handled yourself pretty well against those demons."

Ana grins. "Yeah. I guess I did."

Devon sighs. "Well, I'm heading over to Rolfe's after this. There's so much stuff I still need to know. I want to check out his books, since Mrs. Crandall still won't let me see the ones in the East Wing."

"Let me come with you," Cecily says.

"If your mother finds out . . ."

"She won't!"

"Okay. It's your head in the guillotine, not mine," Devon says.

So D.J. drops them both by Rolfe's after they finish

their pizza. Devon had arranged earlier with Rolfe to meet him at the house. Roxanne is nowhere to be seen; Devon still wonders just what power she has that enabled her to break Isobel's hold over Rolfe. But right now he's focused on something else.

"What do you want to look up first?" Rolfe asks.

"I want to find out what happened to Gisele of Zeeland."

"Why are you so interested in *her*?" Cecily asks, looking over his shoulder as Devon leafs through the first book Rolfe hands him. "Did something go on between the two of you?"

Devon smiles. "Why? Are you jealous?"

"Well, kind of. Even if she did look exactly like me."

Rolfe laughs. "I wouldn't worry about her too much, Cecily," he says. "Whoever she is, she's been dead for almost five centuries."

It's an observation that still seems so bizarre to Devon. All of those people, dead. Long dead. Except Bjorn, of course. But for Devon they had been alive just days ago.

"Here!" he suddenly exclaims. "Here she is!"

" 'Gisele of Zeeland,' " Cecily reads, taking the book from Devon. " 'Daughter of Arnulf of Flanders and Sybilla of Ghent. One of the great Nightwing of the sixteenth century. While still in her teens, she helped defeat Isobel the Apostate in England. Returning to her native country, Gisele discovered a pustulous break between this world and the next—'" She pauses, looking up at Devon. "What's a pustulous break?"

"It's an emerging Hellhole," Rolfe explains. "I've been doing a good deal of reading-up on all this, if I'm to do a good job as Devon's Guardian. One of the things I've learned is that when a Hellhole first forms, it causes the earth to become contaminated—like pus on a human sore."

"Gross," Cecily says.

Rolfe winks at her. "Well, what do you expect when you've got demons eating through the earth's crust?"

"*Any*way," Cecily says, resuming her reading, " 'Gisele discovered a pustulous break between this world and the next and did battle with the creatures therein, sealing off the portal. Later, she helped save many Nightwing children from the catastrophic demonic assault on the school of Wiglaf in 1558. Hailed as a hero, Gisele lived to a very old age, dying at ninety-seven in 1605.' "

She looks up from the book into Devon's eyes.

"I *so* want to be a Nightwing," she tells him dreamily.

He smiles and takes the book from her. It might all seem pretty glamorous to Cecily, but Devon knows differently. He's inhaled the stench of the Hellholes. He's seen the destruction and the bloodshed caused by demons and renegade sorcerers. The destruction of the Nightwing school might seem like the stuff of Arthurian fantasy to Cecily, but Devon *knew* Wiglaf, and it bothers him to think he had to face such a thing.

Would I give it all up? Devon thinks, as Rolfe drives them back to the cliffside staircase. *Would I give up all my Nightwing past the way Mrs. Crandall and Edward did, just so that I might try to live an ordinary life?*

As if it had worked for them.

Devon knows he'd have no better luck.

HE DREAMS of Isobel again that night—except now she's Morgana again—and they're sitting in the back of Stormy Harbor, holding hands. He wakes up flushed and frightened. Why does he keep dreaming about her if she's gone?

It's just going to take a while to forget her, he assures himself. *That's all.*

The next day after school he spends time with Alexander, who's had little to say about his father's departure, pretending it doesn't bother him. Devon drags out a couple of sleds from the garage and the two race each other down the sloping hill behind the mansion, hooting and laughing. Alexander gets the sudden idea to build a snowman at the foot of the hill, which they do, rolling three big balls of snow and placing them one on top of the other. Alexander finds one of his father's old hats from the garage and places it on the snowman's head. Then the boy hops back on his sled and rides smack down the hill into the snowman, obliterating it.

Devon resists the urge to play child psychologist. He just gives the boy a high five.

For supper, Bjorn makes them a terrific meal of roast chicken and gravy. It's just Devon, Alexander, and Cecily at the table. Mrs. Crandall has avoided them all as much as possible since her mother's death. She takes her meals in her room, barely speaking even to Cecily. She seems overcome, not just by the loss of her mother, but by Edward's departure and the sudden realization that she is all alone now, the sole sentinel against Ravenscliff's supernatural past. Devon wonders if she might be softening, if she will relent in her steely determination to keep whatever secrets she holds deep within herself.

Yet if he dares to hope she'll reveal something—*anything*—he is quickly proven wrong. The following night, encountering her on the stairs as he heads up to sleep, Devon finds her pale and shrunken, her eyes lost in deep sockets of sleeplessness. It is the first time she has emerged from her room in days, and she barely acknowledges Devon as she tries to pass him on the stairs.

"Mrs. Crandall," Devon says, stopping her, "maybe it would be easier on you—on all of us—if you told me what your mother tried to say before she died. I'm not just asking for myself. That way you wouldn't have to carry this burden alone, whatever it is." He touches her arm. "Please. Let me help you."

She looks at him without emotion. "Help me? You? No, Devon. You cannot help me." Her eyes move away, seeming to fix on something only she can see. "And I cannot help you."

She continues on down the stairs like some wandering ghost.

That night Devon doesn't dream of Isobel the Apostate, but of his father.

"Beware, Devon! Beware!"

"Dad? Where are you?"

It is dark. There is no light, only heat and darkness.

"You will open the Hellhole, Devon! Beware!"

"No, Dad," Devon cries into the darkness. "I didn't open it. We defeated her! The vision was wrong! I never opened the Hellhole!"

"But you will, Devon! You will!"

He bolts upright in bed. Every night another nightmare. He's drenched in sweat. He rubs his head. Will he ever get a good night's sleep again?

Kicking off his sheets, he's suddenly aware of how warm he is. But it's not just the aftereffects of the dream, he quickly realizes. His room is wickedly hot—and he knows what that means.

"Oh, no," he groans. "Not again."

But he senses no demons present. Just the heat and pressure. He concentrates. They must be in the house somewhere.

In his mind's eye, he sees the portal in the East Wing. It is thrumming with a high-pitched sound and once more is glowing green.

You will open the Hellhole, Devon!

"No," he says, a small voice in the darkness of his room.

What could be causing the disturbance? he asks himself. *Isobel is gone.*

Isn't she?

That's when he hears her laughter.

Gone? But you know that's impossible, Devon!

"Isobel," he breathes, gripping his pillow to his chest.

You saw how I transcended even the flames of death!

Fear takes him by the throat.

Come to me, Devon. It is time you learned the truth of who you are. I will tell you the truth. I will tell you all you want to know.

"She's at the Hellhole," Devon says.

And this time he's really on his own.

Come to the East Wing, Devon. I await you. I await you with the truth.

"But I can't," he says weakly. "I've never been able to get in there—"

The old woman is dead. Her power is ended. You are the Master of Ravenscliff now!

Devon tosses his pillow across the room. "No! You're trying to trick me!"

I will open this portal, Devon, even if it means destroying this house and everyone in it!

Devon concentrates. And he finds Isobel was telling the truth, at least about his ability to get into the East Wing. The way is no longer barred to him. He disappears from his bed and reappears in Emily Muir's cobwebbed parlor. From the inner room the green light glows anew.

Isobel the Apostate waits for him. She is different somehow. She seems strangely transparent. Moonlight shines through her, and when she turns certain ways she disappears entirely from view.

The Hellhole is clear and solid, pulsating and glowing. From behind, disgusting vermin scratch and howl, frantic to be set free.

"We are evenly matched, the two of us," Isobel says. "I cannot force you to open this portal against your will."

Devon faces her. "So why have you called me here?"

"To make a bargain with you."

"I'm not interested in sharing any kind of power."

She smiles. Even with all the horror, Devon still finds her dazzlingly beautiful. Her black eyes dance.

"Not power, Devon," she says. "I know now that's not what you want. You want knowledge. *Truth*."

He says nothing.

"You want to know who you are. Who your parents were. Why you were sent here to Ravenscliff. What is the secret of your past, Devon, and what is your future?"

Still he says nothing.

Isobel smiles cunningly. "I will make an even exchange with you, Devon. The knowledge you seek for your assistance in opening this Hellhole. If you want to rescue the people in this house once you have done so, so be it. You have the power to do so. I will not stop you. Just give me access to the power of this portal and to the creatures within, and I will give you the knowledge you seek."

"So give it now."

Isobel laughs. "Do you think I'm as gullible as that? That I have spent five centuries observing the foibles of humankind to fall for such a trick? I would tell you what you want to know and then you would back out on your part of the deal."

Devon doesn't reply.

She shakes her head. "No, my boy. The exchange will take place simultaneously. You open the door and the knowledge will immediately be yours, there in your mind—as if it had always been there."

He narrows his eyes at her. "You know who my parents were?"

She beams. "You are my blood, Devon. I have watched all my descendants. I know full well the secret Amanda Muir Crandall has been keeping from you."

Devon hesitates.

I could do it. I could learn the truth. And I'm sure I could save Cecily and Alexander from whatever might come out of that Hellhole . . .

"The truth, Devon," Isobel taunts. "Finally the truth."

"The knowledge I seek," he says dreamily, *"for opening the Hellhole."*

"That's all, Devon," Isobel insists. "Just a quick and easy exchange. You get what you want, I get what I want."

"What I want," he mumbles.

"The name of your father," Isobel says. "The name of your mother. Your place in the history of the Nightwing."

"Yes," Devon says.

"Yes," Isobel echoes.

He turns from her and concentrates on the portal.

He feels no fear, just a calm and certain resolve. He did this once before, when he plunged into the Hellhole to bring Alexander back. He knows how to do it. He knows how to open the door between this world and the one below.

"Oh, yes, Devon," Isobel breathes, near ecstasy as she watches Devon concentrate.

Behind the door, the demons are wild. The portal shudders under the force of Devon's mind. The great iron bolt begins to tremble.

He feels his awesome power then, raw and mighty. A magical passion consumes him, and he is no longer a fourteen-year-old boy but an ancient wizard, a Sorcerer of the noble Order of the Nightwing. He takes in a long, deep breath—and the bolt on the door slides easily and smoothly from its place.

"It is mine!" Isobel exults. "It is mine!"

The metal door creaks open to reveal the blackness within.

And suddenly Devon rushes the Apostate. Her face changes then, realizing his deception. All of her centuries catch up to her in that instant. She is no longer young and beautiful, but rather a wizened, hideous crone.

Devon grabs her around the waist and runs with her into the throbbing darkness of the Hellhole. "You wanted them so bad!" he shouts. "Now you'll *be* with them—forever!"

Isobel the Apostate screams as the portal shuts against her.

Devon falls staggering back onto the dusty floor.

He's remembered his lessons from *The Book of Enlightenment.* A sorcerer has the power to open the portal without letting anything out, only letting himself—or someone else—*in.*

He hears her now behind the door, banging against the other side. Her cries are quickly drowned out by a cacophony of angry, frustrated demons, promised their freedom only to be denied, yet again. Devon hears their struggle. In his mind's eye he sees them, scaly and putrid, dragging Isobel away from the door deep down into the bowels of the Hellhole—the only place that will contain her, keep her evil spirit from returning.

"You were wrong, Isobel," Devon says, staring at the portal, once again cool and quiet and still. "We *weren't* evenly matched. You forgot just one important little detail."

He grins.

"I'm the one-hundredth generation from Sargon the Great."

He sits up suddenly. He's in his room, in bed. The night is cool.

Was it all a dream?

Yes, he realizes, it *was* a dream. But that doesn't make his triumph over Isobel any less real. Her power had to be ended, and her power came through dreams—so it's fitting that their final battleground was Devon's mind. Just because he never left his bed doesn't mean he hadn't exiled her to the Hellhole. A Sorcerer of the Nightwing can pick his battles, *and* where he fights them.

He sleeps like a rock the rest of the night.

——◆——

BEHIND THE WALL

BUT YOU COULD have learned the truth from her," Cecily says the next night, after he's filled her in on all the details. "You could've learned who you really are."

Outside the wind is howling. The ravens cry, fluttering their wings, as ever guarding the house. There is no snow tonight, but thunder rumbles in the distance. Another Misery Point storm is on its way.

Devon smiles. "Yeah, but the truth at what cost? Isobel and the demons roving the world isn't something I want to imagine. Besides, who's to say she wasn't planning something as devious as I was?"

Cecily grins. "You really are Johnny-on-the-spot, aren't you?" She reaches over and kisses him. "I'm very proud of you, Devon."

He blushes. "Well, the Voice is confirming for me

that she's gone. We don't have to worry about Isobel the Apostate anymore."

"Mother ought to be more grateful than she is."

Devon shrugs. "I think she's starting to realize keeping secrets from me is a losing proposition. But she's stubborn. She's not going to give in easily."

"Yeah," Cecily agrees. "But then again, neither are you."

She heads up to bed, leaving Devon to sit in the parlor staring up into the oil paint eyes of Horatio Muir. "Thanks for your help," he tells the portrait. "I guess we're destined to meet again. Maybe *you* can fill me in on all the outstanding mysteries of this house. Like who's buried in the grave marked Devon and where I fit in with all of this."

From some far corner of the house he hears it then: the sobbing.

He smirks, keeping eye contact with Horatio. "Oh, and how could I forget? Maybe you can tell me who the heck it is who's hidden away in the basement. Is it a ghost or is it human?" He listens, as the sound grows louder. "And how come whatever it is seems to know *me*?"

You know her name, comes a voice in his head.

Whether it's *the* Voice or someone else's—Horatio's, maybe?—Devon can't be sure.

"I know her name?" he asks.

You know her name.

"Who?" Devon asks the portrait, but the face of Horatio Muir remains flat and mute.

Thunder suddenly crashes directly over the house and the lights flicker. Devon stands and lights a few candles, just in case.

It can't be Isobel. I can rule her out. The Voice says she's really gone.

Then who can it be?

You know her name.

He takes a candle with him as he heads down the stairs into the cold, damp cellar. As he suspects, the lights do go out with the next assault of thunder, and he must use the candle to guide him to the source of the cries. They are louder down here as usual and seem to grow more agitated as he approaches.

He approaches the wall from where the sound seems to originate.

"Tell me your name," he says.

But the sobbing only grows more pitiful.

"Tell me your name and I can help you."

"Devon?" the crying voice asks. "Devon, is that you?"

"Yes. You know my name, now tell me yours."

But there is only silence. Devon sets the candle down on an old trunk, the light flickering throughout the shadowy basement. He feels along the length of the wall. Nothing. No seam. No panel that he can discern.

"There must be a way out," he says. "How else did they get you in there?"

He knocks against it with his knuckle. It's only drywall, maybe a couple of inches thick. It's a hastily built room with seemingly no door. Why had the Muirs built it? What is hidden back there? And who are they hiding it from?

From me, Devon tells himself.

He tries to will himself behind the wall, the way he had in the East Wing. But he is met with failure—odd, given that Greta Muir's sorcery is now gone. What force here is stronger than he is? More than ever, Devon realizes there are answers behind this wall.

Answers to questions about himself.

He looks around the basement. "Well," he says, "if my powers won't do the trick, I'll have to do it with my bare hands."

He spots what he's looking for.

"Stand back," he calls to whoever—or whatever—lives behind that wall. "I'm coming through!"

He raises a sledgehammer over his head.

CONTINUED IN BOOK THREE

ACKNOWLEDGMENTS

Gratitude goes to Judith Regan, for first recognizing the power of the Nightwing; to my smart and supportive editors, Cassie Jones and Brian Saliba; to my industrious agent, Malaga Baldi; to James Rea, designer of www.ravenscliff.com; and, as always, to T.D.H.

And to my readers—whose many enthusiastic responses to Book One were tremendously rewarding. Keep on writing me at HuntingtonGeoff@aol.com.

—G.H.

GEOFFREY HUNTINGTON lives in a house by the sea not far from where the ghost of a pirate is said to eternally walk the cliffs in search of his lost gold. Under another name, he is the author of several acclaimed works of fiction and nonfiction.

www.ravenscliff.com

To receive notice of author events and new books by Geoffrey Huntington, sign up at www.authortracker.com.